THE TRIUMPH
OF
ANGELSCOMBE

A Catholic Novel

HILARY WALKER

The Triumph of Angelscombe

A Catholic Novel

By Hilary Walker
Copyright 2024 Hilary C.T. Walker
Cover Design: 100BookCovers.com

All Rights Reserved

*****

A Special Tribute

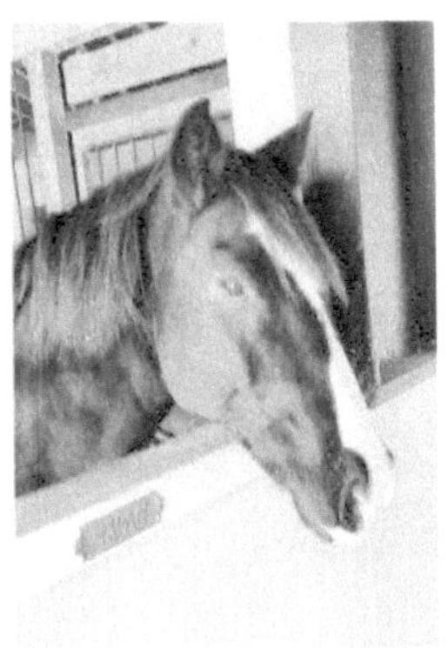

SPRUCE MEADOW ONSLOW
AKA
OZZIE

I owe a great debt to Wendy Wagner for allowing me to ride and compete on her lovely Dales pony, Ozzie, when my own horse was out of commission for over a year.

Her generosity saved my sanity when I thought I wasn't going to be able to ride for all that time, and maybe never even ride my own horse again.

Ozzie is the reason why I used the Dales breed in this book, as a tribute to a wonderful pony who took care of me both physically and emotionally during a very difficult time.

Thank you, Ozzie and Wendy!

TABLE OF CONTENTS

Introduction

Is This the Future of the Catholic Church?

Things are changing rapidly in the Catholic Church, but they are not going in the right direction.

Xavier Reyes-Ayral, a highly respected author on Marian apparitions, said the following in an interview with John Henry Westen on Lifesitenews.com:

"The new false church will be led by a false prophet … It will be under the leadership of a new pope … ignoring all the teachings of Jesus Christ." He goes on to say, "At that time, the Holy Eucharist will be attacked. The liturgy or the consecration of the Holy Host will no longer be valid."

A bleak vision indeed!

A Bishop's Call to Open Our Eyes

Just before this book went to press, Bishop Joseph Strickland, bishop emeritus of Tyler, Texas, issued a new letter to the faithful.

In it, he urges us to "see the corruption and the powerful evil forces" that are moving us inexorably toward a catastrophic disaster. "We MUST open our eyes before it is too late!"

He exhorts us to recognize the attacks on the Catholic Church, Christ's mystical body, so that we can be one with Jesus and "embrace the salvation He won for us on the cross." And we must do all we can to bring others into the fullness of truth, which is only to be found in Jesus Christ, and which His Church is charged with safeguarding.

Bishop Strickland urgently requests that we understand what's manipulating the forces against the Church: "it is no less than the hand of Satan, the prince of darkness."

He cites Cardinal Mario Luigi Ciappi, who read the Third Secret of Fatima, in which the Virgin Mary said that "apostasy would begin from the top." He also mentions that Padre Pio talked of the existence of a "false church" and a "great apostasy" that would occur after 1960.

The Infiltration of Heresies

In his new book, *Flee From Heresy,* (© 2024 Sophia Institute Press) Bishop Athanasius Schneider describes Magisterial Positivism, a heresy which holds that all actions, teachings and commands of both the pope and ecumenical councils are to be obeyed, because they are infallibly true and morally good. He stresses the danger of conferring greater importance on the Magisterium than on Holy Scripture and Tradition, especially when the Magisterium seeks to challenge and weaken the Church's revealed truths, and her sacramental and liturgical practices.

He cites two instances of this heresy by Pope Francis, the latest being in 2023 when he gave permission for the blessing of couples in adulterous or sodomitical situations. (More on that later.)

Bishop Scheider goes on to explain that such heresies are rationalized, among other things, through clever semantics or irrational obedience.

Things Are Moving Fast

On 4th July, 2024, the Vatican excommunicated Archbishop Carlo Maria Viganó for alleged schism.

The archbishop wrote a moving sermon for 7th July, 2024, the Solemnity of the Most Precious Blood of Our Lord Jesus Christ, in which he describes the Church as being "enslaved to the world" and having excommunicated him for openly professing the Faith he was ordered to preach at his ordination.

He goes on to lament, "But how can we even think that it is the *true Church* that strikes its children and its Ministers, and at the same time welcomes its enemies and makes their errors its own?"

Why This Book?

The outline for *The Triumph of Angelscombe* was conceived during the Synod on Synodality in 2023.

That meeting, in which the *process* was deemed more important than the *outcome*, was cause for great anxiety among the faithful. (See **Resources & Notes** for my blog post on the topic.)

Traditional Catholics are being labelled schismatic. But the Vatican welcomes those who rebelliously depart from Christ's Gospel in the name of 'progress' and whose idols are false compassion, fraternity which does not acknowledge God as Our Father, and concern for Mother Earth.

This novel explores the likely impact of these actions on faithful Catholics, both clergy and laity.

Are We Confused Yet?

During the course of this writing, *Fiducia Supplicans* was published, producing further confusion about what is and what isn't doctrine in the Catholic Church.

Its design is to allow the blessing of irregular unions, while pretending not to. It's supposedly blessing the individuals in that relationship, not the relationship itself.

As someone astutely put it, that amounts to blessing the wheels on a bicycle, but insisting one is not blessing the bicycle. It is an attempt to change the custom without openly changing the doctrine. But in the end it amounts to the same thing – blessing sin.

God will not be mocked, and I pray daily for Pope Francis. May he have a change of heart and steer Holy Mother Church back on course before he has to meet his Maker.

Nova Theologica Populi: The People's Theology

The *Nova Theologica Populi* mentioned in this novel is purely fictitious; it is not an actual document.

But it highlights current attempts to demolish the Catholic Church's Traditions and orthodox teachings, which have supported, sustained and created countless saints since Jesus instituted His Church, two millennia ago.

As Jesus asks, in Luke 18:8 : will He find faith on earth when He returns?

The Warning

The end of this book contains information about the Warning, to which I add my own warning: certain artistic liberties were taken with the prophecies in order to fit them into this novel.

Final Words of Comfort

Monsieur Reyes-Ayral rightly says, "We must know that we cannot abandon the Church, which was instituted by Christ upon Peter, for to do so would be to say Christ failed to foresee what the future held. That's impossible."

Jesus has assured us that the gates of Hell will not prevail against His Church. To paraphrase St. Paul in Romans 5:20, where sin abounds, grace abounds all the more.

May we be recipients of that grace in order to serve the Lord, and may we live to see the triumph of His Sacred Heart and the Immaculate Heart of His Blessed Mother!

God bless, and I hope you enjoy "The Triumph of Angelscombe".

Hilary Walker
https://HilaryWalkerBooks.com
Rubesca4@gmail.com

Cast of Characters

MAIN CHARACTERS

Father Terry Talbot, cancelled Catholic priest, horse rider and manager of the Angelscombe Dales Preservation Project

Father Godfrey Hughes, cancelled Catholic priest, close friend of Father Terry and vehicle mechanic

Pastor John Morgan, cancelled Lutheran minister and the farm's vet

Brother Melvin Martin, retired SSPX brother, cook and gardener

Father Oliver Jones, cancelled Catholic priest, accountant and cook

Father Fred Harris, cancelled Catholic priest and farrier

Father Harry Wilder, cancelled Catholic priest and trainer of the ponies to harness

Father Abnus Doyal, Catholic priest in good standing with the progressive New Church and manager of the Lambcot Fell Pony Preservation Project

This book is dedicated to the Catholic priests who are remaining true to the Deposit of Faith.

Their task is daunting.

For our sakes, day after day, they push back against crushing pressure from the Father of Lies to pursue the wide path and depart from the teachings of Christ.

These amazing men are Our Lord's true shepherds and many have been cancelled for their loyalty to Him.

Please support them and pray for them.

Chapter One: Unto Them a Foal Is Born

Sunday, 29th September 2030

The black mare had been circling her large stable for two hours now. She was uncomfortable and sweating, and Father Terry Talbot wanted to stay with her.

But dawn was breaking and Father Godfrey Hughes tugged on his sleeve. "Time for Matins."

It was a reminder of his priestly duty to pray the Divine Office.

"God will take care of Ruby," Father Godfrey reassured him.

Pastor John said, "And your trusty vet is also keeping watch." He smiled wryly. "Even a non-Catholic will do in a pinch, wouldn't you agree?"

Chastened by this gentle reproach, Father Terry said, "Yes, of course, I'm sorry. You're an absolute Godsend and I'm glad you're here."

He meant it.

A month ago, the Lutheran minister had sought asylum at this old monastery, now a project for preserving the endangered Dales Pony breed.

"You've come to the wrong place," announced Father Terry, when Pastor John Morgan appeared at the massive front door. "We're all Catholics here."

"No, this is the right place," was the confident reply. "God sent me here because you need a vet, and I need somewhere to live."

Each resident had to earn his keep by contributing a useful talent. Every penny of the British Government's funds allocated to the Angelscombe Dales Preservation

Project must be accounted for – there was no money to waste on slackers.

Each of the cancelled clerics running the farm brought a different skillset. All areas of expertise were covered, except veterinarian – although *some* priests muttered about the dire need for a replacement cook, too.

When a vet was needed for the ponies, they had to call – and pay – Dr. Tilman from the neighbouring village of Angelscombe.

And now, here on the doorstep, was a vet asking to live with them! He might not be Catholic, but he *was* a Christian clergyman.

Yet why did he need somewhere to live? Had he done something wrong – something illegal? Father Terry curbed his enthusiasm. "What brings a Lutheran minister to our doors?"

"You mean, have I been kicked out for some crime?"

The priest reddened.

"The answer is, no. The same is going on with us as with you: the tolerant progressive Lutheran Church does not tolerate traditional clergy. I am a dinosaur, like yourself, and no longer allowed to poison my congregation with God's revealed Truth."

"*You've* been cancelled, too?" Father Terry was unaware that the plague of removing faithful ministers had infected other Christian denominations.

"Yes." The pastor held out a letter. "Here's the bishop's litany of my many faults."

The list was uncannily similar to that from Father Terry's own prelate. It included familiar words and phrases such as 'divisive,' 'over-zealous in his preaching of the truth,' 'too traditional,' 'lacking in sensitivity towards his parishioners,' 'too much emphasis on sin, and not enough on God's mercy and forgiveness.' It was all there.

He handed it back to the man, who exchanged it for his certificate of qualification as a vet. Father Terry recognised the veterinary college and it all looked in order.

He shook the pastor's hand. "Welcome to the farm! Your arrival is most timely. We have a mare due to foal in four weeks, and could use your expertise."

And now, Angelscombe's Black Ruby, a beautiful example of the Dales Pony breed, was about to give birth to the farm's first foal.

This was a momentous event and proof of the project's success in breeding a new generation of ponies for their originally intended purpose.

Father Terry wanted to witness the foal's arrival, but obedience to God was his first obligation.

"Good luck, Ruby – and you, John!" With a big sigh, he followed his friend to the chapel-turned-hay-barn for Matins.

Once inside the large building, they walked through a narrow gap between several hundred bales of high-stacked hay, taking care not to attract wisps onto their black attire. At the far end, and well-hidden from the casual observer, was a fake wall, painted to look like the rest of the barn.

Father Terry punched in a code and opened the camouflaged door. The two priests entered a small section of the chapel, lovingly preserved from destruction by sealing it off from Bishop Hardy's sight.

Father Terry treasured this sacred space. It raised his spirits from deep sadness at being cast out from his own Church.

The Church's whole course had changed during the latest Synod. The Catholic clergy were outnumbered three to one by non-Catholic ministers and laity, and the focus was on 'dialogue' with anyone who took offense at Catholic teaching.

It alarmed Father Terry that this included talks with sworn enemies of the Church, and that her new duty was to 'pastorally walk' with her foes in the name of 'compassion'.

Traditional priests, who believed true compassion lies in saving souls, by telling them the hard truths of Jesus' Gospel, were labelled 'backwardists' and ideologues.

They were given a choice: either join the New Church, or live in limbo with no active ministry – and no salary – until they saw the light and repented of their waywardness.

Since Father Terry refused to participate in the mutilation of the Church he loved, his bishop had recommended him to lead the new government project within his diocese.

"And here is a list of other local priests who prefer to live outside the Church," he'd said. "You'll need help with running the place."

Choking back his indignation at this description, Father Terry had taken the list and used it to find his new staff.

As he later told them, "The bishop is happy to have us rounded up in one place. It makes it easier for him to keep an eye on us."

And yet, he wasn't unhappy about the work allotted to him. Bishop Arthur Hardy was aware of his riding background and passion for horses, and Father Terry had leapt at the chance to work with the breed, despite its short height.

He was almost six feet tall, and the true Dales pony didn't exceed 14.2 hands – just under five feet. Luckily the powerful breed was capable of carrying a man, and the lean priest was well within its weight capacity.

His legs hung below the animal's belly and looked rather comical, which Father Terry suspected was part of the bishop's intent. However, it was better than not working with equines at all.

And now, as Matins began, he tried to concentrate on the Lord his God, rather than the mare straining to give birth.

After prayers, the priests dispersed to tackle their daily pony chores, except for Father Oliver, the cook. They made their way to the monastery's old cloister, now converted into stables and utility rooms.

They removed their overalls from hooks on the tack room door, and used them to cover their black shirts with the distinctive white dog collar, and long black pants. After exchanging their polished black shoes for brown paddock boots, the priests were dressed for barn work.

Together with Pastor John, they shared the tasks of feeding, watering, leading the animals out to the paddocks, mucking out the stables and distributing hay. With eighteen mares and two stallions on the property, there was plenty to do.

Father Terry collected the full feed buckets and forced himself to finish giving the other ponies their breakfast before visiting the mother-to-be. She would be fed last, as she had other things to focus on at present.

When he arrived with her feed, he found Pastor John speaking soothingly over the stable door.

"There, you can do it! Keep trying!" the vet urged. Upon seeing the priest approach, he put an index finger to his mouth. Softly, he said, "Take a look at the miracle of life, Father."

The priest hurried the last few strides and quietly placed Ruby's bucket on the floor outside. As he peeked into the stable, profound awe overcame him.

A gangly black foal was swaying uncertainly on four long legs, while his dam licked him, nudging him in the direction of her full teats.

"She dropped this little man almost as soon as you left," whispered Pastor John.

"No complications?"

"None, thank the Lord. She slid him out right away and he started breathing as she was cleaning him. Once the umbilical cord broke, I dipped it in iodine to prevent infection, but other than that, I've left the two of them alone."

"Did he stand up quickly?"

"Yes. He's a strong chap. And smart, too. Look, he's already found the milk source."

Father Terry grinned as the colt suckled ravenously after a few failed attempts.

Pastor John patted the priest on his back and chuckled. "Congratulations. You're a *real* father now!"

The priest grinned. "And we got our first foal before the Fell Preservation Project beat us to it."

"The government will be proud," replied the minister.

Both men rolled their eyes. The last thing they cared about was what the government thought. But they were beholden to that institution for their sustenance and should at least appear to want to please it.

"What happens next?" asked Father Terry.

"I now wait anxiously for this little fellow to make his first poop. It's called meconium, and it's important he gets that out to prevent constipation. Otherwise, I have to help him do it, which I don't look forward to."

"How long before he should produce the goods?" After long years as a dressage rider and horse owner, Father Terry was well acquainted with the urgency for a horse to pass manure in cases of colic.

"About four hours."

Father Terry looked at his watch and made a mental note of when to check back with the vet.

"How soon can they be turned out?"

"As soon as that poop has been accomplished, I'd say. The weather's mild and we're not expecting rain."

"I look forward to seeing them outside. Can I give Ruby her feed now?"

"Absolutely. She deserves it!"

Curiosity brought the other three priests over to check on the mare, with Pastor John exhorting them to keep their voices down.

Then, suddenly, the Catholics' mobile phones pinged.

Ruby's head shot up at the noise and they drew back from the stable to see what the emergency was.

Pastor John looked on in bewilderment, not himself having received a message.

Father Godfrey exclaimed, "The pope is dead!"

"I didn't know he was sick!" said Father Fred Harris, the farm's farrier.

Father Harry Wilder, who trained the ponies to harness, read, "It says here that he fainted during yesterday's evening session of the Synod and took a turn for the worse during the night. He died at 2 a.m. this morning."

An Extraordinary Synod was currently in session in Rome, and the priests of Angelscombe were dreading its conclusions.

Father Terry well knew his fellow priests were, like himself, having difficulty thinking charitable thoughts about the late pontiff, who'd allowed their dismissal from active parochial life and had steered the Barque of Peter into perilous waters.

"We'll offer today's Mass for him," he said.

His companions bowed their heads. "Amen."

"I'll come, too," said Pastor John. "He may not have been my superior, but I suspect he needs all the prayers he can get."

In silence they finished their duties before removing their overalls and meeting in the chapel for the Sacred Liturgy, and to pray for the repose of the deceased pope's soul.

Chapter Two: Speculations & Awful Cooking

Sunday, 29th September 2030

Breakfast provided the first opportunity to share their reactions to the pope's unexpected death.

But first they voiced the usual complaints about the food.

Father Oliver's primary area of expertise was accounting, not preparing meals. He was in charge of the Dales project's finances and applying to the government for additional funding, which was rarely forthcoming. But when interviewed for the accounting position, he had recklessly mentioned how much he enjoyed cooking.

He quickly rued that statement when it earned him the additional post of resident chef. His menus were criticised daily, with barely a semblance of good humour. He once bewailed this ill-treatment to Father Terry, who blithely counselled him to offer up his sufferings for the holy souls in Purgatory. Yet Father Terry did feel bad for the poor man.

However, this morning Father Oliver was in for a reprieve. Today's events quickly diverted everyone's attention from moaning about the greasy bacon, quasi-burnt sausages, and runny scrambled eggs.

Their joy over the birth of the first foal on the farm soon gave way to speculation over the pope's death.

"I think God is punishing him for not caring about the salvation of souls during his pontificate," said Father Oliver.

They all nodded, except Father Godfrey. "We mustn't presume to know what was in the pope's heart, or to understand God's actions."

"You're being kind," said Father Harry. "But he spent too much time *accompanying* people and *dialoguing* with them instead of calling them to repentance. Compassion without conversion, and no one can pretend otherwise."

Father Godfrey shook his head sadly. "Let's hope he repented before his death."

"That's assuming he had time to repent," said Father Fred. "*I* think there was foul play." Seeing the others' expressions, he tapped his mobile phone with a forefinger. "I'm not the only one. The Catholic news services are buzzing with speculation about no actual illness being reported before he died, and how he was in reasonable health at the beginning of the Synod. He was issuing daily statements as recently as yesterday evening."

"That's true," said Father Terry, and the others murmured agreement.

Father Fred continued. "Then, *Boom!* He's gone. Doesn't that strike you as a little suspicious?"

"Are they saying that he was murdered?" ventured Father Godfrey nervously.

"Not yet. It's not impossible though, is it?"

"But on what grounds?" asked Father Terry.

"Here are a couple of possible reasons." Father Fred read from his phone. "One is, the pope was old and slow and the Synodal Fathers wanted to wrap up the Synod before the faithful could revolt against its agenda.

"Or, close to meeting his Maker, he changed his mind about the disastrous direction in which he was leading the Church; he was trying to turn things around and undo his betrayal."

"I'd like to think he was," said Father Godfrey.

"We can all hope that," said Father Terry. "But if so, what a terrible shame he was prevented from doing it."

"What worries me," said Father Fred, "is what's going to come out of this Extraordinary Synod. Who's in charge now? Will they suspend it until there's a new pope? Or will the cardinals, bishops and 'select lay persons' presently in the Vatican, hurry to achieve their goal of making the Catholic Church 'more relevant'?" He drew air quotes around those last words.

"Does anyone know what was being discussed before your pontiff died?" asked Pastor John, even though he wasn't personally invested in the outcome of the Synod.

"No, it was kept deliberately vague, with no mention at all of God, or the Holy Trinity or the Deposit of Faith, just like the previous one," said Father Terry. "And who knows what direction it'll take now? I suspect the gloves – flimsy as they were – will now come off."

"I fear you may be right," agreed Father Harry. "While the previous pope promoted ambiguous double-speak, I won't be surprised if the new one feels free to openly promote heresy."

"Surely not!" cried Father Godfrey. "Let's pray for a good, traditional pope."

Father Terry smiled indulgently at his naïve friend, who was always looking for the good in people. He himself tacitly agreed with Father Harry; this did not look good for the Catholic Church, nor for any hope of their small band of cancelled priests being reinstated to active ministry.

Breakfast was finished in despondent silence, broken only by renewed murmurings that 'something needs to be done about this awful cooking.'

All at once, the priests' phones pinged again to announce another important development. Reports were coming through that, since all the cardinals were in Rome for the Synod, a new conclave had already been called.

Father Terry was immediately suspicious. How convenient that the former pope should expire during this second synod, allowing a successor to be elected at such short notice! Could there be any truth to the rumours that the pope had not died of natural causes?

The buzz around the table started up again: who would be the next pope? Would he be a progressive? A traditionalist?

"Perhaps he'll insist on reinstating all the cancelled faithful priests," posited the ever-optimistic Father Godfrey.

Father Terry sighed. "If only!"

Chapter Three: Convictions & Conversions

Sunday, 29th September 2030

Despite this exciting development, the ponies still needed tending to.

Leaving Father Oliver to clean up the breakfast things, the others went to their cells and changed into full barn clothes.

Father Terry, the head rider, put on breeches and paddock boots – an ensemble that would convince any snooping government official that he was performing no priestly offices and was entirely devoted to the Dales project.

The initiative to save the breed had come directly from the pope – may he rest in peace.

The pontiff had agreed with the global elite that Mother Earth was in grave danger from human activities. Convinced that addressing climate change was the real thrust of his pontificate, he had joined the secular powers in deciding that mankind should revert to days of yore, before the advent of the evil motor car.

All efforts must be directed to turning back the clock, and using good old-fashioned horse transport to stop polluting the atmosphere.

Father Terry and his companions privately considered it futile for prideful man to believe he had power over nature. Was he able to prevent earthquakes and tsunamis? Or tornadoes and hurricanes – or even the humble thunder-storm?

Even if it *were* possible to influence the climate, was that the job of the Catholic Church? Surely, she was supposed to be guiding souls to their home in Heaven, not obsessing over preserving their earthly one?

However, things being as they were, the priests cheerfully obeyed their bishop's order to help with this 'important' undertaking, of bringing back the old and less polluted days. They well understood this job was intended to keep them too busy to cause disruption to the New Church's 'progress'.

Father Terry had been tasked not only with managing the resuscitation of the breed, but also with the training of the animals for riding and pulling carriages.

His background was ideal for leading this project. In his youth he'd been an avid competitive dressage rider. He'd kept horses on his home property and was well educated in their care.

It had been hard for him to give up his beloved equines and obey God's call to the priesthood. And when Bishop Arthur Hardy removed him as pastor of Saint Thomas More church in the village of Angelscombe, he began to have serious doubts about the validity of his vocation. If he was no longer allowed to preach Christ's Truth and minister to the faithful, what was his purpose? Had he interpreted God's plan for his life incorrectly? Maybe he wasn't supposed to be a priest, after all?

After praying long hours on his knees for an answer, he received the bishop's phone call. "You have a new job, Terry, one much more suited to your capabilities."

The priest was overjoyed: God was making it clear that *horses* should be his main focus!

After handing him the list of priests 'who prefer to live outside the Church,' Bishop Hardy had told Father Terry, "The government has agreed to support up to ten of you, as long as you reach a base herd of twenty ponies, and produce at least ten foals a year. You have four years in which to achieve this quota."

"Who will supply the ponies to start with, Your Excellency?"

"They are being collected from locations around the British Isles and held in a temporary facility until you're ready to receive them."

Father Terry groaned inwardly. Had those animals been snatched from their legitimate owners in the cause of combatting climate change 'for the common good'?

I promise to take care of your ponies, he silently told the theft victims.

"And where are we to keep them?" he asked his superior.

"The government has just bought a monastery outside Angelscombe, which recently became vacant."

Because the pope drove out the Trappist monks who lived there. His Holiness had ordered them to go out into the world and become useful members of society, instead of lurking in dark cloisters with their traditional prayer books. Enemy forces operating within the Vatican had prevented the pope from appreciating that those devoted monks, and other religious brothers and sisters like them, were keeping the forces of evil at bay through their constant intercession on behalf of wayward humanity.

"I have already desacralised the chapel," the bishop proudly announced. "I'm told it will make an excellent hay barn. And I want you to oversee the conversion of the monastery cloister into stables."

Father Terry had cringed at these orders. *But Thy Will be done*, he prayed. *You have a plan, as always, and I must humbly submit to it.*

While the conversion plans were being drawn up, he had no trouble enrolling the right men to help run the project. This was a rural area, and most of Father Terry's cancelled priest friends had grown up on farms.

His close friend, Father Godfrey Hughes, had a background in vehicle mechanics, which he'd learned from his farmer father. The fresh-faced young man was put in charge of driving the tractor, grading the new riding arena, spreading the manure in the paddocks, and any other tractor-related tasks. He was brilliant at fixing ailing engines and, though not familiar with horses, was keen to learn about them.

"Ponies aren't as big as horses," Father Terry told him, "so they're not so scary."

Ruddy complexioned Father Harry Wilder had grown up driving horses in harness and was a good complement to Father Terry's riding skills. The gentle Dales Pony was a versatile and strong all-rounder, and the two priests would train the animals in both disciplines.

Father Fred Harris was the son of a local blacksmith, who favoured letting horses go barefoot. "That's how God made them," he'd say, "and who am I to improve on His handiwork?" When Father Terry approached the short, weatherbeaten priest to ask him to be the programme's farrier, the latter jumped at the opportunity. "I'll get my dad to teach me how to trim hooves," he said, "and he'll also be close by to help if needed."

The last recruit was Father Oliver Jones, accountant and hapless cook.

The sad day came to talk about turning the chapel into a hay barn. Surveying his co-workers' dismayed faces, Father Terry said, "We are still priests. We therefore need a sacred space to celebrate the Holy Mass and the other sacraments. So I suggest we keep the altar and first two rows of pews."

"But everything's been desacralised! And won't the bishop order us to get rid of the altar and the pews *and* the sacred vessels?" asked an anxious Father Godfrey.

"We'll point out how it will save the government the expense of removing them and finding somewhere else to put them."

"But he'll see they're still in use," objected Father Harry.

That was when Father Terry proposed the solution of building a false wall and secret door. If anyone should discover them, the priests would say that it had been cheaper to leave the desacralised altar to gather dust forever behind the permanent wall, and hope no one insist they seal up the door.

For this part of the project, Father Terry was able to employ a faithful Catholic builder, who swore to keep the deception secret.

Thus, on his inspection visit, the bishop saw only a large converted chapel full of hay.

"But," asked the ever-scrupulous Father Godfrey afterwards, "shouldn't we have told him that we have access to the altar?"

"We might as well tell him outright that we're saying Mass, Godfrey," replied Father Terry. "You can be sure he already suspects us of it. But it would be a travesty to create a makeshift altar elsewhere, when we have a beautiful one right here. It's still been desacralised; we haven't reversed that, and we can't do it anyway without the bishop's permission.

"And we're within the limits of Canon Law Article 932.1 by using this chapel remnant for its original purpose."

Father Godfrey frowned. "Are you sure?"

"Yes." Father Terry pulled out his phone and read from the Code of Canon Law: "'The eucharistic celebration is to be carried out in a sacred place unless in a particular case necessity requires otherwise.'" He looked at his fellow priests. "I think we can call this a particular case, since the chapel was previously a sacred place, and hasn't been used for any profane activity since its desacralisation.

"And, as priests, we *are* within our rights to reconsecrate the holy vessels."

The others were comfortable with that explanation, except Father Godfrey, whose conscience was more sensitive than the others'. He nodded slowly. "I'll pray that Our Lord doesn't mind."

When the cloistered colonnade, bordering a large square of lawn, was turned into individual stables, Father Terry had the original flagstone floors covered with sand and rubber matting. For he secretly wished to preserve the stones trodden over the centuries by holy Trappist monks as they walked around the quadrangle, deep in prayer. He hoped one day this monastery would be restored to its proper use.

The extensive grounds were divided into large paddocks, and a full-size riding arena was created.

The priests cheered when, at last, eighteen elegant Dales mares and two proud Dales stallions were unloaded from several large horse boxes and led under the high arch over the grass to their new stables in the old cloister.

Father Terry beamed; his life's work had truly begun.

Chapter Four: Candlesticks & Brother Melvin

Sunday, 6th October 2030

With the arrival of the first foal, Father Terry became convinced that his primary job was to protect this breed of pony, come what may.

While, of course, preserving his priesthood, as best he could under the circumstances.

During the week since the birth, he'd been bombarding Pastor John daily with questions about the colt's progress.

The animal had provided the vet with the precious first poop, and was turned out daily with his dam. But Father Terry found plenty of other reasons to fret. Did Ruby have enough milk? Was the foal developing as he should? Was he carrying enough weight?

The Lutheran minister shook his head on seeing the priest approach the mare's stable yet again, after Sunday Matins. "You're worse than a new human mother, Father! They're both doing *fine*."

"But when I was watching them in the paddock yesterday, I noticed the baby trying to eat grass, and he was doing the splits like a giraffe. Is he supposed to do that? Isn't that bad for his tendons?" Father Terry had only ever been around adult horses and had no experience of baby ones.

Pastor John laughed. "He's a week old now, and trying to copy his mum, that's all. He can't *actually* eat grass yet, and will need her milk for a good few months. But what he's doing is normal. Stop worrying so much!"

"I'm sorry, John. But there's a lot riding on this little guy."

"Maybe it'll help you relax if I tell you that two other mares are getting close to their due date."

"That's wonderful news!"

The minister chuckled. "Then you can be a helicopter mum to three foals, instead of one."

"Mock all you like. At least I care."

"I certainly can't fault you on that. And there's one pony we *do* need to keep an eye on."

"Oh, no. Which one?"

"Our older lady, Trudy. I think she has Cushing's."

In Cushing's Disease, more properly known as PPID (Pituitary Pars Intermedia Dysfunction) there is an overproduction of certain pituitary hormones. In its advanced stages, the animal loses top line muscle, drinks and urinates more, holds onto his winter coat and either sweats abnormally much or little, among other issues. His attitude becomes dull and he can't tolerate exercise.

"Ugh!" responded Father Terry. "What signs is she exhibiting?"

"She was slow to shed her winter coat this year. And recently, she's been drinking a lot more than usual and sweating for no obvious reason."

"Do we need to test her for it?"

"The test is very expensive and can be inconclusive. I'm sure she has it, and at her age it won't hurt to manage her as if she does." The pony was twenty years old.

"Poor thing! That means no morning grass because of the high sugar content, doesn't it? And a grazing muzzle. I hate those things."

"We'll try to avoid using the muzzle by reducing her grazing time, and feeding her hay soaked for 30 minutes to lower its sugar content. We'll do all we can to keep her happy and healthy."

"That does explain why she didn't take when she was covered last autumn," said Father Terry. "Dales ponies aren't considered old at age twenty and the other mare of that age is doing fine with her pregnancy."

Pastor John nodded. "Yes. Cushing's mares are often infertile."

"I'm worried the government will find out that we have an unproductive mare here. Who knows what they'll do to her."

"Let's keep her condition between ourselves, Terry. If the others don't know about this, they can't accidentally blab to outsiders. That would seal her death warrant."

"Mum's the word, John."

Father Terry was unhappy about Trudy's need for extra hay. He was already concerned they might not have enough for the coming winter; more funds were needed than the coalition between the government and the Catholic Church was willing to give him, despite Father Oliver's repeated requests.

He'd been mulling over what he could sell to obtain extra money. That valuable second pair of gold candlesticks on the altar wouldn't be missed. Mass could be said without them, and their sale would be for a good cause – the Lord's cause.

He'd recently run this idea past Father Godfrey, his sounding board in difficult spiritual decisions.

His friend was dead against such a course of action. "You want to go back on your promise to Our Lord to keep everything on the altar safe?"

Father Terry couldn't recall having expressed a promise in *quite* those words, but had taken his friend's advice to heart and held off selling the candlesticks.

Until now. This news about Trudy brought a greater sense of urgency to the plan.

As he went about his pre-Mass morning chores, his heart was heavy with worry over keeping the old mare's condition secret, and whether Pastor John could treat her without expensive medication. He didn't look forward to telling Father Godfrey that he needed to sell those candlesticks after all.

He was approaching the feed room when Father Oliver ran up to him. "Father Terry, there's a man in the main entrance wanting to talk to the person in charge."

Father Terry checked his watch. "At *this* hour of the morning? What on earth does he want?"

"He didn't say, just kept insisting he talk to the person in charge."

"Do you think you could help with feeding the ponies for me?"

Father Oliver, dressed for Mass in his immaculate blacks and white collar, looked horrified at the suggestion.

But Father Terry was already taking off his overalls. He thrust them into the hapless priest cook's hands. "Put these on. Pastor John will tell you what to do."

"But I might get bitten by a pony!" Father Oliver protested.

"And you might be struck down by a bolt of lightning if you *don't* help out," countered the other. He patted Father Oliver on the back. "Just kidding. And the ponies don't bite – I promise you."

Father Terry strode towards the main building, brow furrowed. *Lord, please don't let him be a government inspector.*

He then laughed at the idea. Not even the most zealous of inspectors would come out this early in the morning.

A green Morris Minor, relic from the distant past, was parked in the driveway, and by the front door stood an old man, who appeared to be in his eighties. His back was slightly stooped and he wore a black soutane and white collar.

Definitely not a government inspector, unless they were descending to new lows in their search for rebels against the New World Order.

Brother Melvin watched the tall priest walking towards him with confident strides; this must be the man in charge.

He hoped he wouldn't be mad at him for coming at this hour, but he'd been anxious to slip out of the home for retired clergy without being noticed. He didn't want anyone there to know about his mission unless it was successful.

He put on a winning smile and extended his right hand. "Hello, I'm Brother Melvin."

To his relief, the priest shook it and smiled back. "I'm Father Terry. What can I do for you?"

"I'm hoping I can be of as much service to you as I trust you'll be to me, Father. Is there somewhere we can talk?"

Father Terry checked his watch. "I don't have long. Mass begins in twenty minutes. I'm sure you understand..."

"Absolutely. Maybe I could be permitted to join you in the Liturgy?"

He saw a flicker of suspicion cross Father Terry's face.

Father Melvin clarified. "I'm not an ordained minister, Father, but I am a Religious Brother of the Society of Saint Pius X. Like you, I have to say Mass daily."

Father Terry's face relaxed slightly. "Then please step into my office."

Brother Melvin followed, grateful for the slow pace set by the priest in deference to his age.

Soon he was seated in the visitor's leather chair, and from the other side of the desk Father Terry again asked how he could help.

"As I mentioned, I'm a Brother of the SSPX. I'm eighty-six, but was useful to my community until very recently. My expertise is cooking, you see, and they had difficulty finding someone to replace me."

"Cooking, you say?" The priest's eyes brightened.

"Yes, and, dare I say, I was very good at it. Which is why it was hard to find someone willing to take over the oven, so to speak."

"Where did you go after that?"

"I was sent to a local home for retired clergy."

"But you are no longer there?"

Brother Melvin blushed at the stinging memory of his dismissal. "I've – er – just been cancelled, if you can do such a thing to a retired minister."

"What on earth for?"

"I was considered subversive, you see. I thought being retired gave me the freedom to speak God's Truth to the unfortunate old priests in there who've swallowed the liberal theology besetting the Church. I wanted to save their souls before it was too late. But I was wrong to believe it was allowed. And I was already suspect because of my background."

"I can believe that," said Father Terry. "As a member of the SSPX, you're the most traditional of the traditionalists."

Brother Melvin nodded.

"So, it was just a matter of time before they found a reason to expel you."

"Quite. Two days ago I was given my marching orders and told to find somewhere else to live."

"How did you find out about us?"

"My niece is mad about ponies and was aware of your programme here at Angelscombe. She encouraged me to ask if you would give refuge to a retired brother."

"Forgive me for asking, but how can I be sure you're not a government or New Church mole?"

Brother Melvin coughed delicately. "My niece is Lady Rowland, the daughter of Archbishop Gregory's sister. She'll vouch for me." Archbishop Gregory was one of the few prelates publicly speaking out against the heresies being ushered into the Church, and attempting – with filial deference and unsuccessfully – to correct the former pope. Brother Melvin added, "In case you're wondering why I don't go and live with her, it's because I want to be with a community of traditional priests to whom I can be of service, rather than take her charity. My whole vocation has been to minister to the SSPX priests' nutritional needs."

"And you're sure you want to cook for us Novus Ordo priests?" Father Terry gave a half-smile.

"Absolutely!" Brother Melvin chuckled. "I need to be back in the kitchen, where I belong. Unless that will tread on your present cook's toes?"

"Not at all!" came the quick reply. "Quite the contrary. But how do you feel about ponies? Do you have any equine experience? Will it bother you to be around them?"

Brother Melvin shook his head. "I love horses, although from a purely artistic point of view. I think they're magnificent animals."

Father Terry nodded approvingly. "Being in the kitchen, you won't be expected to help out with them. But it certainly helps if they don't make you nervous."

"I'm sure they won't." The brother smiled. "Would you like me to cook today's breakfast? You could see if I pass muster before you make a decision about me."

"Our resident cook would appreciate the help."

"When do you usually eat?"

Father Terry looked at his watch. "Mass is over by 8 a.m. We change into our horse clothes after that to allow time for cook to burn our bacon and sausages."

Brother Melvin laughed. "Let's see if I can improve on that." He saw a flicker of doubt cross Father Terry's face. "If you're uncomfortable with my coming to Mass until you've spoken to Lady Rowland, I can wait in my car until it's over." He had a sudden thought. "Unless you have a kitchen garden for me to potter about in?"

"Thank you for your understanding, Brother Melvin. We can't be too careful these days. As it happens, we do have a kitchen garden – although it has seen better days. Let me take you there."

Three minutes later the SSPX brother was standing in the middle of what had once been a magnificent fruit, vegetable and herb garden.

"I'll be back to fetch you after Mass," said Father Terry. "I hope I can trust you to stay here until my return?"

"Of course." Brother Melvin chuckled. "You're welcome to lock me in, if you like."

"That won't be necessary."

Brother Melvin was surprised when Father Terry returned. "Have you really been gone thirty-five minutes?"

"Yes, why?"

"It feels as if you just left. I've been having the most wonderful time exploring your amazing herbs."

"I take it you know your sage from your basil?"

"Learned it from a herbal book written by one of the monks who lived in this very monastery."

"Are you serious?"

"Dead serious. It's called *The Useth of Plants in the Treatment of Human and Animal Ailments.*

"It was written by the Cistercian monks of Angelscombe in 1534, and the book's margins are filled with intricate illustrations of herbs and other plants that were in this garden. They're all described by Hugo Dujardin, the monk and cook who tended it.

"As the title suggests, the book prescribes herbal remedies for animals, including some for horses. In these dark times, when medication is hard to come by, we might be able to treat your ponies with what's here."

"That would be wonderful!" cried Father Terry. "We could use your help with one of our ponies right away."

"Oh? What's wrong with it?"

"I'll leave it to our resident vet, Pastor John, to explain it to you. But first, I think you agreed to make us breakfast?"

"Lead me to your kitchen!"

Chapter Five: Herbs & Horses

Sunday, 6th October 2030

Father Terry kept Brother Melvin out of sight in the kitchen, helping Father Oliver prepare breakfast. The latter was sworn to secrecy about a second chef's involvement, until the verdict was in about his cooking.

When, in the refectory, Father Oliver served sausages done just right in the oven; crispy, non-fatty bacon, and eggs scrambled to perfection, the priests looked at him with surprise and admiration.

"What's got into you today?" asked Father Fred. "This smells divine!"

"Did you finally find the recipe book?" derided Father Harry.

Even Father Godfrey spoke up. "I must say, you've outdone yourself this morning!"

Father Oliver glanced uncomfortably at Father Terry, who said, "Actually, gentlemen, we have a new cook. Or rather, someone who would like to be our new cook, if we agree to let him join our community."

"I'll fetch his suitcases!" said Father Fred.

"I'll show him to his new bedroom!" yelled Father Harry.

The others laughed. "So will we!"

"Then I take it he's welcome to reside with us?"

"Does that mean I'm fired from the kitchen?" Father Oliver asked hopefully.

"If you wish," Father Terry said gently. Surveying the men around the trestle table, he added, "Gentlemen, let him answer for himself, if you don't mind."

Father Oliver grinned. "That wonderful old man is the answer to my prayers!"

"Then please fetch him out and we'll introduce him to everyone. And tell him to bring a plate, so he can eat with us, if you would." Father Terry turned to the others. "But first, I must check his credentials and make sure he's not a mole from the New Church or the government. So please, no talking about sensitive issues in front of him."

"You're right, of course," said Father Godfrey. "But we do hope he'll be a permanent fixture."

A slightly stooped and smiling Brother Melvin came into the refectory, with Father Oliver carrying a spare plate.

"I give you Brother Melvin," said Father Terry, and everyone cheered.

Father Oliver led him to an empty chair and encouraged him to fill his plate.

Father Terry left briefly, and returned ten minutes later to whisper into the new brother's ear. "I hope you don't mind, but I telephoned the archbishop to establish his relationship to Lady Rowland and verify her details before calling her, and she has vouched for you." In a louder voice, he said, "Welcome aboard, Brother Melvin."

Everyone cheered, and the elderly man beamed. "Thank youl. I'll do my best not to let you down."

"That would be very difficult, after the cooking we're used to," said Father Harry, eliciting a ripple of laughter.

"I'm glad to wash my hands of you lot," Father Oliver said good-humouredly. He clapped a hand on Brother Melvin's shoulder. "Good luck, they're a tough crowd to please."

"I like a challenge," came the reply.

Father Terry turned to Pastor John. "Brother Melvin has a book from the time of Henry VIII, written by a monk who used to live here. It includes herbal remedies for horse issues."

"That's wonderful," said Pastor John.

Father Terry looked meaningfully at the minister, then said to the new brother, "Perhaps we can meet in my office after breakfast and go over what ailments your herbs can heal?"

"I would be most grateful for your input," Pastor John replied.

"I'd be happy to share what information I have," Brother Melvin said.

A short while later, several priests had fulfilled their offer to carry his suitcases into the monk's cell nearest the kitchen, and Brother Melvin was again sitting with Father Terry in his office. This time with Pastor John present.

On the large desk sat *The Useth of Plants in the Treatment of Human and Animal Ailments,* a large tome with heavy leather-bound covers.

Father Terry asked Pastor John, "Would you like to explain Trudy's situation?"

Brother Melvin listened as the minister told him about the old mare's signs of Cushing's, then began flicking through the pages of his ancient tome. "Hmm," he said, "the ailments are listed here in alphabetical order, but I don't see anything under Cushing's. Does it have other names?"

"PPID, or pituitary pars intermedia dysfunction," said Pastor John.

"That doesn't sound very medieval," replied Brother Melvin. "More likely it's a recently diagnosed disease." He pulled out his mobile. "Let me see what I can find out."

Sure enough, Cushing's was first discovered by the American neurosurgeon Harvey Cushing in 1912.

"That's disappointing," said Father Terry. "Then there won't be a herbal remedy for it."

"I'm sure there will," said the old man. "We simply need to conduct a little research."

The priest and minister waited hopefully while Brother Melvin typed into his phone.

"Voilà!" he said. "Oh, this *is* interesting. The herb used for Cushing's is definitely in my book. It's called monk's pepper – and I saw it in your kitchen garden."

"Makes sense, given the name," remarked Father Terry.

"More sense than you know." He grinned. "It was used to subdue the monks' libidos. Another name is chasteberry and it's Latin name is *vitex agnus castus*."

Pastor John frowned. "Can it really be used for Cushing's?"

"If the internet says so," replied the brother, with a chuckle. "Don't worry, there are several studies cited here, with respectable names attached to them. Let's be grateful that we have the herb on hand. While I have the book open, are there any other health concerns with your ponies?"

"Do you have anything to encourage milk production in our nursing mare?" asked Pastor John. "It wouldn't hurt to help her along a bit."

Brother Melvin rifled through the book and prodded one of the pages with a stubby index finger. "Here we are! Marigold, aka calendula. I'd be surprised if you have that growing on purpose in the garden, but it's bound to be growing wild on the property."

"Brother Melvin," exclaimed Father Terry, "you're going to be a real asset to our community!"

The brother gave a small bow. "I'm happy to hear it, Father. One always wishes to be of use." He closed the large tome and coughed delicately. "While you do have a wonderful kitchen garden, it *is* rather suffering from neglect. I was wondering …"

Father Terry said, "You'd like some help with weeding and such?"

"It would be most appreciated. I hate to play the age card, but there comes a time when bending over to pull out weeds, as well as picking herbs and vegetables on a regular basis, isn't quite what the doctor ordered."

"No problem. I'll make up a roster of helpers. Your cooking prowess will guarantee no resentment among the volunteers."

"You are most kind, Father. Thank you!" The old man took out a large white handkerchief and wiped his watery eyes.

His reaction made Father Terry glad he could give the elderly brother a home here at Angelscombe – and he looked forward to some wonderful meals.

Chapter Six: Brother Melvin Muses

Sunday, 6th October 2030

Brother Melvin's effects included two large statues, which he asked the priests to carry into the kitchen garden.

The five-foot Jesus was placed where He could keep a vigilant eye on the fruits and vegetables, while Mary, a few inches shorter than her Son, would reign supreme over the herb section.

However, the two figures arrived in disguise. Even more so than the cancelled priests of Angelscombe, Brother Melvin knew what it was like to live under the scrutiny of tyrannical progressives in the New Church. For many years, his society had been hounded for adhering to Catholic tradition, and he'd consequently learned to hide precious religious objects from the regime's spies.

And so the statues came into the garden masquerading as Father Time and Mother Earth. The waterproof camouflages fit snugly over the Sacred Heart of Our Lord and Immaculate Heart of Our Lady. The back zippers of the covers weren't noticeable after Brother Melvin placed tall bushy plants behind them.

He registered Father Oliver and Father Fred's puzzled expressions as they carried in these secular images, but they didn't ask for, and he didn't volunteer, an explanation. They'd find out the truth soon enough.

When the priests had left, Brother Melvin sat on the stone bench next to Father Time and gave a happy sigh. He was finally alone in this wonderful and expansive walled sanctuary; back in his element and his true calling. He loved the satisfying balance between cultivating God's plants under the broad Cotswold sky, and preparing the harvest in the kitchen.

He took the cover off Our Lord, and walked over to remove Mother Earth from Our Lady. Back on the stone bench next to Jesus, he folded the pagan outfits on his lap.

With a Sign of the Cross, he smiled first at Jesus, then His Mother. "Thank you both for my successful application to live here.

"At last I don't have to worry about being reported on for my traditional beliefs. What a relief to be among like-minded clergymen!

"Of course," he confided to Jesus, "it *would* be nice if they said the Latin Mass. But one can't have everything."

During breakfast, he'd discovered that the cancelled priests had only learned to celebrate the Novus Ordo Mass, the new Mass in the vernacular, against which the SSPX fought so hard. But he was heartened that they weren't averse to the Traditional Latin Rite; perhaps he could introduce them to it one day?

However, that would put them in more danger than they were in already; best to abandon that hope.

Surveying the weeds sprawling among the rows of carrots, parsnips, cabbages, strawberries and rhubarb, his thoughts wandered to his previous SSPX garden. An habitual worry returned to plague him; had he made a difference to *anyone at all* during his years of humble service to that community?

Granted, people enjoyed the food he prepared, but being a good cook hardly counted as aiding priests and brothers in their spiritual life – even if it were true that the way to a man's heart was through his stomach.

And here he was, in yet another post as cook. Nothing had changed, except that, unlike with those progressives at the retirement home, here he could share his 'backwardist' views.

He understood that he was supposed to evangelise through humble service. But how could he know whether he'd made a positive difference in anyone's life?

Chopping vegetables in the kitchen and picking herbs from the garden wasn't really spreading the Gospel. No one was ever going to walk up to him and say, "Brother Melvin, your wonderful food has brought me closer to God," or "Brother Melvin, your amazing meals have enriched my priestly life."

How he yearned to see the fruits of his efforts!

But God had assigned him the new task of nourishing this marginalised community, and he was grateful to escape that awful retirement place and put his skills to good use again.

"Jesus, Mary, please inspire me! Help me make their meals more interesting. Let me at least be thought of kindly, even if it's not for any spiritual reason."

Chapter Seven: Forewarned in a Dream

Sunday, 6th October 2030

Father Godfrey lay in bed that night after the first decent dinner he'd eaten since arriving at Angelscombe.

It wasn't that Chef Melvin, as they'd already dubbed him, used new and exotic foods. All the ingredients were familiar. It was how he prepared them which made the difference.

The roast potatoes were crisp and not swimming in grease: the carrots and Brussels sprouts were al dente, instead of a soggy mess, and the lamb was roasted to perfection.

For dessert, instead of watery rice pudding, they'd had sticky toffee pudding and custard – hot, not tepid.

The whole meal had looked and tasted divine.

As a result, Father Godfrey's stomach wasn't growling, as it usually did, from being unable to finish Father Oliver's offerings. Within ten minutes of sliding under the covers, he fell into a deep sleep.

Most of the time, his dreams were a jumble of disconnected events, that may or may not have any bearing on what had happened during the day. But tonight was different.

He was standing outside under a charcoal sky, admiring the beautiful full moon amid a million twinkling stars.

Suddenly, the stars vanished and the sun appeared, huge and menacing. Father Godfrey watched it hurtle with a wide, fiery tail towards the moon, which had morphed into another sun. He realised with horror that the two celestial entities were about to collide in a cosmic crash – right above him.

He was desperate to dive for cover and avoid the fallout from the impact, but he couldn't move his legs. Neither could he avert his eyes from the impending catastrophe.

The sun and moon-turned-sun smashed into each other. In the massive explosion, the smaller orb was crushed into tiny pieces, while glowing flares shot out at high speed from the still intact sun.

Father Godfrey used his hands to shield his face from the solar flames and shards plunging towards him with frightening velocity.

When he gathered the courage to peek between his fingers, the space debris had disappeared. The remaining sun was morphing into a massive Cross and, from the holes where the hands and feet of the Saviour were pierced with nails, great beams of light shone down upon the earth.

The ground shook violently beneath the frightened priest and he fell to his knees.

A deep voice spoke from the suspended Cross. "Godfrey, I am Jesus, the Risen Lord. Listen to what I tell you!"

"Here I am, Lord," the priest replied in a strangled whisper, echoing the words of Samuel.

"You are to warn your fellow priests, and everyone you encounter, about the imminent visitation of My Mercy upon the whole of mankind."

"But, Lord, I am not worthy! I'm not pure enough to be Your messenger!"

"Godfrey, I, the Lord, have chosen *you.*"

The priest was in a panic. He didn't have the strength for this mission! No one would listen to naïve Father

Godfrey. They'd say he was hallucinating – he'd be the laughing stock of the monastery.

"My Grace will be sufficient," the Lord replied to his unspoken fears.

Father Godfrey sighed; he had no choice in the matter. "Thy Will be done," he said meekly. "May I ask how we will know that Your Visitation is at hand?"

"Through the signs you just saw. Then the skies will peel back like a roof and reveal the flames of My Divine Mercy.

"Those fiery rays will penetrate every human soul and their sins will be shown them. They will see all their wrongdoings and insults toward their neighbours and Me.

"Give them to understand that this is not the Day of Judgement, it is a *Warning*, a last chance to let them know their sins can and will be forgiven, *if they repent and ask for forgiveness.* My Father in Heaven is permitting this Miracle, to ensure as many people as possible are able to enter My New Kingdom.

"This will be a cleansing. It will wake up My children and many will allow themselves to be enveloped in My Love.

"I will extend My Mercy to all who acknowledge the black state of their souls during the Warning, and *ask for It.*

"Alert everybody, Godfrey. Do not keep this knowledge to yourself!"

The priest swallowed hard. "I will do my best, Lord."

"Tell people to prepare. They must go to Confession every two weeks, keep blessed candles in the buildings and store enough food and water for ten days.

"Tell them to sprinkle every corner of their homes with Holy Water, to wear a Benedictine Cross and keep their Rosary beads close by.

"Pray also to St. Michael the Archangel, and keep holy objects in the home."

That's easy, Father Godfrey thought, *we already have those things at the monastery.*

"Godfrey!" boomed the Voice, "remember what I told you: this information is not only for you and your brother priests. You must spread the word to others!"

"Yes, Lord, I'm sorry."

"Trust in Me, Godfrey, and all will be well. I now leave you My Peace."

Father Godfrey slowly crossed himself as the Risen Lord and His massive glowing Cross faded away.

The fully restored moon returned to the sky, together with all the stars, and Father Godfrey rose from his knees, able to walk again.

He woke up covered in sweat.

Although he had read about the Great Warning, he'd never been sure it was something Catholics, especially priests, were allowed to take seriously.

But this dream was too vivid to be taken lightly. God was telling him to get ready, and prepare others, for His coming Visitation.

Clutching his Rosary, he made the Sign of the Cross again and began to recite the Our Father and Hail Mary to calm himself down. At the same time, he begged for the graces needed for the difficult task ahead.

Then he opened the notes app of his mobile, and wrote down every detail of the phenomena in the sky, and Christ's words.

Preparation for the Warning would include stocking enough food for the Dales ponies, too, he reflected.

For sure, the others would scoff at him when he told them about this. But Noah was laughed at, too, and Father Godfrey knew he must do his duty and alert everybody to what was coming. After that, it was up to them whether they heeded God's Words.

A sudden frisson of excitement ran through his body; this was his chance to be a hero! He longed to perform heroic acts for Christ, even to the point of martyrdom, in reparation for his daily struggle against mortal sin.

The moment had come to achieve his dearest wish, and this thought strengthened him.

Chapter Eight: Lucius II
Monday, 7th October 2030

Fired with enthusiasm to deliver Jesus' message, Father Godfrey was brimming with courage when he entered the refectory for breakfast the next morning.

Time was of the essence, for he knew his bravado would dwindle the longer he left the job undone.

Fortified by the tantalising aroma of expertly cooked sausages and bacon, he sat down and waited for everyone to be seated before announcing his big news.

But instead of quietly taking their places, they were talking excitedly about another news flash from the Vatican. A new pope had been elected overnight!

While Father Godfrey was dreaming about the Warning, it appeared his brother priests had been avidly checking their mobile phones for the latest from Rome.

Embarrassed at being out of the loop, he said nothing until Father Terry asked him outright, "You're very quiet, Godfrey. What do *you* think about our new pope?"

He hedged. "Isn't it a bit early to speculate?"

Father Terry chuckled. "Always fair-minded – an admirable quality."

Father Godfrey squirmed at this unmerited praise. "What do we really know about him?"

"That's just the thing, isn't it?" said Father Terry. "No one has ever heard of the man. Was he even a cardinal before the conclave met?"

"What do you mean?"

"Well, surely we'd know about this guy if he'd been a cardinal for any length of time. Especially if he was papal material – don't you think?"

Father Harry, the harness trainer, nodded. "*I'm* worried about his choice of name. *Lucius* is a little too close to *Lucifer* for my liking, and the election was conducted during the hours of darkness. Don't you find that rather alarming?"

"Interesting you should say that," said Father Fred. "Have you seen this unconfirmed report about what happened when this pope's election was announced?

"Lightning struck the chimney over the Sistine Chapel as the white smoke was rising out of it. I'd say that supports your worries about the new pope."

"But we've already had a Pope Lucius," Father Godfrey protested, "so he will be Pope Lucius II. The name does come from the Latin word for light, after all. Maybe, following the darkness the last pontiff spread over the Faith, this one will be a beacon of light?"

Father Terry frowned deeply. "Gentlemen," he said slowly, his eyes on his mobile. "I don't think the new pope will be a beacon of light – rather the opposite. He's wasted no time in setting the tone of his pontificate. Only two hours after waving to the crowd in St. Peter's Square, he signed a papal document allegedly resulting from the deliberations of the current synod."

"What's in it?" Father Godfrey asked anxiously. Could things get any worse for the Catholic Church?

"I've just pulled it up, too. *Nova Theologica Populi*," said Father Harry. "This is appalling!" he cried.

"And look at this!" exclaimed Father Oliver. "There's a report going round that at the very moment Pope Lucius II signed the document, two bolts of lightning struck the halo of St. Peter's statue in the Basilica *and* the hand holding the keys to the Kingdom. They were both knocked off!"

"Didn't that statue suffer damage under the previous pope?" asked Father Harry. "If I remember correctly, the halo and hand have come off before."

"Yes," replied Father Oliver. "It says here that he had them replaced after they 'mysteriously' fell off. But supposedly, that previous incident was witnessed by hundreds of visitors to the Vatican. It happened at 3 p.m. on a clear day when two bolts of lightning came out of nowhere and did the damage."

"This recurrence has to be rather embarrassing for the new pope," said Father Harry. "He has three weird incidents to explain away."

"I'm sure he'll find someone to scientifically rationalise them," Father Fred said. "In the meantime, we can be sure he'll push this awful new document of his."

Father Terry said, "Before we examine it in detail, let's eat our breakfast, so lovingly prepared by Brother Melvin. We'll go through the articles on a full stomach. And plenty of coffee."

The clergymen nodded soberly.

As they ate in nervous silence, Father Godfrey felt this was not the moment to bring up the subject of the imminent Warning. He hoped Jesus would forgive him for the delay.

When breakfast was over, and the plates were cleared and the dishwasher was running, everyone, including Pastor John and Brother Melvin, sat at the trestle table with a second cup of coffee.

Father Terry suggested they each pull up the papal document on their phones and read it through calmly and quietly, before sharing their views.

Even Father Godfrey, who tried to see things in the best possible light, could find nothing positive in it.

His misgivings began when reading the summary.

NOVA THEOLOGIA POPULI

1. **The Pope is Infallible in Everything He Says and Does**
2. **The Church is a Democracy**
3. **Everyone Is Saved.**
4. **Denying This Truth Is Hate Speech**
5. **Prohibition of Evangelization**
6. **Revised Teaching on Sin**
7. **Conservation of Mother Earth**
8. **Abolition of Daily Mass**
9. **Abolition of Priestly Celibacy**
10. **Abolition of the Novus Ordo Mass**
11. **The New Role of Confession**
12. **Women's Role in the New Church**
13. **On Keeping the Sabbath Holy**

No one spoke for a full fifteen minutes, and Father Godfrey knew he wasn't alone in his consternation at this radical departure from the teachings of Mother Church.

Everything he'd been taught and held dear his whole life was being obliterated by the new pope, who'd only been in office a matter of hours!

Could Father Terry be right? Had the previous pope been eliminated by the Vatican hierarchy to make way for a new regime that wearied of waiting for him to pass their progressive reforms? Had this document been drawn up days, even weeks, ago and been rejected by the now deceased pope, leading to his hastened demise?

And what audacity to call it the 'people's new theology'! The people weren't consulted in drafting this

– nor *should* they ever decide what constituted Catholic theology.

It was the non-Catholic pastor who spoke first. "This is clearly the work of the Devil."

"Pope Paul VI did warn us that the smoke of Satan had entered the Vatican," remarked Father Oliver.

"Now it's way more than smoke," Father Terry said. "All the fires of Hell seem to have been set ablaze in there."

There was a general murmur of "Hear, hear!"

Brother Melvin said, "Surely, there'll be a backlash? The faithful aren't going to take this lying down."

"Don't you see?" said Father Terry. "The faithful have been carefully softened in preparation for this. First came the plague, as a dummy run to see if the world population could be cowed into submission by the secular authorities. And then, we Catholics were told it was 'charitable' to take abortion-tainted vaccines.

"After that, almost all the bishops closed down the churches and refused to administer the sacraments, even to the sick and dying, for fear they themselves would die. Where was their faith in Jesus? Why did they cling to this life instead of shepherding their flock and saving their souls for the next? They turned their backs on the faithful, and on the Sacraments which we have always taught are indispensable.

"And now, having got the faithful used to the idea that they're *not* that important, it's been an easy step to persuade them that non-attendance at Sunday Mass isn't a mortal sin, and from there, to believe sin and the Devil don't exist at all.

"And here we are, per Article 13 of this document, only expected to attend state services once a month.

"What was good is considered evil, and vice versa.

"And, by the way, no one was granted attendance at the current Extraordinary Synod, unless they'd taken this latest round of 'preventative' medicine."

Pastor John said, "This time around, freshly aborted foetuses are being used to produce *each* batch."

Brother Melvin added, "There'll be even more injuries and deaths than last time." He tapped his mobile. "In connection with that, just look at Article 7, Conservation of Mother Earth: 'The Church is obligated to lead the way in reducing the human population by several billion, to allow Mother Earth to restore herself and recover from the iniquities imposed on her by man.'

"Tell me that isn't a thinly veiled justification for killing off as many people as possible."

Father Godfrey winced. He didn't feel comfortable criticising his Church superiors – even if he suspected there was an element of truth in what was being said.

"This business of the pope being infallible in everything he says and does in Article 1 is most worrying," said Father Fred. "Where is his humility? As a human being, he isn't infallible at all, and he's supposed to be the servant of the servants, in the service of God the Father, not a dictator."

Father Fred snorted in derision. "And yet in the next breath he says the Church is a democracy!"

"And how can this be the Church of Christ when the obligation to go to Mass on Sunday has been removed?" wailed Father Oliver.

"And now even the new Mass has been destroyed!" cried Brother Melvin.

"And what about Article 13 which says these articles are subject to revision from time to time, to address 'more errors from the Old Church and accommodate the everchanging needs of the people'?" Father Harry held his head in his hands. "What have they done to our One, Holy, Catholic and Apostolic Church?"

Father Terry sighed. "You know what this means, don't you? There's no longer any hope of our being reinstated to our parishes with this man in charge."

Father Godfrey shook his head mournfully: the future looked bleak indeed.

Lord, these men are already so dispirited. How can I broach the subject of the Warning now? It's going to be even harder than before for us to safely spread the word about it under this new pope.

Chapter Nine: Preaching through Ponies

Monday, 7th October 2030

A despondent Father Terry left the breakfast table with Pastor John and Fathers Godfrey, Fred and Harry to don barn clothes and continue their pony chores.

The clergymen came to the bigger stable that housed the new foal and his dam. On seeing the vet, the mare looked up and nickered.

The minister laughed. "Yes, Ruby, I have treats for you as a reward for being such a good mother." He fished in his overalls pocket and drew out a piece of apple, which she delicately removed from the palm of his hand.

He rubbed her forehead. "Ready to go out and enjoy the sunshine?"

Father Terry stood back with the others to let the pastor go into the stable and put on the mare's halter. Then he led her out across the grass courtyard towards the paddocks.

With a high-pitched whinny and a little buck of protest, the colt ran after her. Ruby answered with a reassuring nicker and he settled down on her right side.

Father Terry could tell the other priests were as enchanted by the sight as he was. It gave him great joy to see such an innocent soul follow the parent he trusted so completely.

The same way we are supposed to trust You, Lord, he mused.

Pastor John released the mare into the field. With a backward glance to make sure her foal was at foot, she trotted around the perimeter fence, neighing as she went.

Some ponies answered from their stables, where they were waiting to be let into the adjoining pasture.

The colt kept up with his mother, long spindly legs striding out and little head high.

"He's showing off!" cried Father Fred.

"He has a lot to be proud of," replied Father Terry. "Our foundation foal."

"I assume he'll be kept entire?" said Father Harry.

"That's the plan," said Father Terry. "Unless he shows some undesirable characteristic, we'll keep him for breeding."

"But Dales ponies don't normally have undesirable traits, do they?" Father Godfrey said. "I thought that was their main asset – apart from their strength, that is."

Pastor John said, "You're right. This breed is known for its good work ethic, courage and playfulness – even when older. And they're docile and eager to please."

More whinnies from the occupants of the loose boxes reminded the men they had work to do.

Soon all the ponies were out at grass. The feed buckets were washed, evening meals made up, the water buckets refilled, and hay piled onto wheelbarrows to distribute to the animals and supplement the nutrition-poor winter grass.

When all these tasks were completed, the men reconvened in the tack room and sat around the scruffy coffee table in the middle. Upon it lay a manila folder containing details of that day's scheduled activities.

Father Terry opened it. "Father Godfrey, you'll be giving young Tony Brenton a lesson on Black Pepper."

Father Godfrey nodded.

"How far have you got with his Catechism?"

"We're onto the Third Commandment."

Private riding lessons were the perfect opportunity for giving surreptitious religious instruction, when parents allowed. The Catholic hierarchy had scrapped the Catechism of Pope St. John Paul II several years ago. It was deemed too rigid in its interpretation of the Ten Commandments, and was in the process of being overhauled.

Unfortunately, the definition of 'too rigid' continued to expand, and the Vatican was having a difficult time coming to a consensus on exactly *how* the Commandments ought to be understood. Since the process was an ongoing work-in-progress and showed no sign of being resolved, the priests of Angelscombe had taken the opportunity to fill the void with the true Deposit of Faith.

Using activities with the ponies as cover for transmitting traditional Catholicism, the priests at Angelscombe quietly continued to do the work of saving souls they had been ordained for.

There was always the risk of a progressive parent posing as a traditional Catholic and reporting on them to the bishop. But this did not deter them, and so far had not happened.

However, with the signing of this new and disturbing document by the freshly-elected pope, the consequences of being discovered in the act of transmitting the truths of the Catholic faith were more severe than before.

The wording of Article 5. Prohibition of Evangelisation left no room for doubt as to the animosity of the Vatican towards actual teaching of the Faith: 'Any attempt to force the old religion on anyone will be punishable to the full extent of New Church Law.'

And yet, as had been the case with many declarations of the previous pope, the wording was confusing. What constituted 'forcing'? If a child was willing to be taught, surely that couldn't be considered forcing. But Father Terry knew the parent would be accused of forcing the child and the priest would be blamed for aiding and abetting the crime.

And what was understood by 'the old religion'? Pre-conciliar Catholicism? Post-conciliar Catholicism, prior to this papal declaration? The religion from the days of the Latin Mass, or of the suddenly defunct Novus Ordo Mass?

One thing was sure; whatever religion he and his group of cancelled priests adhered to would automatically be rejected as old.

And what exactly *was* the punishment under "the full extent of the New Church Law"? No definition was given, but one wrong move and the priests at Angelscombe would quickly find out.

Father Terry groaned. Their work of evangelisation was even more difficult, now that the new pope and his henchmen had publicly joined the New World Order and subscribed to a New World Religion. In their minds, the Catholic Church founded by Christ was dead.

Yet they were mistaken. Man had attempted to murder Catholicism for over two thousand years. Man murdered her Founder, too. But the Catholic Church is His Body – and therefore indestructible; she continues to rise from the ashes, just as He did.

Father Terry wondered; were he and his cohorts destined to be burnt to ashes? Then so be it. Until that time, they would continue to spread the Gospel through any means available.

Father Godfrey cut into these deliberations. "Terry, how do we navigate the new pope's statement that our Sunday Mass obligation has morphed into a duty to attend official Church services once a month? And what about the electronic tracking system they plan to implement to make sure – sorry, 'let us know' – we've fulfilled our monthly requirement? That's going to apply to us, isn't it, as well as everyone in the village?"

Pastor John said, unhelpfully, "This is where being Lutheran comes in jolly handy."

The other priests groaned at him.

"How nice for *you*," said Father Harry. "We still have our *daily* Mass obligation, let alone weekly. But are we going to clock in once a month to the official service? And should we submit to electronic tracking?"

Father Terry sighed. "Gentlemen, I suggest we give ourselves time to think about these new rules in private first. We'll get together later and thrash out a plan of action.

"Meanwhile, let's continue as we have in the past, teaching the traditional truths of our faith." He turned to Father Godfrey. "Little Tony will continue to be taught his Catechism." To Father Harry he said, "Three parishioners have volunteered to help you muck out the stalls. The first one is coming at 10 o'clock."

'Mucking out stalls' was the cover for administering the Sacrament of Reconciliation. The penitent stood in the stable, pitchfork in hand, looking busy if anyone should walk by, while confessing his or her sins to the priest, who was scooping up the soiled bedding and throwing it into a wheelbarrow. Except, of course, when it was time to grant Absolution.

Father Harry nodded.

"Father Fred, you have an appointment at 10:30 with Jacob Masters for another trimming lesson."

Jacob Masters owned a couple of horses which he wanted to transition from shod to barefoot, and Father Fred was showing him the ropes on the Dales ponies, which were all barefoot.

Jacob was also going through a very painful period in his life, and these sessions were an opportunity for clandestine spiritual direction.

Father Fred smiled. "Very good, Father."

"Pastor John, I think you wanted to look into that herbal remedy you discussed with Brother Melvin?"

"Indeed I do, Father. He's going to show me how to recognise and prepare the herb he was talking about."

"Good. Father Oliver, since you no longer have kitchen duty, I was hoping you'd prepare another begging letter to the government for more funds. We need extra hay for the winter."

"Happy to do it," he replied, "although we know it's unlikely to be successful."

Father Terry grimaced. "I agree. But we have to give it one more stab before I sell something valuable to get the money we need."

"I hope you don't still have your eye on those candlesticks," warned Father Godfrey.

"I may have no choice. Let's just hope Father Oliver's letter is persuasive enough." He looked down at the folder. "My main task for today is afternoon tea with Mrs. Prince." She was an elderly lady in Father Terry's old parish, still devastated by his removal as her pastor. She invited him regularly 'to tea', that is, to say Mass in her living room, attended by a few trustworthy friends.

"Just before that," he said, "I'm going to introduce young Drumbley to the saddle."

Drumbley was a three-year-old Dales, ready to commence her education as a riding pony.

"O.K. gentlemen, we have our starting orders," declared Father Terry. "May God bless our efforts today and grant us success in glorifying Him."

Chapter Ten: Sounding the Alarm

Monday, 7th October 2030

Father Godfrey walked alongside the fifteen-year-old Dales pony named Black Pepper. Ten-year-old Tony Brenton was on board and, true to her breed, the mare was showing enormous patience with her rider.

The priest expended as much effort on getting the young man to stop pulling on Pepper's mouth as on teaching him the *Fidei Depositum*, outlined under Pope St. John Paul II in the Catechism of the Catholic Church.

The child's mother was leaning against the arena railings in rapt attention.

"What is the Third Commandment of the Decalogue?" he asked Tony.

"What's the Decalogue?"

"Last week we said 'decalogue' is a word combining the Greek for 'ten' and the Greek for 'word'. It means 'the ten words'. By which is also meant the Ten Commandments."

"But there are more than ten words in the Ten Commandments," the astute boy responded.

"You are absolutely right, young man. But think of each of the ten words as meaning each of the Ten Commandments. Pepper is not going to turn left if you yank on her left rein. Remember how I told you the proper way to do it?"

Tony thought for a moment, then opened the inside left rein – without pulling back, the priest was happy to note – and let the outside rein rest on the right side of the pony's neck, while looking in the direction of the turn.

Pepper quietly moved as required, and Father Godfrey said, "So what is the Third Commandment of the Decalogue?"

A look of concentration crossed the boy's face, then he said triumphantly, "Keep the sabbath day holy!"

"Good man! And what day is the sabbath, for Catholics?"

"Sunday!"

"Excellent! Put your hands together again and keep light contact with Pepper's mouth. Don't keep them rigid. And how do we keep the sabbath holy?"

"We go to Mass and we don't work."

"Very good! And why do Catholics go to Mass on Sunday, not Saturday, the original sabbath day of the Jews?"

"Because it's the day when Jesus rose from the dead," came the prompt reply. "Can I please trot now?"

Once the lesson was over and Tony had brushed off the pony, turned her out, and left with his mother, Father Godfrey's thoughts returned to that awful document signed by Lucius II.

Here he was, teaching young Tony the Third Commandment, while the new pope was busy getting rid of it.

He could feel the Lord telling him that He wasn't going to delay the Warning much longer. Father Godfrey needed to get the word out.

As always. before an important undertaking, he retired to the chapel to pray for help from Our Lady as well as her Son.

He slipped behind the high stack of bales by the back wall of the hay barn and punched in the door code. Making sure no one from the outside world was watching, he entered the chapel and closed the door behind him.

An immediate sense of peace flooded him while he walked up the short aisle to genuflect in front of the golden tabernacle. It contained the consecrated hosts and rested in a niche carved out of the massive stone slab behind the magnificent altar.

Above the tabernacle, chiselled into the stone, hung Christ Crucified, with Mary on His left and the Apostle John to His right. On either side of the Cross were six Apostles, including St. John. The magnificent ensemble was based on the altar in the Sacré-Cœur Basilica in Mont Martre.

Since it was against the back wall, the priests faced *ad orientem* when celebrating the Novus Ordo Mass.

Father Godfrey knelt in the first pew and made the Sign of the Cross, fixing his eyes on the Crucifix.

Lord, I am not worthy to deliver this message, but may it be done according to Thy Will. Please grant me the words to be persuasive!

He gazed at Mary's statue in an alcove to the left. She stood radiant in a white robe and blue veil, holding the Child Jesus in her arms.

Most Blessed Virgin Mary, please shelter me under your mantle and keep me strong in my resolve to carry out your Son's mission!

The lunch bell rang: it was time.

The clerics stood behind their chairs in the refectory, staring in amazement at their replete plates, and fully meant their prayers of gratitude for the meal when Father Terry led Grace.

Father Godfrey couldn't wait to dive into the food presented so artfully by Brother Melvin, and emitting such delicious aromas. Roast mutton with mint sauce, roast parsnips, carrots, and potatoes dauphinoise greeted his hungry gaze.

As they sat down, Father Terry said, "Brother Melvin, you're spoiling us."

"But please, don't stop!" Father Fred quickly added.

Brother Melvin's face glowed with pleasure.

This wonderful repast is putting everyone in a good humour, realised Father Godfrey. *They'll be more receptive to my message.* He offered a prayer of thanks to Our Lady for smoothing his path.

Once a few mouthfuls had been eaten, he cleared his throat.

Father Terry looked at him. "Did you want to say something?"

Feeling like a child about to tell his parents he'd just seen a Yeti in the garden, Father Godfrey swallowed hard to calm his nerves.

"What is it?" his friend persisted.

"I know this is going to sound rather bizarre, but last night I had a dream. Actually, it was more like a vision."

He had everybody's attention now.

"Go on," said Father Terry.

"It was about the Warning. The sun clashed with the moon, which had turned into a second sun, and a huge, luminous Cross appeared in the heavens. Jesus spoke to me from that Cross, telling me to warn you that the Illumination of Conscience is coming very soon."

"We all know that a thousand years are like one day for God, and vice versa," said Father Harry kindly. "But I don't suppose Jesus gave you an actual date, did He?"

"Unfortunately not." Father Godfrey shook his head miserably.

"What were His exact words?" asked Brother Melvin.

"'You are to warn your fellow priests and all whom you encounter about the imminent visitation of My Mercy upon the whole of mankind.'"

"That puts a different complexion on it," said Father Terry. "When the Lord says imminent, He doesn't just mean 'sometime in the future'."

Father Godfrey looked at him gratefully. "Don't you find it interesting that I should get this message at the very moment when the Catholic Church has moved into an even more perilous state than before, with that declaration of the *Nova Theologica Populi*?"

"You're absolutely right," said Father Oliver. "God is patient, but at some point, His Patience runs out."

Father Godfrey continued, "Our Lady has recently said that the present times are like the days of Noah and Sodom and Gomorrah put together. And look what happened to *them*!

"But in His Loving Kindness, Christ is giving us one more chance to repent and acknowledge Him as Lord."

The priest explained how fiery rays of Divine Mercy were going to fall from the sky and penetrate every human soul, revealing their sins to them – *everything* they had done against God and their fellowmen.

"Jesus stressed that it would be a warning, not the Day of Judgement, and a chance to know that, *if we repent and ask for forgiveness*, our sins can and will be forgiven.

"Jesus promised to extend His Mercy to anyone who, during the Warning, accepts the black state of their soul and asks for His Forgiveness."

The men around the table had stopped eating.

Pastor John said, "Did He say anything else?"

Father Godfrey nodded. "Yes. In preparation, we need to go to Confession every two weeks and keep blessed candles in the buildings. We must sprinkle every corner of our homes with Holy Water and wear a Benedictine Cross, as well as keep our Rosaries nearby.

"And we also have to store enough food and water for ten days."

"That means for the ponies, too," Father Terry said. "You said we are tasked with spreading this message?"

"Yes. We are under obligation to warn everyone we know."

"Then there is no time to lose, my brothers in Christ. For we can be sure that Satan will do all he can to prevent us."

Chapter Eleven: Father Abnus Doyal

Monday, 7th October 2030

The clergymen finished their meal in pensive silence and Father Terry shifted uncomfortably in his seat. How black was his soul?

Brother Melvin gathered up the plates to take into the kitchen and Father Terry said, "Let's think about ways to get the word out to our parishioners, without our enemies finding out. We can discuss ideas over supper this evening."

They dispersed to perform their afternoon chores, and Father Terry asked Father Godfrey, "Do you have anything pressing right now? I need some help backing young Drumbley before I visit Mrs. Prince."

"I'm happy to lend a hand," his friend said.

"Thank you. It should be straightforward."

To keep Drumbley's mind off Father Terry, who was on the mounting block leaning across the saddle, Father Godfrey offered the pony small cubes of sweet potato.

The black animal didn't care at all about the weight on her back, so Father Terry said, "Time to get on, I think."

There was still no reaction from the pony as Father Terry swung gently into the saddle. He held the reins lightly, while Father Godfrey took the lead rope, attached to the halter resting over the bridle, and led Drumbley around the sand arena without touching her mouth. Rein contact would come later, when the pony was comfortable carrying a rider.

While Father Terry was sitting quietly, in order not to upset the Dales' balance, he became aware of a figure standing by the arena fence, wearing a black jacket and cleric's white collar.

"Godfrey, who's that, watching us?"

"I've never seen him before." He led the pony and rider over to the man.

"Can we help you?" asked Father Terry.

"I hope so. I'm Father Abnus Doyal. I've just been appointed manager of the new Fell Pony Project, your sister programme a few miles down the road in Lambcot. Is either of you the manager of the Dales Project here?"

"That would be me," said Father Terry, from the saddle. "Forgive my not shaking your hand, but it's my first time riding this pony, and I don't want to startle her."

"That's quite alright." The man stretched out his hand to Father Godfrey. "Pleased to meet you. I understand you've just bred a new foal."

"That's correct," said Father Godfrey.

The priest continued to address him. "I'd love to see it, if I may?"

Father Godfrey appeared uneasy. "I'm sure we can arrange that sometime soon."

"Well, since I'm already here, perhaps we could do it now?"

Father Terry didn't know why, but he took an instant dislike to this visitor. Coughing delicately to prise the priest's attention away from Father Godfrey, he said, "It will be quite a while before we're finished with this backing session." He also wanted the man out of the way so he could visit Mrs. Prince in secret.

"Oh, I can wait. I've nothing urgent to do."

"I'd have expected you to have a lot on your plate, if you've just taken over the management of the Fell Project," Father Terry said, in a not-so-friendly tone.

Father Doyal gave him a brilliant smile. "I have wonderful staff, whom I trust completely. They've got everything under control."

Then why do they need you? Father Terry was tempted to ask. But out loud, he said, "Then we'll get on with our work. Father Godfrey, let's see how Drumbley copes with a few gentle turns."

Helped by frequent strokes on her nose and neck, the pony remained calm throughout the next five minutes, after which Father Terry could no longer stand Father Doyal's skulking presence. "Godfrey, she's been very good. Let's call it a day. I'll see if she'll let me slide off her back in here."

His friend stood by the pony's head, ready to intervene if the animal showed signs of nervousness. But Drumbley didn't move while Father Terry pulled his feet out of the stirrups and slowly leaned forward, before pivoting to the right and leaning across the saddle in order to slide softly to the ground.

There was a ripple of applause from Father Doyal. "She's a cracking little pony," he said. "What a good girl."

Irrationally annoyed by this comment, Father Terry forced a smile. "Yes, she's a good example of her breed."

He ran up the stirrups and loosened the girth. Walking alongside Father Godfrey towards the arena gate, which Father Doyal opened for them, Father Terry caught a whiff of aftershave as he passed the visiting priest. It was thoroughly inappropriate in a man of the cloth.

Ashamed of his judgementalism, he prayed, *I'm sorry, Lord, I don't know this man, and I'm sure I'm being unfair. He's a child of God like all of us.*

Determined to be more civil, he said, "Give us five minutes and we'll be ready to show you our new foal."

Father Doyal followed them back to the barn and offered to help Father Godfrey with untacking the pony.

"There's no need," said Father Godfrey.

"I like to be useful," Father Doyal replied with a half-smile.

Father Terry was grateful the man didn't ask to help him brush down the pony and pick out her feet. But he did make a comment on Drumbley's lack of shoes.

"All our Fell ponies are shod at the front," he said in a reproachful tone.

"Why's that, then?" said Father Terry.

"I'd have thought it was obvious. To protect their feet from hard surfaces."

"But God gave them hooves for that. They don't need extra help from us."

"God didn't intend them to carry the weight of a rider on their back, thus increasing the burden on their front hooves. They need metal shoes for added support."

Father Terry gave him an insincere smile. "It looks as if our perspectives differ."

"But surely, there can only be one right perspective?"

"I completely agree."

"So you see it my way, then?"

"No." With a slight chuckle, Father Terry said, "Let me show you the new foal."

The priest looked around. "Father Godfrey, you're coming, too, I trust?"

The priest could not refuse without being rude. "Of course," he said.

As the three men walked to the far paddock, Father Doyal said, "Have you seen the document from our new pope yet?"

"Yes, we saw it this morning." Father Terry's words were suddenly guarded.

"What do you think of it?" The question was directed more to Father Godfrey.

"How do you mean?"

Father Terry was glad to note that his friend also understood the need to tread carefully with this stranger.

"Some of the decrees have been a long time coming."

"Such as?" challenged Father Terry.

"Well," said Father Doyal, "for example, Article 6: the revised teaching on sin."

Father Terry saw Father Godfrey's face redden at this allusion to 'sins below the waist,' which had been demoted from mortal to venial by the new pope.

"Is that revision a good or a bad thing?" Father Terry asked.

"Surely, it has to be a good thing! And number 9; the abolition of celibacy for priests. It was about time that got changed!"

Father Terry's ire was rising as Father Doyal continued. "But I forgot, your community is made up of cancelled priests, isn't it? So you're not really bound by the Catholic Church's teachings anymore."

Father Terry fought hard to keep his temper. This man was not one of them; he was obviously a progressive and avid member of the New Church.

Mild-mannered Father Godfrey saved his friend from saying something he might regret. "Father Doyal, I assure you, that although we've been cancelled, we are still faithful priests, and dedicated followers of the traditions of the Catholic Church."

Father Doyal gave him a benevolent smile. "But, my dear Godfrey, isn't that precisely why you've been cancelled?"

Father Terry bristled at this familiarity and felt for Father Godfrey, who was blushing at Father Doyal's accurate assessment of their status.

Unabashed, Father Doyal continued, "But if you embrace the new pope's theology, you can be reinstated. Surely, you realise that?"

"Thank you for clarifying the situation for us," said Father Terry, without a trace of sarcasm. They'd reached the far paddock. "Now, let me show you our first breeding success."

"Wonderful!" said Father Doyal.

For someone who'd supposedly come to see the new foal, he spent very little time admiring the little fellow, who was suckling off his dam and happily flicking his short, fluffy tail from side to side.

He did, however, have the grace to say, "He's a healthy-looking chap, isn't he?" He then looked at Father Godfrey and changed the subject. "By the way, I hear your kitchen garden was very famous in its day. Any chance of taking me to see it? I might get some ideas for one at our place."

Father Godfrey pointed him in the direction of the main building. "It's in that walled area, to the left."

"Aren't you going to show it to me?" The disappointment in the priest's voice was unmistakable.

"I must get on, I'm afraid, Father Doyal," Father Godfrey replied. "I'm already behind on my chores."

"Another time, perhaps?"

Father Godfrey gave him a wan smile.

Father Terry positioned himself slightly between the two men. "This is a very busy farm, Father, and we have much to do. Enjoy your visit to the garden. I hope it inspires you."

Father Terry watched the man's receding back, not wishing to see him again. There was something not quite right about his interest in Father Godfrey.

Chapter Twelve: Stirrings

Monday, 7th October 2030

Father Godfrey also felt relief at Father Doyal's departure. He disliked the priest's air of self-congratulation at not being cancelled like the Angelscombe clergy.

In addition, he belonged to the progressive sect that was destroying the traditions of the Catholic Church and creating havoc for faithful priests like himself.

Which made it even more distressing to Father Godfrey to discover he was physically attracted to the man.

He bade Father Terry a swift farewell and walked with resolute strides to the hay barn. He urgently needed to talk to Our Lady about this; the afternoon tasks would have to wait.

He was pleased no one else was in the chapel; he wanted to be alone with his shame.

He genuflected and slid into the second pew. Ignoring the kneeler, he sank to his knees on the bare flagstones, and folded his hands in prayer, without allowing himself to rest his arms on the back of the pew in front.

Mary, I'm so sorry! I've let you down. I've succeeded for so long in squashing my attraction to other men and now look at me! A priest comes along who is a clear enemy of the True Church and arouses passions in me that I thought I'd overcome!

The more his patellae complained about the hardness of the floor and his back hurt from staying upright without any support, the longer he was determined to stay in that painful position. He must atone for his wickedness. Maybe, Our Lady would accept his suffering in mitigation for the punishments due to him for his base emotions, and intercede for him to Jesus?

Please, O Virgin Mary, I offer this small sacrifice to You and Your Son, and beg You Both to help me overcome the evil inside me.

Then sudden new hope flickered. Maybe Pope Lucius II's new decrees really *were* in line with Catholic teaching, and God really *was* loosening up His tight rules? How wonderful it would be to give into his inclinations without remorse!

But Father Godfrey well knew that the Truth is unchangeable and unchanging. God hadn't changed His Mind; Man was changing *his* mind about obeying Him.

He recognised that Satan was attacking him right here in the chapel, deliberately diverting his attention away from prayer and toward immorality.

Forgive me, Lord! You know that I seek martyrdom in expiation for this sin of attraction – and especially attraction to a man who is not a good priest! Please, help me!

Ten minutes later, a different guilt accosted him: he was shirking his duties on the farm. He rose and rubbed his sore knees, still hoping his time on the floor would count for something with Jesus and His Mother.

As he exited the chapel, he tried his hardest to push the image of the handsome and dangerous Father Doyal out of his head.

Father Abnus Doyal strolled towards the kitchen garden whistling a tune to himself. He'd have liked the young and good-looking Father Godfrey by his side, and yet his visit to Angelscombe wasn't a total loss.

He'd enjoyed rattling the two traditional priests. Everybody knew that the cancelled clergymen had been given the job of preserving the Dales pony breed to keep them busy doing something useful for Mother Earth, instead of bellyaching about their predicament in the public sphere and creating schism within the Catholic Church.

And, being in charge of government funds, they had to account for every penny. Woe betide them if there was even a whiff of misappropriation! And Rome would happily take any other opportunity to defrock them, and probably excommunicate them into the bargain.

It had been fun to see the priests' reactions when he mentioned the *Nova Theologica Populi*. He knew full well how it upset their precious morals. Serve them right for being so sanctimonious, with their slavish adherence to an outmoded ''Deposit of Faith'.

But the icing on the cake was meeting Father Godfrey.

It was a long time since Father Doyal had encountered such a desirable man. His parents, both atheists, had known about his proclivities early on and suggested he join the priesthood, where he could act on them in a sheltered environment.

When he'd protested that he didn't believe in God, they told him neither did most of the men in the seminary. He would be in good company.

And so it had proved. Those formative years had been glorious fun.

Then he'd been sent to a tiny parish as the only priest, and the fun stopped. His parishioners were widows and old men, and he longed for his old seminary buddies.

It wasn't long before the church was closed for lack of parishioners and as part of a general 'consolidation' of churches in the diocese to pave the way for the New Church.

Father Doyal needed a new job. Bishop Hardy, using the example of Angelscombe, had cosied up to the government and got a grant to start a Fell Pony Protection Programme. This second earth-saving project would put the bishop in further good standing with the pope.

Father Doyal was put in charge. But, to his dismay, instead of cancelled priests hired to staff it, a bunch of pony-mad girls and women had been brought in. The place was swimming with them! The only male was an ancient and very ugly gardener. This was worse than being a parish priest!

Therefore, news of the birth of the first foal at Angelscombe had been the perfect pretext for visiting the men at the neighbouring farm.

And there he found Father Godfrey!

How fortunate that he should meet this Adonis just when the Holy Father had seen the light – as befitted his new name – and reduced the severity of 'sins below the waist' to venial. What a timely gift from God!

Father Godfrey was so innocent and naïve; it shouldn't be difficult to win him over.

All that prudish nonsense about same-sex attraction being the cross that some people have to bear, and declaring that acting on it was a mortal sin because it went against the laws of nature – all that had finally been put in its place.

True, the God of the Old Testament had hurled fire and brimstone on Sodom and Gomorrah, *allegedly* because of such behaviour.

But He was the old God of Justice; the God of the *New* Testament was the God of Mercy. As our deceased pope, rest his soul, was fond of saying, Jesus meets us wherever we are and walks with us in love. Unlike those backward traditional Catholics, *He* has no desire to condemn us.

Maybe 'sinning below the waist' – the previous pope had such a clever way with words! – was not totally pure behaviour. But the highest authority in Rome had made it official that Jesus was prepared to look the other way. Same sex relations would not bar entrance to heaven – despite what that homophobe St. Paul wrote. That saint was a mere human. Jesus was – and is – God.

Father Abnus Doyal grinned: the path was clear for him to pursue Father Godfrey.

He looked forward to the chase and whistled even more loudly.

Chapter Thirteen: A Garden Pest

Monday, 7th October 2030

"Yes, Father Terry, I appreciate the warning." Brother Melvin returned his mobile phone to the deep pocket of his black soutane, and could already hear a tuneless whistling outside the garden wall.

In haste, he covered the statues of Our Lord and Our Lady. When the whistling stopped and several sharp raps sounded on the old wooden door, he picked up a hoe. Thus looking the part of a gardener, he opened to a young, good-looking priest with a smug grin on his face.

"Hello, I'm Brother Melvin." He stretched out his right hand. "Can I help you?"

Father Doyal shook it heartily. "I do hope so. I hear you have a famous garden within these walls, and I was hoping for a tour."

"By all means, I'll be glad to show you around. Follow me." As he closed the heavy door, Brother Melvin heard murmurs of approval from his visitor, and turned to see him admiring the statue of Mother Earth.

"Bravo!" said Father Doyal. "I see you've already embraced the spirit of the latest Synod."

Brother Melvin nodded, seeking a way to answer without lying. "I don't think anyone can argue with the need to take care of the earth, do you?"

"Definitely not. But we're getting a lot of pushback from *some* clerics, who don't understand that reverence for Mother Earth should be front and centre in the Church today. Mankind is ruining nature!"

Brother Melvin bowed slightly. "As the gardener here, I'm most fortunate to be in a position to do my modest bit to rectify that."

"Then I take it you're pleased with the *Nova Theologica Populi*?" Father Doyal asked.

"We've only just received the document," the brother deftly replied. "We've not yet had time to examine it thoroughly."

Father Doyal nodded. "Someone of your advanced years is bound to appreciate the Church's softening attitude. Although, I'm surprised to see you're still active in the community. Surely, life would be easier for you in a retirement home?"

Restraining a desire to throttle the young man, Brother Melvin said, "I like to stay busy, Father, and keep up with developments in the Church."

"Then you'll find the *Nova Theologica* most stimulating. Remember when Pope St. John XXIII wanted to let a little fresh air into the Church?"

Brother Melvin nodded, forbearing to say that it wasn't certain the saint *had* pronounced those words.

"You'll see – this document does the trick." The smug smile returned.

Brother Melvin longed to say that, if the saint had indeed said those words, he had a very different kind of fresh air in mind. But Father Terry's phone call had warned him that Father Doyal belonged to the enemy camp, and everything he'd said so far supported that judgement. The SSPX brother must tread with caution.

"Of course, if, on inspection, you *don't* feel comfortable with the *Theologica's* precepts," continued the priest, "perhaps you should retire? St. Dymphna might be a good fit."

Brother Melvin gave a start. Named after the patron saint of mental illness, St. Dymphna's Retirement Home for Elderly Clerics was a notorious institution. Older clergy were sent there to end their days if they had 'psychological issues'. A widespread rumour suggested the unfortunate inmates weren't permitted to live out those days in peace. The recent lax laws on euthanasia were rigorously applied to anyone who became too much trouble, or when a bed was needed for a new rebel priest.

Was this a veiled threat from Father Doyal? If so, did he have power within the Church to enforce it?

Brother Melvin gave a nervous chuckle. "I trust I'm not yet ready to be carted off, Father."

Father Doyal smiled benevolently, but Brother Melvin saw an evil glint in his eyes. "What are your views on euthanasia, Brother?"

"I see the need for it with animals, in some instances."

"But not for people?" The priest feigned surprise.

"Life is sacred, Father, a God-given gift. It is not for us to snuff it out."

Undeterred, Father Doyal replied, "But there comes a time when old people need to make way for young, *useful* people."

Once more, Brother Melvin choked back his ire. "I think I *am* still useful, despite my age. The residents here would have nothing to eat if I didn't grow their food or cook for them, and the ponies would have no access to herbal treatments, either.

"By the way, I thought you were interested in a tour of the garden?"

Father Doyal glanced at his watch. "Goodness! It's later than I thought. I must be going. Another time, perhaps?"

Brother Melvin bowed. "I'll show you out."

A shiver ran down his spine as he closed the heavy wooden door behind the man.

Snake in the grass! I wonder if the Serpent in the Garden of Eden looked like him? The brother glanced heavenwards. *I'm sorry, Lord, but You have to admit, he's not a nice man. He came here to make us all uncomfortable and anxious because we don't subscribe to the progressive agenda for the Church. That can't make <u>You</u> feel comfortable, either.*

Making the Sign of the Cross, he pulled the Mother Earth cover off Our Lady's statue. *I apologise for this undignified camouflage, but I hope you agree how necessary it is to protect ourselves from enemies of the true Church.*

He walked over to Father Time and unzipped the disguise. As he removed it, he said, *Lord, I do hope you're not trying to tell me through that man that I should retire? I've only just got this job! If it be Your Will, please don't let him persuade the others that I'm past my sell-by date. Or that I need carting off to the funny farm, to get put down like a sick dog when it suits the powers that be. Make me useful to You, even if it's just as a humble cook, for the remainder of my days.*

Hiding the two covers under a massive upturned flower pot in the greenhouse, Brother Melvin resolved more firmly to become totally indispensable to the residents of Angelscombe through his culinary skills.

They'll be expecting a really tasty dinner tonight, after today's lunch!

He cast an eye over the vegetables, lovingly protected by the Sacred Heart of Jesus, together with rows of fruit.

I'll roast a pork sirloin with Brussels sprouts, almonds, and Parmesan cheese; butternut squash, creamy sweetcorn for colour contrast, and roast potatoes. Then finish it off with rhubarb pie and custard. That should do it.

The men would appreciate this hearty meal after a long day labouring outside with the ponies. It would also convince them that he was completely *compos mentis*, despite anything that serpent might insinuate to the contrary.

The wheelbarrow was tipped upside down by the greenhouse to prevent rainwater filling it. He donned his gardening gloves, righted the barrow, and placed the basket containing his fork and trowel inside. Wheeling it over to Jesus' statue, he proceeded to dig up the fruit and vegetables he needed for that evening.

The work usually brought him peace, but as he toiled, he couldn't shake off a growing foreboding. That so-called priest meant trouble for Angelscombe. Definitely for him, but likely for all of them. Father Doyal had a very dark side, and he enjoyed causing discomfort.

The SSPX brother's spirits needed lifting.

I know, I'll pay Ruby and her foal a visit. That'll cheer me up: they're not plotting to get rid of me.

He left the barrow inside the wooden door and stepped out of the garden to contemplate the idyllic scene of mare and foal under the afternoon sun.

Drawing near the paddock, he noticed Ruby was holding up her left foreleg as if afraid or unable to put weight on it.

He walked towards her as fast as his aged legs would allow and, as he drew alongside the black pony, he exclaimed, "Oh, you poor thing!"

Chapter Fourteen: Troubled Dales
Monday, 7th October 2030

Blood was oozing from a long gash inside the mare's leg, from the knee down and Brother Melvin had to stop the bleeding.

But how?

"I'll be right back!" he told the pony, and forced his body into a painful jog to the barn for help.

He found Pastor John sitting in the tack room, making up the herbal blend for the Cushing's pony. He leaned his exhausted body against the doorway, breathing heavily.

The Lutheran jumped up. "Brother Melvin! What on earth's wrong?"

Clutching his sides, the brother forced out the words, "Ruby – hurt – badly."

The pastor led him to a chair. "Sit here. Can you tell me what's wrong?"

Brother Melvin whispered hoarsely, "Gash on leg – holding it up."

"We can't bring her to the barn, then?"

"No – can't – walk."

The minister nodded. Hastily, he threw items into a medical bag then half-filled two buckets with hot water.

"Can you assist me in treating her? Or would you prefer I call Father Terry?"

Having now caught his breath and anxious to prove his usefulness after that encounter with Father Doyal, Brother Melvin said, "I'd like – to help." He rose wearily out of the comfortable chair and straightened up. "Can I carry anything?"

Pastor John threw four towels over the brother's arm and handed over his medical bag. "Yes, please take these." Then he lifted the two buckets of water.

Brother Melvin struggled to keep pace with the minister's long strides and was relieved when Father Terry noticed them hurrying out of the barn.

"What's up?" the priest shouted.

"Ruby's gashed her leg," Pastor John replied.

"Can I help?"

"By all means!"

When Father Terry took a water bucket from the vet, Brother Melvin knew the priest would take over from him in assisting the pastor. But at least he'd shown his willingness to help and could stand by, holding the towels, even if he was no good for anything else.

He trailed behind the two younger clerics on their way to the paddock, where, despite her pain and having to stand on three legs, the dutiful dam was allowing her son to suckle.

Pastor John stroked her face over the fence. "You're a great mum, Ruby. We're going to fix you as quickly as possible."

Still balancing the towels on one arm and holding the vet's bag, Brother Melvin opened the gate with his other hand, to allow the two men through, and closed it behind him.

The mare was now resting the hoof of her wounded leg on the lower fence rail, to obtain relief after holding it up so long.

Pastor John put his bucket of warm water next to her and asked Father Terry to follow suit with the other one. He motioned to Brother Melvin to hand him his bag, and took out a bottle of iodine. He poured some into one of the buckets then drew out a roll of cotton wool.

"Father Terry, would you please put on Ruby's headcollar? We'll see if she'll stand still while I tend to her."

The priest took her halter off the peg outside the gate and gently placed it over the mare's head. "Good girl, you know we're here to help, don't you?" he told her, stroking her nose.

"Thank you, Father." Breaking off a large piece of cotton wool, Pastor John dipped it into the disinfected mixture and lightly wrang out the liquid. He approached the leg from the mare's right side, where he could better see the wound.

The black Dales was still resting her hoof on the lower rail and Brother Melvin sent up a prayer that she would let the vet reach under her belly to clean the gash. *Please don't let her crush him!*

"There, there, Ruby," Father Terry was saying, "we know you trust Pastor John. Now's the time to show it."

The vet-turned-minister said, "I'm going to see if I can reach in between her front legs first, just to test how well she'll tolerate having the wound cleaned."

"That's a very good idea!" said a relieved Brother Melvin.

The vet inched himself between the fence and the mare's chest, and reached down to the long wound.

Starting with soft dabs, he cleaned the surface. Ruby shifted uneasily as she felt the first sting, but with Father Terry's ministrations and her foal's insistence on suckling, she settled down and allowed the vet to continue.

Pastor John applied pressure. "Brother Melvin, would you pull another large piece off the cotton roll and immerse it in the disinfected water, please?"

The brother handed him a new piece of soaked cotton, and exchanged it for the used one, which he dropped on the ground outside the paddock fence.

During this switch, Ruby placed her wounded leg on the ground.

"That's a good sign," said Pastor John. "The bleeding isn't as bad as I feared, and I don't see any debris in the wound."

He slowly drew away from the pony and threw the used cotton piece next to the other one. "Father Terry, could you please bring the other water bucket and my bag around to this side?"

Pastor John took a bar of disinfectant soap from the bag and poured a little clean water over it. This time he reached under Ruby's belly and gently washed the wounded area with the damp soap. "This is where the famous Dales temperament comes into its own," he said, when the mare stood stock still for him.

"Amen to that!" agreed Father Terry. "This is one of many reasons the breed is worth preserving."

"I must admit, I never thought I'd see anyone safely crawl under a horse's belly like that," Brother Melvin remarked.

With a grin, the vet retreated from below the pony. He took another, larger piece of cotton out of his bag, dipped it into the bucket of clean water and began rinsing off the wound.

"How on earth did she get injured?" asked Brother Melvin.

"Who knows?" came the reply. "Horses are geniuses at wounding themselves, even when there's no obvious cause."

"Just in case, we'll check the fence line once we've got her sorted," said Father Terry, "and look for anything sticking out, like splinters or nails."

"That's a good idea," the minister said. "She might have stuck her foot between two rails and caught it on something sharp when she pulled it back."

"I can do that, while you gentlemen treat the patient," Brother Melvin volunteered.

Pastor John pulled away from the pony and straightened his back. "Yes, please. Thank you. I'm going to dry the area, then bandage the leg. After that, she'll be able to walk around again. I'll change the dressing every day to make sure it's healing properly."

"I can give you some comfrey to put on it, once you're sure there's no infection. It does wonders to speed up the healing process."

"Thank you, Brother. That sounds wonderful. I'll let you know tomorrow if it's ready for your magic potions."

A smiling Brother Melvin began a slow and methodical tour of the paddock. But it yielded no clues as to how Ruby had hurt herself. He went round twice, to make sure he hadn't missed anything, even rubbing his fingers along the fence rails to feel anything sharp sticking out. But he reported no findings on his return to the now bandaged pony.

"Don't worry," said Pastor John. "As I said, that's not uncommon."

"Let's hope she has the sense not to repeat the incident," Father Terry said. "Are you sure she's going to be O.K. if she stays out? Shouldn't she be in her stall until that wound heals?"

"I don't believe in keeping a horse inside unless it's absolutely necessary. She'll heal faster if she keeps to her normal routine and is allowed to move around. It's better for her colt, too."

"But supposing she runs around and that wound gets worse?"

"Unfortunately, since she has a foal at foot, I can't give her even a mild sedative as it'll go into her milk. If she does act up, I'll revise my plan accordingly."

"If you don't need me anymore, I'm off for my 'tea' with Mrs. Prince," said Father Terry, "now that Father Doyal has left."

"Thank Goodness!" said Brother Melvin. "I'm glad he's gone."

Pastor John looked confused. "Anything I should know?"

"Hopefully not," replied Father Terry.

Brother Melvin didn't feel the need to elaborate.

Chapter Fifteen: Revisitation

Wednesday, 9th October

Two days later, Father Godfrey was again instructing young Tony on the ever-patient Black Pepper.

It was 10 a.m. and Tony's mother had left to go food shopping. The priest was under less pressure without her constant presence, and her son seemed to feel the same way. He was more relaxed in the saddle, and not so inclined to haul on the pony's mouth.

"You're doing exceptionally well today, Tony. If you tell me what the Fourth Commandment is, I'll let you do a round of trot before we talk more about it."

Tony smiled broadly. "Yippee! You hear that, Pepper?" He frowned for a few seconds before coming up with, "Honour thy father and thy mother!"

"Well done, young man! Alright, prepare Pepper properly, then off you go."

Spurred on by this praise, the youngster surprised Father Godfrey by visibly letting the pony know, through his aids, that he was going to ask for trot. The result was a smooth upward transition and an active working trot.

Before their circuit of the arena was complete, the priest called, "Come across the diagonal and trot once around on the other rein."

Beaming, Tony complied, with good preparation in the corner before changing direction.

"Bravo!" cried Father Godfrey in excitement.

"Bravo!" came an echo from the arena fence.

Father Godfrey's heart sank when he saw Father Doyal leaning on the top rail, and all plans vanished for the day's catechesis; he'd have to continue with a normal riding lesson.

He hoped Tony wouldn't ask awkward questions about it. But what boy would request more religious education and less riding time?

With a cursory wave at the intruding priest, Father Godfrey told Tony, "Keep going, you're doing really well! One more change across the diagonal, then come back to a walk and we'll talk about how to canter." That should make the boy happy and stop him wondering about the change of course content.

Tony's face lit up. "For real, Father?"

"Absolutely," came the reply. "You've earned it. I haven't seen you yank on Pepper's mouth one time today. Keep it up!"

Father Godfrey hadn't intended to add canter during this lesson, but it would encourage the boy's enthusiasm for riding and be a good carrot to dangle in future sessions when he didn't want to attend to his catechesis.

Father Doyal showed no signs of leaving. Instead, he cheered on young Tony and threw out comments to his instructor. "You're a very good teacher, Godfrey. You missed your calling."

Forbearing to reply that he hadn't missed it at all, as was clear from the fact that here he was, teaching – or that he should be addressed as *Father* in front of his pupil, Father Godfrey smiled wanly in response and turned his full attention to Tony.

Lord, please make him go away!

Although that didn't happen, the boy's mother showed up at the conclusion of the lesson and took the focus off Father Godfrey for a few moments. He opened the arena gate to allow the dismounted Tony to lead Pepper out, and Father Doyal rushed to open the car door for Mrs. Benton, who blushed at this handsome priest's gallantry.

"Thank you, Father!" She waved at her son. "How did it go today?"

Father Godfrey prayed that she wouldn't ask about the catechesis, and God answered him.

Tony couldn't get the words out fast enough, as he talked about the wonderful ride he'd had and how he'd cantered today and how Father was very pleased with him and how he couldn't wait to have another lesson.

His mother laughed. "Well, he doesn't *usually* act that way after a lesson!" she exclaimed. "I don't mean any offense by that, Father," she quickly added.

"None taken, Mrs. Benton," Father Godfrey responded. "It was a real pleasure working with him today."

"I must say, I was very impressed with your son," said Father Doyal. "And Father Godfrey handles him so well."

Mrs. Benton was visibly pleased at this praise for her offspring, and appeared not to catch the sly wink Father Doyal gave Father Godfrey.

Anxious to get rid of him, the latter said, "And now we need to unsaddle Pepper and brush her off. Come along, Tony. It's been nice seeing you, Father."

But Father Doyal said, "I actually came to pick your brains about the breeding programme here."

Father Godfrey shook his head. "I'm afraid I'm rather busy. You need to make an appointment with Father Terry for that sort of thing."

Not to be put off, Father Doyal said, "I have a better idea. Why don't I shadow you while you're doing your chores? That would give me a good idea about how you run the place."

Father Godfrey's insides were churning. He desperately wanted this man gone! And he didn't want him around young Tony, either.

But he could think of no good way to make the priest leave. He would have to grin and bear it as best he could.

Jesus, Mary and Joseph, come to my aid!

"If by shadowing, you mean you'll let me go about my business unhindered," he managed to say, "then fine. But only until we've given the ponies their lunch. Agreed?"

Father Doyal looked at his watch. "When is that?"

"At noon. That gives you an hour." Father Godfrey was surprised at his own forcefulness. While hoping he didn't sound rude, he nevertheless needed this man to know he couldn't stay here all day. Otherwise, he'd get ideas about coming round whenever he felt like it. Boundaries must be set.

With a quick glance to see that Mrs. Benton was paying attention to her son leading Pepper to the barn, and not to this exchange, Father Doyal leaned towards him and said, in a low voice, "I didn't have you pegged as a man with such backbone."

Blushing at the man's forwardness, Father Godfrey pulled away from him. Without answering, he marched off behind Tony and his mother.

He could feel the man's eyes boring into his back. *Lord, please make him go away!*

He busied himself with helping Tony remove Pepper's tack. But when he pulled off the saddle, Father Doyal was quick to remove the saddle blanket and follow Father Godfrey to the tack room.

"Where should I put this?" he asked.

Father Godfrey fairly snapped his reply. "Over there, in the laundry basket."

"Do you wash the saddle blankets after every ride?"

"Yes." Father Godfrey placed the saddle on a rack and walked swiftly out of the room. He did not want to be alone in a confined space with this priest.

Tony had removed Pepper's bridle and was washing off the bit.

"I can brush the pony down for you," offered Father Doyal to the boy.

Father Godfrey cut in. "No, thank you. You're shadowing, remember?"

"But I may as well make myself useful," the other said.

"Tony is learning to take care of the pony by himself," came Father Godfrey's sharp reply. "It's part of his lesson and we don't want to get in the way of that, do we?"

Father Doyal raised a hand in truce. "No problem. I'll just stand in the shadows as we agreed."

You'd better! thought Father Godfrey.

He was sorry to see Tony and his mother leave ten minutes later; their presence had provided a useful barrier. As soon as they left, he walked resolutely out of the barn, to join the other priests about their work.

Father Doyal followed him to the feed room, where Father Godfrey was relieved to see Father Terry. He sensed his friend didn't like this man and maybe he could make him leave the premises for good?

He saw Father Terry's scowl, at the sight of Father Doyal walking behind Father Godfrey into the room, change quickly into a false smile of greeting.

"You're back," he said. "What can we do for you?"

"Father Godfrey invited me to shadow him while he did his chores, as research for my own project."

Father Godfrey, whose back was to the priest, put on a desperate expression, which Father Terry thankfully interpreted correctly.

"I can't allow that, I'm afraid," he told Father Doyal. "We're not open to the public and really are very busy."

"Oh, surely you can make an exception for a fellow priest? I'm not the public."

Father Godfrey rolled his eyes in defeat. "Father Doyal agreed to leave by noon."

Father Terry pointedly checked his watch. "No later."

Father Godfrey turned and saw their visitor take this warning calmly. He knew neither priest could throw him out; he was in good standing with the New Church – they weren't. He had power over them, and Father Godfrey was certain he would wield it whenever he wanted.

Chapter Sixteen: The Visit Continues
Wednesday, 9ᵗʰ October

Father Doyal couldn't conceal his smugness. Those priests didn't have a leg to stand on; he could stay as long as he liked.

But today he would do as they asked, in order to keep in Father Godfrey's good books.

He stood patiently by the door and watched him make up the feeds. Then he walked behind him as he wheeled a barrow of hay to the paddocks and began throwing large amounts over the fence of the first one.

"I can help you with that," Father Doyal said, as two ponies ran up to them. He noticed the priest putting out three batches. "Why are you dividing it up like that?"

"Because, as you'll quickly see, the ponies are very food aggressive. It's important to put it in several piles, so each one has a chance to eat without being pushed away."

Sure enough, the first mare to reach the pile was quick to shove her companion out of the way. As soon as the second mare started eating from the next pile, the first one came over and pushed her off that one.

"That's why I give them a third one, so the musical chairs finally stop and they settle down to their own hay."

"That's very smart," replied Father Doyal. "I need to check that the ladies at my project do that for our Fells. Are you sure I can't help you?"

"Very sure, thank you." Father Godfrey lifted the wheelbarrow handles and pushed it towards the next paddock.

"Then while you're working, let me ask you something."

Did I just hear Father Godfrey groan? Wondered Father Doyal. *Whatever.*

He continued. "I'd like to get your honest opinion on the revised teaching on mortal sin."

"What about it?"

"Well, specifically, that sins below the waist are no longer considered mortal, and may not even be sinful at all."

Father Godfrey ignored him and threw a large armful of hay over the fence. Immediately, two black mares roared over from the other side of the paddock, manes and tails flying.

As the priest fetched more from the barrow and turned to throw it into the field, Father Doyal grabbed his arm. "Did you hear what I said?"

Father Godfrey shook him off. "Yes, I did." He walked to where the pony, who'd been pushed off the first hay pile by her companion, was waiting for the next portion to arrive.

Father Doyal brushed up against the priest, almost knocking the hay out of his hand, as Father Godfrey stepped forwards and hurled it over the fence, close to the expectant pony.

"Well, what *is* your opinion?" Father Doyal asked again.

"My opinion? My opinion doesn't concern you." He strode back to the barrow for a third armful of hay.

Feisty! thought Father Doyal. *I didn't know he had it in him. This is going to be more fun than I'd hoped.*

"But you aren't going to go against our new pope, are you?" he goaded.

"As I said, it's not your concern."

"But it'll become my concern, if I find that fellow priests are threatening the unity of the Catholic Church by refusing to accept the teachings of her pontiff."

Father Godfrey carried the final load of hay to the paddock and threw it as far in as he could. Before it even landed, the alpha mare had trotted over to claim it for herself.

The young priest returned to the wheelbarrow red-faced. Was that from physical exertion, wondered Father Doyal, or was he trying to hide his attraction to him? Hopefully, the reason was the latter.

Picking up the barrow handles, Father Godfrey looked straight at Father Doyal. His face was back to its normal hue, and his voice measured. "I accept the teachings of Christ." With that, he pushed the barrow towards the next paddock.

Father Doyal quickened his steps to keep up with the angry priest. "But the pope is Christ's representative on earth. As such you have to obey him."

"Only when he speaks God's Truth."

"You don't think he is doing that?"

"Do you?" It was said with a calmness that Father Doyal found infuriatingly alluring. This priest had hidden strengths. Where did he get them from?

"He must be," continued Father Doyal. "He's speaking in his capacity as the head of Christ's Church."

"So you see no need to exercise a spirit of discernment when he pronounces a teaching contradictory to that preached by the Catholic Church for two millennia?"

"Ha! So you *do* have a problem with what he's saying!" Father Doyal cried.

Father Godfrey didn't bat an eyelid. "I didn't say that." He filled his arms with hay. "I merely said we can't take everything a pope says as Gospel. We have to test it, as St. Paul admonishes us to."

Father Doyal registered Father Godfrey's words 'a pope' not '*the* pope,' being careful not to incriminate himself. But Father Doyal knew full well the man was an inveterate traditionalist.

That would make his downfall even more rewarding.

"Pope Lucius II is the Holy Father, our shepherd and earthly leader. Think about it, Godfrey. Think of the doors this document opens for men like you and me! Oh, don't deny it, I know you're one of us. You've repressed your natural desires for too long. Do you think God made you this way simply to torment you? Is that what a loving God would do?"

Father Doyal saw his words shoot home, and was amused by the wretched expression on Father Godfrey's face as the poor man struggled to deal with them. He didn't even try to deny that they were both of the same ilk, Father Doyal noted.

It would soon be time for the kill.

Chapter Seventeen: Making an Enemy

Wednesday, 9th October

While Father Godfrey's arms were carrying hay to the next paddock, his heart begged Heaven to hear his pleas to stay strong and not cave into this man.

Three ponies rushed towards him as he dropped the forage in a large pile by the fence. The lead mare lowered her head and began to eat as the other two crowded in on her. She snaked her neck around to threaten first one then the other.

"Hey! Cut that out!" cried Father Godfrey, swiftly fetching more hay from the wheelbarrow. He distributed it in two heaps far away from the bully mare, then collected more, and the rebuffed ponies trotted over to the safer piles.

He was glad of this diversion from his inner conflict. Father Doyal's presence was becoming unbearable.

The man was Satan incarnate. Never before had Father Godfrey been so tempted to commit the mortal sin he'd succeeded in resisting his entire life – a sin that Father Doyal now reminded him was venial under the New Church rules.

Part of Father Godfrey wanted to shut him up; but the other part was enjoying the attention. So used to being the unseasoned priest whose opinion was often disregarded, he was being singled out and pursued for *himself*. And by someone who understood him only too well.

He was becoming dangerously close to letting Father Doyal know that, yes, he did reciprocate his interest. How glorious it would be if the Church's new teaching really had changed due to inspiration from the Holy Spirit! What a blessed release that would be!

Briefly, he wondered whether he could cave in to this seductive man without the others finding out? But the very fact that he wanted to keep the relationship secret told him this was wrong. It had always been wrong, and always would be wrong. Sodomy was one of the sins crying out to heaven for vengeance; that had not changed.

Even if he managed to sneak behind the back of his fellow priests, he couldn't escape God. What had he himself said earlier to this serpent? 'I answer to Christ.' Did he really mean that?

He needed to get away from Father Doyal.

Ignoring the evil man, he continued to throw hay to the remaining ponies, then pushed the empty wheelbarrow back to the barn and the safety of the other priests.

Still without talking to Father Doyal, he parked the barrow and looked at his watch. Time to distribute feeds in the stalls before bringing the ponies in for lunch.

Father Doyal offered to help carry the buckets, but Father Godfrey replied with an angry scowl. The man continued to walk behind him, even coming in to each stable as Father Godfrey tipped the bucket contents into the corner mangers.

No matter how the priest tried to shake him off, Father Doyal stuck to him like Velcro, making him feel sleazy and unclean, and in desperate need of a shower.

Then, as Father Godfrey was pouring feed into the manger of the last stable, Father Doyal closed the upper and lower doors behind them. He pulled the bucket out of the priest's hands, grabbed his shoulders, and swung him round.

"What are you doing?" cried Father Godfrey in shock, as Father Doyal backed him into the far corner.

He recoiled at the power emanating from the man and the sharp smell of his aftershave.

Father Doyal slowly placed a palm against the wall on either side of the hapless priest and leered into his face. "Don't be such a prude, Godfrey!"

Father Terry was worried. He'd been watching Father Doyal shadow Father Godfrey, and knew this would not end well.

Although he'd always been aware of Father Godfrey's struggle against same sex attraction, he'd never let him know, and greatly admired him for giving no sign of how greatly he suffered because of it.

He saw Father Doyal enter the stables with Father Godfrey, and watched in alarm as both doors of the last one were closed.

Swiftly, he walked down the line of loose boxes. Not wanting to embarrass his friend, yet anxious for his soul, he stood outside listening.

On hearing Father Doyal's words, he stormed in. "What is going on here?" he demanded, horrified to see his friend pinned in the corner by the monster.

He saw a look of relief on Father Godfrey's face.

Father Doyal pulled back from his intended victim, and with an expression of sheer hatred, glowered at the tall man who'd thwarted him. "You will sorely regret this!" He roughly pushed against Father Terry as he strode out.

Pale and shaking and almost in tears, Father Godfrey leaned back against the wall. "Thank you, Terry, from the bottom of my soul! I dread to think what might have happened if you hadn't walked in!"

"Glad to help, Godfrey. That man is dangerous and I've just made an enemy of him. Unfortunately, I don't think we've seen the last of him."

Father Godfrey groaned.

"God is on our side. We *will* win," insisted Father Terry.

Father Godfrey hung his head wearily. "I wish the fight were already over!"

Father Terry smiled gently. "We must all carry our crosses, if we want to win the crown."

Chapter Eighteen: Brotherly TLC
Wednesday, 9th October 2030

"How's Ruby doing?" Brother Melvin asked, as he handed a brown bag containing dried eyebright herb to Pastor John in the kitchen garden.

"I applied the comfrey you gave me and her wound is already beginning to heal," the Lutheran minister replied. "I have to say, I'm very impressed, and in high hopes that this – " he held up the paper bag " – will help Poppy just as quickly."

Poppy the pony mare had a mild case of conjunctivitis, and Brother Melvin had suggested eyebright tea.

"How do I apply this?" he asked the old man.

"Boil half a pint of water in saucepan and add a couple of teaspoons of eyebright herb. After letting it steep for fifteen minutes, put the liquid through a tea strainer into a container. Use it as a compress to put over Poppy's eyes. Even better, see if you can get some of it into her eyes. She should start improving within a couple of days, but keep it up for a week."

"What exactly does it do?"

"It reduces the inflammation and will make her feel more comfortable. Let me know how she does."

"Thank you very much!"

"My pleasure. Glad to help."

Brother Melvin closed the heavy garden door behind his visitor. With a feeling of satisfaction, he walked over to the Sacred Heart of Jesus statue. "Thank you, Lord, for the opportunity to help people with my knowledge of herbs."

It was two o'clock in the afternoon. Lunch had been another success, although it worried him that Father

Godfrey hadn't finished his meal. The others had eaten all of theirs, so he concluded it was nothing to do with the food, but an unrelated problem. Which would make sense, for the priest looked out of sorts.

Brother Melvin was pottering happily in his greenhouse, checking on the progress of some poinsettias he was growing for Christmas, when he heard a loud rap on the tall door of the walled garden.

Lord, please don't let it be that dreadful Father Doyal!

Arming himself with the hoe, he was pleased to see Father Godfrey instead. "Hello, Father! Can I help you?"

"Good afternoon, Brother Melvin. I was rather hoping I could do something to help *you.*"

"I can always do with help, but what about your pony duties?"

"I'm caught up for the time being," said Father Godfrey, eyes lowered. "I need a serener activity for a while."

Did this have anything to do with why the priest hadn't emptied his plate? But it was none of his business. The most useful thing he could do was give the man something to occupy his hands, and time to think through whatever was bothering him. Although it was strange that he hadn't sought peace in the chapel.

Perhaps the sight of the poinsettias might cheer him up? Their upper leaves were just beginning to turn a brilliant red. "How do you feel about watering greenhouse plants?"

"Sounds wonderful!"

"Then follow me."

Brother Melvin gave him a green watering can with a long spout. "It doesn't hold much, I'm afraid, so you're going to be walking back and forth to the hose for refills."

"I'm happy to do that."

"Thank you. It'll save me from exercise that I don't enjoy a whole lot at my age. Perhaps you could start with the poinsettias?"

"Gladly." Father Godfrey pointed to half a dozen long stems with exquisitely formed white flower petals, gracing the far end of the glass building. "Are those orchids?"

"Yes. They were in very poor shape when I arrived, but with a lot of TLC they've made a comeback."

"Do they serve any medicinal purpose?"

"Apparently one of their effects is help with sleeping. I was thinking of asking if anybody would like one in their cell, to find out if it's true."

Father Godfrey's expression brightened. "Sign me up! I'd love to be your first candidate."

"Then, please take one when you leave."

"If you tell me how to take care of it."

"Absolutely. And now I'll leave you to your watering while I contemplate which vegetables to dig up for tonight's dinner." He paused a moment. "I noticed you weren't happy with your lunch today. Is there anything in particular you'd like me to prepare this evening?"

"It had nothing to do with your cooking, Brother Melvin, I promise you. Please don't let me influence your dinner menu."

"Are you're sure?"

"Very sure."

"Well, if you change your mind, I'll be with Our Lord, asking Him for ideas." He chuckled. "And if you feel inspired to help me with that, please come out and do so."

With that, Brother Melvin exited the greenhouse and sat next to the Sacred Heart. Together they surveyed the rows of produce spreading out in front of them.

Lord, something is really troubling that young man.

He got no insights from Jesus regarding Father Godfrey, but did receive some menu ideas. He pulled a notepad and pen from the deep recesses of his soutane pocket and scribbled them down.

He usually knew what meat he was going to cook – or fish, if it was a Friday or other day of abstinence. But he preferred to let the accompanying dishes be more impromptu, as he found this method encouraged his creative side.

Examining the ripe vegetables at his disposal, he wrote down a list of candidates that would go well with this evening's roast mutton. Of course, mint sauce was a must, and perhaps he could ask Father Godfrey to pick the mint leaves for him? Their wonderful aroma might also serve as a refreshing pick-me-up for the priest.

The thought had barely formed in his mind, when he saw Father Godfrey approaching.

Brother Melvin beamed at him. "I hope you've come to share some culinary insights."

"I'm afraid not. I was hoping you'd be able to share your insights with me." Father Godfrey gave him a shy smile. "I don't mean culinary ones."

"Sit down, and we'll see if I have anything worthwhile to offer."

The priest took a seat and remained silent for a few moments. Assuming he was more in need of companionship than speech, Brother Melvin left him in peace and continued to let the vegetables in front of him quietly suggest ideas for side dishes.

He was jotting down 'glazed carrots', when Father Godfrey said, "Brother Melvin, when one is fighting the same temptation over and over again, is there any chance it will finally let up? Is there any way to persuade God to take it away?"

"In such situations, I've found my only recourse is to trust God will continue to give me the strength to overcome it."

"But don't you ever tire of battling? Don't you sometimes want to give in?"

"I find it very tiring. But we're called to persevere to the end, Father.

"Satan lures us into sin with the promise that it will feel good. But he is the Father of Lies. He wants you to give in, not because you'll be at peace from no longer fighting the temptation – because you won't be – but so he can reproach you for being weak and spineless, and make you feel an abject failure. Remember, he is also the great Accuser.

"Believe me, you'd feel way worse after caving than if you didn't. Your remorse would far outweigh any transient pleasure from allowing the temptation to lead you into sin. I assume we're talking about mortal sin here?"

"That's just the problem! I'm not sure we are."

Brother Melvin frowned. "I don't quite follow."

Father Godfrey gave him a worried look, as if afraid of having said too much.

Brother Melvin said soothingly, "You don't have to say anything more, if you'd rather not. Perhaps pray to Our Lord, here?"

Father Godfrey made as if to get up, then changed his mind. He remained sitting and made the Sign of the Cross.

Brother Melvin picked up his pen and notepad, and they sat without speaking for a few minutes.

Suddenly Father Godfrey said, in a petulant voice, "What are we supposed to do when the pope keeps changing the rules? One minute something is a mortal sin and we must avoid it at all costs. The next, it's been demoted, and almost *encouraged* by the Vatican. The pope's supposed to lead us with clarity, as Christ did. But instead, he's sowing confusion and blurring the distinctions between good and evil."

Brother Melvin said, "By their fruits you shall know them, Father. And we all know who the Father of Confusion is."

"Thank you! That's exactly what I needed to hear!" The priest leapt up from the bench. "Do you mind if I go? I must visit the chapel."

"Of course!"

"I'll be back later for my orchid." He hesitated a moment, then turned to face the brother. "Would you give me a blessing, please?"

"Gladly." Brother Melvin rose from his seat as Father Godfrey bowed his head. "May you go in the peace of Our Lord Jesus Christ, and may He strengthen you to resist any and all temptations."

He then made the Sign of the Cross over the priest.

"Brother Melvin, I can't thank you enough for helping me with this! I shall say a prayer for you."

"And I'll be praying for you, my son."

Brother Melvin opened the door for Father Godfrey, who departed with a radiant smile on his face.

As he returned to his seat next to Jesus, the SSPX brother whispered, "Lord, if I'm right about the temptations besetting that young priest, he is in dire need of prayers."

Chapter Nineteen: Pondering Payback

Wednesday, 9th October 2030

Father Abnus Doyal was livid.

Eyes forward, he marched past the do-gooder priests taking care of their precious ponies and opened the driver's door of his new electric car – one of the few the government had allowed to be produced that year.

With the emphasis on saving Mother Earth, there'd been a forced move away from petrol vehicles, and also a decline in electric cars – for the power for them had to come from somewhere, too. Only a privileged few were allowed to purchase new vehicles.

The rest of the population were making their current transport last as long as possible, before they had no choice but to follow the government mandate and switch over to literal horsepower. Only the elite were permitted to continue using motor powered conveyances.

Father Doyal had been put forward by Bishop Hardy as one worthy of such a car. In good standing with the Catholic Church and undertaking valuable work at the Fell Pony Preservation Project, he needed conventional transport.

He hoped the residents of Angelscombe noticed it. For sure, those cancelled clergymen were struggling to keep up the maintenance on their old vehicles.

He sniggered to himself. One day their antiquated motors would gasp their last and the self-righteous priests would be forced to ride their hairy Dales ponies throughout the countryside. Preferably in the pouring rain, or, even better, icy sleet and snow.

The image brought a smile to his face.

But then he remembered the ignominious discovery of him with Father Godfrey by that straight-jacket, Father Terry.

Father Doyal had been so close! Father Godfrey was ripe for the taking. He'd given all the signs of having suppressed his desires for a very long time; he was vulnerable and ready, even eager, to give in to Father Doyal's advances. But, just as things were getting interesting, Father Terry the Pious had barged in and ruined everything.

The manager of Angelscombe had appointed himself as Father Godfrey's protector, and the young priest was easily influenced by him. Now that Father Doyal had shown his hand, Father Terry would be on the look-out for more threats to his ward.

If only he weren't so tall and muscular! He was far superior in strength and Father Doyal could never hope to win a physical challenge.

Yet these obstacles only made Father Godfrey the more desirable.

He got into his car and drove away, trying to shake off the shame of having his true colours discovered and knowing those two backwardists were laughing about him.

His failed attempt on Father Godfrey meant he no longer had a pretext for visiting Angelscombe. He must find a way to remove Father Terry and clear the path to Father Godfrey – but it would have to be very subtle.

The key was to find Father Terry's Achilles heel. He had to discover something the tall priest valued, and put it in serious jeopardy. Something he could use to blackmail him.

As he drove the few short miles back to his own pony farm, it dawned on him what that weakness was.

The Dales ponies!

They were Father Terry's *raison d'être* – both in the eyes of the Catholic Church and the government. Lose the ponies and his job at Angelscombe, and he would be out on his ear, with no status, however precarious, within the Church; no money and no accommodation. He would be ruined. And all because the prig wouldn't let Father Godfrey loosen up and follow the new rules promulgated by Pope Lucius II.

Father Doyal chuckled to himself. "Gotcha!"

Chapter Twenty: A Brief Reflection
Wednesday, 9th October 2030

The eagerness with which Father Godfrey left the kitchen garden dissipated when the stables came into view.

The walled enclosure of the garden and Brother Melvin's kindness had created a holy refuge from the evil world outside. But, in order to reach the chapel, he must go past the location of his shameful encounter with Father Doyal.

The other priests were busy about their work, yet he was sure they knew what had happened, and were sneaking furtive glances at him as he walked by.

They were decent men who would not make him feel bad about it, but still; *They Knew,* and it was horrible. How could he ever hold his head up in the community again?

But it wouldn't do to slink by them in humiliation; he must act naturally.

Forcing himself to wave in greeting to anyone who happened to look at him, he made his way to the hay barn and entered the chapel through the concealed door.

He almost ran to the first pew and knelt on the stone floor, holding his head in his hands, and not daring to look at the tabernacle where the Eucharist resided.

"Lord, I am not worthy, Lord, I am not worthy," he kept repeating. When his knees could stand the pain no longer, he sat on the pew seat.

His heart beat faster, as he remembered being cornered by Father Doyal in the dark stable, reliving the man's strength and smelling his aftershave as his handsome face drew ever nearer.

How close he'd come to giving in – after so many years of self-discipline! And how fortuitous that Father Terry had rescued him! Father Terry, the good shepherd, had saved the lamb from slaughter. He'd acted as God's true representative; Father Doyal represented the Devil.

How interesting that temptation incarnate should appear now, redirecting Father Godfrey's efforts into fending off unchaste advances, just when he was supposed to be alerting the faithful about the coming Warning. Satan's hand was indeed all over this and he thanked God for his rescue by Father Terry. "Lord, you *are* watching over me, after all."

Then he prayed five decades of the Rosary, asking Our Lady for chastity in thought as well as deed. "Please! Never let me be tempted like that again! Keep that man away from me!"

Should he have any more dealings with Father Doyal, he was resolved to make himself as undesirable as possible.

Chapter Twenty-One: Difficult Decisions

Wednesday, 9th October 2030

Father Terry noticed Father Godfrey had no appetite at lunch time.

It was hardly surprising, after the events of the morning. If not for swift intervention, his friend might have done something he'd regret for the rest of his life.

Father Doyal was an emissary of the Devil, and Father Terry needed to watch for any more attempts to corrupt the suffering priest.

Pope Lucius II had a lot to answer for, encouraging the clergy to go against the clear teachings of Scripture and the Catholic Church. Because of him, millions of souls were 'falling into Hell like snowflakes' to quote St. Teresa of Avila.

It was hard to imagine what pretext Father Doyal might find to come back to Angelscombe. Nevertheless, another visit from him could occur at any time, which meant cloaking their evangelical activities in even more secrecy than before. That man had made their lives harder than they already were.

Without letting the others know what had transpired between Father Doyal and Father Godfrey, he must let them know this visitor was dangerous and to be regarded as Satan's spy.

He hoped the Warning would indeed come soon. Father Doyal must understand the need to turn his life around and follow God's narrow path to Heaven, instead of the broad road to eternal suffering.

Despite these extra restrictions on their efforts to minister to the faithful, the priests must still alert them to the Warning before it was too late.

The only way this could be done without rousing suspicion was still through the ponies. More than ever, Father Terry was convinced God was telling him that his top priority was protecting and caring for the Dales.

And those ponies had to eat, which meant buying enough hay to see them through the winter.

Which meant selling those candlesticks.

His heart sank. Father Godfrey would be upset, and he was already devastated by Father Doyal's attack. Would this send him over the edge?

Father Terry argued the pros and cons of letting Father Godfrey know in advance about his plan.

The problem was, they needed the money urgently. Father Oliver had been unsuccessful in his attempts to persuade the government to supply more funds. He had let them know that a new foal had arrived, another two were imminent and a couple more mares were heavily pregnant. Thus it was clear they were fulfilling their mandate to produce more ponies, and would require more food to feed them. Yet the powers that be insisted there was no need until the babies were weaned in six months' time. 'Then please feel free to reapply.'

The question was, would Father Godfrey be more upset at discovering after the fact that the candlesticks were gone, or at being told now?

Still unsure, he went to his office and drafted an advertisement for the sale of two magnificent gilded candlesticks, 'a fine adornment to any dinner table or mantelpiece'.

He passed Father Godfrey coming out of the haybarn on his way to the chapel to take photos of the two items. The young priest smiled at him and appeared in much better spirits.

Father Terry decided to bite the bullet. "Godfrey, can you spare a moment?"

"Of course."

"I think you'll agree that, thanks to our infernal visitor, we're going to find it much harder to do our job of spreading the Faith, and more pressingly, to let everyone know about the Warning."

"Most definitely."

"Our only chance of transmitting the message is through the ponies. Which means we have a moral duty to take the best care of them that we can."

"No argument from me there, Terry."

"Good. Because what I'm about to say next will be hard for you."

"You're not back to selling the candlesticks again, are you?"

"Can you think of anything else we could sell that will bring in enough money for extra winter hay?"

Father Godfrey shook his head miserably. "No."

Father Terry suddenly thought of a solution. "Brother Melvin has good connections with Lady Rowland." He wasn't free to explain their real relationship without prior consent. "She is the daughter of Archbishop Gregory's sister and a staunch Catholic. Supposing I offer the candlesticks to her first? She is very well-to-do and we could ask her to keep them safe for us until we have the money to buy them back."

Father Godfrey nodded enthusiastically. "That would keep them in the community, in a certain sense."

"Excellent, thank you. I will deconsecrate them until we have them in our possession again. Wish me luck!"

After taking the photos, Father Terry returned to his office and phoned Lady Rowland.

As agreed in that conversation, he texted her three photos of the items from different angles, with details of their height and provenance, and waited.

Half an hour later they had agreed on the sale.

Father Terry texted Father Godfrey with the news and received a thumbs up emoji in reply.

Chapter Twenty-Two: A Chance Encounter

Saturday, 12th October 2030

The now deconsecrated candlesticks were paid for promptly in cash to Father Oliver two days later, enabling Father Terry to visit the feed shop that very Saturday and order the extra hay.

It could have been done over the phone, but the priest wanted to make sure the bales were of good quality. Sometimes a few of them were mouldy from being out in the elements, or weeds were mixed up in it, or it was simply not the best cut.

Father Terry wanted to be a good steward of the project's resources and make sure he got the best for the ponies.

"Good morning, Father!" said Mr. Browning, who ran the shop. "What can I do for you?"

"I'm here to order your best Timothy hay."

"Very good, Father. I'll take you round back and show you what we have."

The priest followed him through a connecting door behind the counter to a huge storage area filled with hay bales stacked in separate sections.

Mr. Browning led Father Terry to the far end. "This is our best stuff, Father. Mind you, it costs quite a bit more than the rest."

"I know," sighed the priest. "But it doesn't pay to cut corners on quality with horses and ponies. You only end up spending more on vet bills later."

Mr. Browning nodded. "Try explaining that to your fellow churchman down there." He pointed to a man standing next to the worst hay. "I told him it was only good for cattle fodder, not horses, but he wouldn't listen."

Even from the back, the man was recognisable as Father Doyal. Surely he was supposed to be buying, if not the best, at least good quality hay for his Fell ponies? What was he thinking?

It was none of Father Terry's business. Or was it? Those animals would suffer if he didn't say something. And he didn't owe that excuse for a priest any consideration for his feelings, after his attack on Father Godfrey.

"Mind if I go over and have a word? But I would like two hundred bales of this hay delivered to the monastery, please. After my little chat, I'll come to the front register to pay."

Mr. Browning doffed his flat cap to the priest. "Sounds good, Father. Hope you have better luck with him than I did."

Trying to quell his twofold anger over the cleric's malicious behaviour towards Father Godfrey and now the cheap stunt he was attempting on the ponies, Father Terry used the element of surprise.

Father Doyal spun round when he felt a tap on his shoulder. "You!" he hissed.

Father Terry grinned. "Yes, me." He leaned into the stack of hay and smelled a musty bale. "Ugh! This is awful! Are you getting this for your Fells?"

"So what if I am?"

"Don't you know anything about feeding ponies?"

"If I didn't, I wouldn't be the manager, would I?"

"Then I assume you know this hay would be fatal to your herd."

Father Doyal's eyes became shifty. "What makes you think I'm buying *this* hay?"

"Why else would you be standing here?"

"Why are *you* standing here?"

Father Terry pointed to the bales at the other end. "Because I've already ordered the best hay for my ponies, whose welfare is very dear to me, and I'm anxious to prevent a brother priest from making a grave mistake in *his* hay purchase."

"I wasn't going to make a mistake in my hay purchase. Not that it has anything to do with you."

"I'm glad to hear that, although I understand you didn't heed advice on the matter from a member of the staff here. Then I presume you're buying the same hay as me?"

"You presume correctly."

"Good, because I would hate to have to inform the government that you are using the money they've entrusted to you, to make the ponies under your care very sick." Father Terry leaned forwards and peered closely into his eyes. "But if you leave Father Godfrey alone, I shan't need to breathe a word of this matter to anyone, and neither will the staff here."

Father Doyal's ugly expression betrayed a deep longing to harm the priest.

Father Terry continued. "Just in case you're tempted to change your mind, I'll witness you making your order."

Undisguised hatred clouded his face, as Father Doyal thrust Father Terry aside and marched through the door to the front of the building.

"Good decision," said Father Terry, following him to the cash register.

Father Doyal was livid; Father Terry actually had the gall to breathe down his neck, while he put in an order for fifty bales of obscenely expensive Timothy hay.

The man was right, of course. His intention *had* been to buy the cheap stuff. No one would have been any the wiser. Those ponies were fine eating anything that was thrown at them; they weren't called a hardy breed for nothing.

But holier-than-thou Father Terry ordered the good stuff, forcing Father Doyal to do the same. He'd counted on adding the saved money to his growing stash from cutting corners elsewhere on purchases for the Fell Project.

Now that Father Terry had his suspicions, Father Doyal would have to be careful for a while. He needed ammunition against that do-gooder and it wouldn't do to give the man ammunition against *him*.

He must strike soon, before he lost his cushy job. The women ran the place without his help, and the project wouldn't suffer if he were removed. In fact, the opposite would be more accurate.

Not only must he be squeaky clean in his financial dealings for the foreseeable future, but staying away from Father Godfrey was the added price for Father Terry's silence.

What could he do to stop that priest from blocking his every move?

He then recalled how, just moments ago, Father Terry had given away the fact that the Dales ponies' welfare was – how had he put it? – 'very dear to me'. So Father Doyal was right: the animals *were* the priest's Achilles heel.

Think, man, think! There has to be a way to use those ponies to get your revenge.

Chapter Twenty-Three: Tea in the Village

Wednesday, 16th October 2030

Father Terry sensed Father Godfrey was gradually regaining his inner peace. There had been no visits from Father Doyal over the past few days, and his friend was eating normally again.

It was time to spread the word about the Warning; that harbinger of evil Father Doyal must no longer be allowed to prevent it.

On Wednesday afternoon, Father Terry took Father Godfrey with him to 'tea' with Mrs. Prince. With her were the usual three friends, eager to take part in the Holy Sacrifice of the Mass, and receive Communion from what they called 'real priests'.

The clergymen arrived wearing long overcoats to hide their Mass robes. Several months ago, Mrs. Prince had draped all her windows with thick lace curtains, so no one could peer in through them and see Mass being said in the living room.

She ushered the two men into her sitting room with a brilliant smile of welcome. The lights were dimmed, the fire in the hearth had been quelled, and the wide mantelpiece was now an altar. Draped across it was a long white cloth, edged in lace, hand-made by the lady of the house. At each end stood a simple wooden candlestick, holding a blessed candle.

From his leather briefcase, Father Terry drew the large gold ciborium, covered in a pristine white cloth and containing the hosts for consecration during the Liturgy, lovingly made by the village baker and brought to the farm under the regular bread, to avoid detection. Father

Terry unwrapped the ciborium with reverence and placed it on a large side table, hung in a cloth matching the one on the altar. Mrs. Prince had already placed the cruets of red wine and water on it. Next to them were a pewter lavabo, a finger towel, and a small jug of water, for pouring over the priest's hands.

Mrs. Prince kept a gold paten and chalice under separate lock and key in a cabinet along the sitting room wall. They were a spare set from the Angelscombe chapel, entrusted to her by Father Terry.

She put these on the table next to the water and wine, while Father Terry brought the linens out of his briefcase. He now placed the purificator – a long white napkin – between the chalice and the gold paten. After placing the large host on the paten, he rested the pall over it.

The pall was a square pocket-shaped piece of linen, made stiff by a cardboard insert. During Mass it would cover the chalice to prevent dust or other matter falling into it. Finally, the corporal, resembling a small folded napkin, was placed over the whole.

During Mass, this last piece of linen would be spread out on the altar, as a kind of table cloth. The chalice would be placed on it, and the Sacred Host would also rest upon it for a short while.

The Roman Missal containing all the prayers and rituals was open on a wooden recipe rack on the altar, and Father Terry made sure the ribbons were in the correct pages for each part of the Holy Mass.

A music stand facing the room served as the ambo, and supported the lectionary.

Both sacred books were the property of Mrs. Prince, and carefully hidden away with the paten and chalice after every Mass.

Father Terry lit the two altar candles, while the ladies took their seats in the dining room chairs brought in for the occasion. He made sure the book on the music stand was open at the correct readings of the day, then walked to the back of the room, ready to begin Mass with Father Godfrey.

The ladies rose as he rang a little dining bell placed on the bureau by the door, and the two priests processed past them to begin Mass.

After the Gospel, read by Father Godfrey, Father Terry sat down with Mrs. Prince and her friends to hear his sermon.

"My brothers and sisters in Christ," began Father Godfrey, "I have an important message for you this afternoon. A message that I, Father Terry, and all the priests at Angelscombe urgently need you to spread to everyone you know – Catholic or non-Catholic, Christian or not."

The ladies shifted uneasily in their seats; they were used to keeping their religious beliefs strictly secret, for fear of reprisal from the progressive element, both within the Catholic Church and from government authorities. What Father Godfrey was suggesting sounded dangerous.

The two priests had talked at length about the best way to word their plea, and Father Terry hoped these good women would be receptive.

Father Godfrey continued, "But before I begin, I don't need to tell you that we must be more vigilant than ever. The Devil is trying, by all means possible, to prevent us from bringing souls to salvation.

"Some of you will have read our new pope's *Nova Theologica Populi* which makes it clear who is in charge. The Devil has infiltrated the Vatican and we, who adhere to the One, True and Apostolic Faith, are now the official enemy of Rome. But our allegiance is to God, not man, and our mission to save souls from the wickedness and snares of the Devil has become more pressing."

As promised, Father Terry had overseen a lively discussion at Angelscombe about how to navigate the new rules of the pope's document.

In the end, the priests decided to wait until each diktat was enforced, rather than worry about them all at once. The timeline for implementation was sufficiently far off – or, in some cases, not even specified – so why agonise over each one now?

Father Godfrey continued his sermon. "Many souls have been led astray. They no longer believe in Satan or the existence of sin. Therefore, we must do everything in our power to be God's instruments in bringing His Word to the lost sheep.

"Yes, it's a dangerous undertaking, and this document has made it all the more so. But Our Lord didn't promise us a comfortable life here on earth. His apostles certainly didn't lead one!

"Bearing this in mind, I need to alert you to an event that is coming soon."

Father Godfrey went on to describe his dream.

Father Terry stole a glance at the four ladies to gauge their reactions. He was pleased to see them all listening with rapt attention.

"Now, I'm not asking you to wear placards in the streets – " titters from the audience " – but whenever you get the opportunity, let people know something called the Warning is coming soon. You can say you heard a rumour about it, if that makes things easier. But I want you to plant the notion in the minds of everyone you meet, that God is about to force them to see themselves as He does, as they really are.

"Please pray hard about this. Don't forget, God will be showing us the state of *our* souls, too. And whether or not we did our best to let our fellow men and women know what was coming, will feature heavily in His assessment.

"This is not the time to be shy. Be prudent, yes, but use all means at your disposal to start people thinking about the Warning. The choice to accept or reject the truth is up to them, not us. God asks us to be faithful, not successful. Ultimately, the success belongs to Him. We are asked to do our part, that's all.

"I will be available for questions after Mass.

"God bless."

When Mass was over, everyone was ushered into the dining room and Fathers Terry and Godfrey carried the chairs back to the dining table. The ladies laid out a Victorian sponge cake, a Bakewell tart, and cucumber sandwiches with the crusts cut off.

They all sat down. Mrs. Prince poured tea into six cups and handed them round. Everyone filled their plates and Father Terry was applied to for the blessing.

They made the Sign of the Cross and he said, "Lord, we thank you for the gift of your Holy Mass this afternoon, and this wonderful food. Bless us Lord, we pray, and keep us safe as we endeavour to carry out Your Will this day and throughout our lives. Amen. In the Name of the Father, and of the Son, and of the Holy Spirit. Amen."

"Amen," repeated the others.

"Dig in!" said Mrs. Prince.

An appreciative silence ensued while the first few bites were taken, then Father Godfrey said, "Any questions about tackling the mission I talked about?"

The two priests left an hour later, pleased with their time at Mrs. Prince's home. The call to action had been taken seriously, with many good questions asked.

To encourage the ladies' efforts to warn fellow neighbours of the impending event, it was suggested they go out in twos, like the disciples sent to the villages by Our Lord. That would assure mutual support and lend weight to their message.

"As I mentioned earlier, you can say something like, 'Have you heard the rumour … ? '" Father Terry suggested. "But do it when you're not the only faithful person in the group, without giving away that you're a traditional Catholic. Otherwise you run the risk of being reported to the authorities as subversive."

Father Terry and Father Godfrey well knew what a daunting task they were laying on their parishioners' shoulders.

"We must do more," said Father Godfrey, as they were on their way back.

"You're right, Godfrey. Since Father Doyal seems to be leaving us alone, we can continue our daily evangelising through the ponies, and this time include word about the Warning."

"That would ease my conscience," said his friend. "I feel I've been slacking, thanks to – well, you know."

Father Terry was driving the farm's old Land Rover, which mercifully they were still managing to keep on the road despite its high mileage and occasional engine hiccups. He turned to his fellow priest with a gentle smile. "Let's hope that's all behind us."

That hope was short-lived.

Back at Angelscombe, they were greeted by Father Oliver, who held out a letter to Father Terry. "This was hand-delivered for you this afternoon, by that creepy priest who came round a few days ago."

"Thank you, Father." With a worried glance, Father Terry gingerly took the letter and said to Father Godfrey, "Let's go to my office."

Seated at his desk, with the door closed, he drew a sheet of paper from the envelope. It was covered in flamboyant handwriting and he wrinkled his nose at the familiar, obnoxious aftershave. Holding the letter away from him, he began to read:

"You are cordially invited to bring a selection of your Dales ponies to an upcoming event at the Lambcot Fell Protection Farm.

"I am preparing statements for us to read, openly expressing our allegiance to Mother Earth according to #7 of the *Nova Theologica Populi*. This occasion will create publicity for our two preservation programmes, and is a wonderful opportunity to show off your new foal."

Father Terry dropped the page on his desk and buried his head in his hands. Father Doyal was challenging them to prove they were fully behind the new regime, or forfeit their status as preservers of the Dales Pony.

Thus far, they had succeeded in to treading the fine line between being cancelled and being useful, for the work they were doing was not against their consciences.

But if they refused to accept this invitation, the residents of Angelscombe risked losing their accommodation and their income – their whole means of survival – and gone would be their ability to secretly save souls.

He explained this to Father Godfrey, who groaned, "I'm so sorry! This is all because you stopped him from propositioning me, isn't it?"

"Only partially."

"What else could be the reason?"

"I'm not at liberty to tell you. But I assure you, it's something completely unrelated. Don't blame yourself for this. Father Doyal would have stirred up trouble for us regardless of our actions."

"Thank you for that. But are we going to accept his invitation?"

"We need to pray about this, and ask God to give us a way out."

Chapter Twenty-Four: Oh, *What* a Shame!

Wednesday, 16th October, 2030

Father Terry was trapped. If the priests at Angelscombe didn't attend the event with their Dales ponies, Father Abnus Doyal would denounce them to Bishop Hardy for refusing to subscribe to the *Nova Theologica Populi*, thus disobeying the new pope.

They'd already been removed from active ministry; the next step would be to defrock them. And what was to stop Lucius II from going further, by excommunication, to make an example out of them?

Father Terry didn't want to burden his friend with these worries; it was better to keep them to himself. Time would tell if he was right about the consequences of non-compliance. There was no point upsetting Father Godfrey further, since he still blamed himself for this situation, despite Father Terry's attempts to persuade him otherwise.

"I'm going for a walk to clear my head," he said. "Then a visit to the chapel will be in order, I think."

"I'm going there now," replied Father Godfrey. "Maybe God and Our Lady will have some words of inspiration."

"Amen to that! I'll catch you later. And Godfrey, we won't tell anyone else about this until we absolutely have to."

"Understood."

Father Terry's steps took him towards the kitchen garden and Brother Melvin's two statues. The weather was warm enough for spending time outside with Our Lord and Our Lady.

Receiving no answer when he knocked on the tall wooden door, he turned the handle and walked in. The two statues were uncovered, and he hoped Brother Melvin wouldn't mind him chatting with Jesus and His Mother uninvited.

He sat by Christ and pondered his predicament.

Should he go to that infernal event and play the role of dutiful servant of the new regime? Or should he obey his conscience and refuse to take part in any of it?

He was split in two; God had asked him to protect the ponies, but his mission as a priest was to remain faithful to the Deposit of Faith. Which was more important?

Lord, is there any way to accomplish both?

Even as he prayed the words, he realised he was trying to serve God and mammon.

Furthermore, he himself had handed Father Doyal this method of retaliation on a platter. At the feed store, while he was triumphantly shaming the priest, Father Terry had given away how much the ponies meant to him. Father Doyal had lost no time using that weakness against him.

He stared across the rows of fruits and vegetables, and recalled the bitter struggles he'd suffered before accepting a vocation to the priesthood.

Young Terry Talbot was being noticed in the world of dressage. He'd won numerous high-level competitions on Major, his home-schooled warmblood. There was even talk about trying out for the British Olympic team, and he had high aspirations of success as a professional rider.

He and his cousin Vincent had no siblings and each young man felt an obligation to make his parents proud.

The boys' families were fiercely Catholic, so Vincent's mother and father were elated when their son went into the seminary. Terry had a nagging feeling that Mr. and Mrs. Talbot regarded their son's worldly career with horses greatly inferior to the spiritual trajectory of his cousin.

Vincent was two short weeks away from ordination, when a speeding lorry crashed into his sedan and killed him instantly.

Terry watched his aunt and uncle, and his own parents, grieve over God's decision to take Vincent before he'd managed to save a single soul.

The young horseman was acutely aware that *his* death would have been the lesser loss to humanity – and suspected the others thought so, too. The guilt in surviving his worthier cousin became unbearable and his riding suffered as a result.

Was God calling him to step into his cousin's shoes? Was He asking Terry Talbot to walk away from horses and join the priesthood? Would He protect a future Father Terry from danger, and ensure that he didn't die before his ordination?

Terry wrestled mightily with this alternative direction in his life. But the prospect of a priest in the family, after all, would overjoy his parents. They would be so proud of him!

Their certain happiness at his change of career gradually eclipsed the pain of the sacrifice it would entail. He began to believe that he owed it to his dead cousin to take over where he had been prematurely cut short.

His duty was to fulfil the dreams of both sets of parents and renounce horses forever.

But it wasn't easy. Even after his ordination and while in active ministry, he frequently endured diabolical attacks on his holy commitment. Did God *really* want him to be a priest? Was he up to the task?

These vicious doubts redoubled after he was cancelled. Satan was right: he'd made a terrible mistake. Guilt over his cousin's death was hardly the proper foundation for a vocation to the priesthood, and would have faded over time.

Then came the bishop's directive to manage the Dales Pony Project at Angelscombe. God was smiling on him after all, by allowing him to secretly save souls while preserving a pony breed, and thereby indulge both his passions.

But now he was being asked to give one of them up. Had he been showing too much interest in the ponies and not enough in God? Had the ponies become his idol?

Father Terry squinted up at the statue of the Sacred Heart of Jesus.

Lord, why did You let me return to my first love, if You were only going to take it away from me again? What are You asking of me? If I don't do as Father Doyal wants, not only will the ponies go to someone else, but <u>everyone</u> *here at Angelscombe will lose their livelihood – and means of saving souls – not just me. Surely, that can't be what You want?*

He'd just finished this prayer, when the garden door opened and Pastor John's voice called, "Brother Melvin, are you there?"

Father Terry replied, "He's not here, John. He might be in the kitchen." The Lutheran looked agitated. "Is anything wrong?"

"We have a case of strangles in the barn. I was hoping Brother Melvin had a cure for it, to save calling the vet."

Father Terry almost burst out laughing.

God had answered his prayers! Strangles was not normally life-threatening, but was highly infectious. Father Terry couldn't possibly take his ponies off the property to attend that event of Father Doyal's. In fact, Angelscombe would be off limits to visitors for the foreseeable future.

The priest knew enough about the disease to be aware that the pony infected with strangles must be kept separate from the others. It was a distressing illness for the afflicted animal; the lymph nodes swelled and pressed on the upper respiratory tract, causing laboured breathing. If they formed abscesses, swallowing would be difficult and the animal would lose its appetite as well as run a fever.

"I assume you've isolated the pony?" he said to Pastor John.

"Yes, but there's no telling whether any others are infected. It takes two to three days to show itself."

"Then we'll pray it's confined to the one animal."

Father Terry was now less elated and more concerned for the ponies' welfare.

"We can't let them off the property for at least six weeks," continued Pastor John. "But I'm banking on the fact that Dales ponies are hardy animals, and will get through this with minimal discomfort."

The garden door opened and Brother Melvin walked in. "Hello, you two! Am I late for a meeting?"

"Not at all," said Pastor John. "I was hoping you had something to give a pony with strangles."

"Oh, dear, I'm sorry to hear that. What are the pony's signs?"

"Fever, nasal discharge and general low spirits."

"Let's attack it with cut echinacea root, and see if that knocks it on the head without resorting to antibiotics."

"Great. They're better off developing natural immunity. Using antibiotics risks reinfection.

"I've put the pony in isolation, and will keep her feed and water buckets separate from the rest." Pastor John turned to Father Terry. "Maybe we should disinfect a wheelbarrow, shavings fork and shovel for her personal use, too? As a precaution."

Father Terry nodded. "I'll pass that on. I should also inform Dr. Tilman that we have strangles on the property."

"Thank you. I expect we'll have more cases soon," said Pastor John, "but hopefully none of them will be serious."

"Amen to that!" agreed the priest. "As you said, these ponies are very hardy."

Back at his desk in the main building, Father Terry had the great pleasure of responding to Father Doyal's invitation. He wrote with small, even handwriting, in deliberate contrast to the other's showy penmanship; he remembered being told that small handwriting was a sign of intelligence.

My dear Father Abnus,

It is with great regret that I must inform you of a case of strangles in one of our ponies.

As you are doubtless aware, this devastating disease is highly infectious and for the next two months our ponies will not be allowed to leave the property.

Therefore, much as I would have enjoyed attending a joint event with you, I must decline your kind invitation.

I hope that despite our absence, it will, nevertheless, be a success.

Yours in Christ,

Father Terry Talbot

Chapter Twenty-Five: Returning the Favour

Friday, 18th October, 2030

Father Abnus Doyal was livid.

Father Terry lived a few short miles down the road, and could have delivered his answer by hand that same afternoon. Instead, he made Father Doyal wait two whole days, by posting it via Royal Mail.

And now, after looking forward to the priest's capitulation, it turned out the man had a cast-iron excuse for not attending the event.

He phoned the vet, just to make sure Father Terry wasn't lying. But the practice's secretary assured him it was true. "We've alerted all our clients, Father. I'm surprised you didn't already know about this."

Embarrassed, he gave a snippy response.

He crumpled Father Terry's letter into a tight ball and aimed it at his waste paper basket.

It missed by three feet.

"Aaargh!"

Clutching the sides of his head with clawed fingers, he forced himself to concentrate.

There must be another way of getting Father Terry to cave; he just needed to calmly think it through.

But instead of forming sensible plans, his churning emotions created colourful ways to physically hurt Father Terry. Yet obviously a Catholic priest couldn't go around harming people on purpose – especially not other priests. Even his protective bishop would be unable to prevent justice being served in such an instance.

But he badly wanted to see Father Godfrey again!

The Dales ponies couldn't leave their farm, but that didn't mean Father Doyal couldn't set foot on the property. Maybe an opportunity to remove Father Terry would present itself while he was there?

He enjoyed the looks of consternation on the priests' faces when he parked by the Angelscombe barn later that morning. He'd chosen this time of day knowing he would find them all busy making up feeds and cleaning out stables.

He was getting out of his vehicle when Father Terry strode towards him. "Abnus! I'm surprised to see you here. Aren't you afraid of carrying strangles back to your barn?"

"People can't carry strangles, Terry. In case you didn't know, humans don't get it."

Father Terry smiled. "No, but they carry the bacteria on their clothes when they've been in contact with an infected animal. You'll have to change when you get back and wash your clothes."

Father Doyal did not know that. "Then I'll make sure I don't come in contact with an infected animal."

"Unfortunately, we can't guarantee that you won't. The disease may be incubating in ponies who aren't yet showing signs of it."

"Then I'll stay away from the ponies," Father Doyal replied.

Father Terry's grin widened. "But you've already been in contact with me, and *I've* been in contact with the ponies. So I might be carrying the bacteria."

Father Doyal was losing patience. He wasn't going to let this feeble attempt to shoo him off the premises succeed, and folded his arms across his chest. "I'll take my chances."

"Suit yourself." Father Terry turned on his heels and went back to the barn.

Father Doyal followed him to the saddling area where Father Godfrey was tacking up one of the ponies.

"Hello, Godfrey."

The young priest nodded, and blushed deeply as he did up the girth without looking at him.

Since Father Terry was wearing breeches and Father Godfrey was in overalls, it was clear the former would be riding. While he was in the saddle, access to the younger priest would be that much easier.

But Father Terry seemed to have read his mind. "Father Godfrey, I'd really appreciate it if you could accompany me in the ring today. Betsy can be a little unpredictable at times."

"I thought the Dales pony was famous for its level-headedness?" sneered Father Doyal.

"It is," replied Father Terry. "But this is only my third time on this mare, and she's still very green."

"Has she shown any signs of skittishness?"

"Horses are flight animals, Abnus. Surely you know that? Riding always carries a risk."

"But does anything in particular bother her?"

"As I said, this is only my third time on her, so I don't know yet. If you'll excuse me, I need to get going."

Father Doyal stood back a few steps to let the priest lead the pony out to the arena, together with Father Godfrey, who stroked her head soothingly as Father Terry mounted lightly into the saddle.

Father Doyal leaned on the fence and observed the priest take up rein contact and quietly urge Betsy forwards with a slight closing of his legs.

The black pony moved off calmly and Father Godfrey sat down on the mounting block in the middle of the arena to watch.

After ten minutes of quiet walk in large circles and loops in both directions, Father Terry said to Father Godfrey, "Time to try her in trot, I think."

"I agree!"

He closed his legs again, with encouragement in his voice, and the pony transitioned into trot. It was a little ungainly, for the animal was still adjusting her balance under the weight on her back. But Father Terry scratched her reassuringly on her withers and she remained calm.

Following along the fence perimeter, the pair came towards Father Doyal. He sneezed loudly and the pony lost concentration on her rider.

"You're fine, sweetheart," said Father Terry, stroking her neck.

Just as she came level with him, Father Doyal shook a large white handkerchief over the fence, in preparation for blowing his nose.

Spooked by the white cloth waving in front of her, Betsy shied violently and lost her balance. Father Terry was pitched forward and put his arms around her neck. But the added weight on her front end made the mare stumble and she fell on her right side, taking the priest with her and pinning his right arm underneath her heavy frame.

Delighted at his success, Father Doyal ducked through the fence boards and made a show of rushing to the priest's aid, as the pony struggled to her feet and ran off, reins trailing.

Father Godfrey cried out to him, "Please catch her! I need to call an ambulance!"

Father Terry was writhing in agony on the ground, his arm an unnatural shape.

Making no move to catch Betsy, Father Doyal bent down and whispered in Father Terry's ear, "Stop protecting Father Godfrey." Peering into the injured man's eyes, he considered adding persuasion by twisting the broken arm. But other priests were running into the arena and they would have seen him do it.

In an tortured voice, Father Terry cried, "Get thee behind me, Satan!"

His eyes narrow slits, Father Doyal hissed, "Think about what I said, or I'll bring real harm on the ponies, too."

Chapter Twenty-Six: Assessing the Damage

Saturday, 19th October 2030

Father Terry woke up in a hospital bed to find his right arm covered in a cast below the elbow, and Father Godfrey hovering anxiously over him.

"Where am I? What's happening?"

"You had an accident yesterday, remember? Betsy fell and pinned you underneath her."

Clarity slowly replaced fogginess. Recalling the incident, Father Terry said, "That was no accident. Father Doyal deliberately caused Betsy to panic. He *wanted* me to get hurt."

With a sigh, Father Godfrey sat down in the cheap plastic chair next to the bed. "I have to agree, it did look deliberate."

Father Terry glanced at the priest. "Did you hear what he said to me?"

"No, I was busy calling an ambulance."

"He threatened to harm the ponies next."

"What? He's got to be stopped! But first we have to get you sorted."

"I assume my arm's broken?"

"In three places, I'm afraid."

Father Terry tried to flex his right hand. "Godfrey, this is infuriating! I can't move my fingers."

Father Godfrey coughed apologetically. "There's no easy way to say this, Terry. The doctors say you'll never get back the use of that hand."

"That can't be true!"

This was awful news! Father Terry lay back on the pillows and squeezed his eyes against the tears welling without his permission.

The consequences of this on his ability to serve were too horrible! What was God playing at? How could He let Father Doyal do this to him? How could He let evil win?

Without opening his eyes, he groaned, "How can I be a priest now, Godfrey? I can't hold up the host and paten, or the chalice or wash my hands …

"I can't even help with the ponies. I'm useless now."

"What a ridiculous assumption!" said Father Godfrey. "That's the shock talking. The doctors could be wrong, for a start, and in any case, you wouldn't be the first priest to say Mass without full use of his hands."

"Oh, really? Name just one!"

"What about Saint Isaac Jogues, who was missing two fingers?"

Father Terry opened his eyes and said reproachfully, "He still could use the rest of his hand."

"You know we'll all help you. We'll say Mass together in the chapel and," he lowered his voice, "go in twos to 'have tea' in the village, like last time."

Father Terry was only somewhat mollified by this idea. "I could never be a parish priest again. And what about helping with the ponies? I can't ride anymore, I can't train anymore, and I can't help with chores anymore. As I said, I'm useless!"

"You'll still be valuable as an administrator."

Father Terry looked daggers at him.

"O.K., O.K.," said Father Godfrey. "Look, it's going to take time to get used to this situation. Let your bones heal before you make any pronouncements about your future. We'll all be praying for you to get back the full function in your hand, and you need to do the same."

"I know you're right, but this is hard!"

"I've brought your Breviary, so you can keep up with the Divine Office. And your Rosary."

"You're determined to keep me busy while I'm in here, aren't you?"

"It won't be for long. They expect to release you tomorrow."

"Why can't I leave today?"

"It was a bad break and they want to make sure you're stable before you leave."

"I doubt whether I'll ever be stable again," quipped the priest.

Father Godfrey chuckled. "Good to see you returning to your normal self. I need to go, but I'll be back this evening to see how you're doing and find out what your time of release is. Perhaps we can say the Liturgy of the Hours together?"

"God bless you, Godfrey – something to look forward to."

But as soon as his friend left, Father Terry sank back into the pillows, fighting off despair.

Was God telling him he shouldn't have become a priest after all? And yet, He seemed to be saying he shouldn't be involved with the ponies, either.

What *did* He want from him?

Sunday, 20th October 2030

That night the hours dragged on and on; Father Terry wasn't even granted the temporary mercy of sleep.

He'd been abandoned by God, the God Whom he'd willingly served – even when his own church kicked him out for over-zealous adherence to the true Faith.

He prayed Into the darkness, *Lord, what is Your plan for me? What do You want me to do?*

But there was no reply.

When he was a parish priest and people came to him experiencing spiritual dryness, he would comfort them by saying, 'Jesus is closest to us when He seems the farthest away'.

How hollow those words sounded to him now!

Jesus, why aren't You answering me?

Nothing.

Lacking divine assistance, his mind sank to devising methods of retaliation against Father Doyal. How sublime it would be to give him a dose of his own medicine!

That man should never have been allowed into the seminary, let alone ordained. He was a minion of Antichrist, anxious to help his masters destroy the precious traditions of the Catholic Church.

Father Terry had a vison of Father Doyal being mown down by a herd of his own Fell ponies. Crushed under their weight, and losing the use of both legs, so he would never walk again. Or, his hand was caught in the machinery of a combine harvester ...

He knew these fantasies were from Satan, but the strength and will to ward them off were fast ebbing.

Yet these imagined scenarios appalled him. He begged forgiveness for indulging in them, and asked for help in finding a better way to handle his infirmities and discover a new purpose in life.

By the next morning, he'd decided that his only chance of banishing despair and repelling evil thoughts was engaging in physical activity. He needed to do something that would take his mind off his woes.

At 10 a.m. Father Godfrey brought him the Eucharist, and prayed with him, before driving him back to Angelscombe.

On the way, Father Terry asked for suggestions on what to do to stay sane.

"I have *one* idea," said his friend. "It may not be exciting enough, but it might be a good way to ease you back into community life."

"Let's hear it."

Chapter Twenty-Seven: A Watering Lesson

Sunday, 20th October 2030

Later that morning, Father Terry was standing next to Brother Melvin in the greenhouse. His right arm rested in a sling and an overcoat was draped around his shoulders against the cool October temperatures.

The SSPX brother was explaining how to water his poinsettias. "They can easily become oversaturated – which is the most common way of killing them, by the way. We want the soil to be moist, but not soggy."

Father Terry had trouble showing interest in this conversation. But Brother Melvin had generously agreed to take 'help' from the crippled priest and, painfully aware that he'd be more of a hindrance, Father Terry knew he should show gratitude towards the elderly man.

The way to do that was to listen and learn.

"I'd like to put you in charge of these beauties, Father. They are destined for great things by adorning our altar over the Christmas season, and they need to look their best."

Father Terry suppressed a smile; Brother Melvin was obviously playing up the importance of this job. But he nodded gravely. "I see. It's up to me to make sure they are ready to greet Baby Jesus on Christmas Day."

Brother Melvin nodded enthusiastically. "And for several weeks thereafter. They are needed throughout the whole of the Christmas season."

"Do they need fertiliser or anything?"

"Not right now, no."

"I assume you have other duties for me besides watering the poinsettias?"

"Oh, my, yes! This is just the beginning. But I'd like you to start with these. Let me show you where the watering can is, and we'll sort out how you can fill it."

Father Terry followed him to the greenhouse entrance, where the water hose was coiled around a holder decorated with a cross. One end was attached to a water tap.

Brother Melvin picked up a small green watering can with a long slender spout and handed it to the priest.

"Here you go."

Without thinking, Father Terry reached for it with his right hand – but his fingers refused to open. With an embarrassed glance at the brother, he took the can in his left and returned the slinged arm to his side.

"Good!" said Brother Melvin. "Now, can you fill it with water?"

The question was humiliating, but natural. Father Terry put down the can and tried to turn on the tap with his left hand. Being the weaker one, it took several attempts.

"I'll be careful not to close it so tightly in future," Brother Melvin said. "Sorry about that."

"Don't be. This hand will get stronger soon. It has no choice!"

The sound of water pushing through the long hose was strangely comforting to Father Terry. Turning on the tap was a tiny task – but he'd accomplished it on his own, and that was huge.

The next step was more problematic. He had to open the hose nozzle and get it into the can before water gushed everywhere. Not only that, but he would need to reverse the process when the can was full.

Anxiety rose in him at the thought of not even being able to fill a watering can.

Brother Melvin must have registered his panic, for he lifted the nozzle off the ground. "Let's do this a different way. Can you get the open nozzle in the can and hold it down with your right hand? We'll turn on the tap afterwards."

Father Terry switched off the water, then bent to open the hose nozzle with his left hand, pressing his right foot down on it to keep it steady.

He then placed it in the watering can, and tried to keep it there by leaning on it with his right hand in its sling. But it was painful and his recovering arm probably shouldn't be in use just yet.

Changing tactics, he leaned against the greenhouse and balanced on one leg, placing his other foot on the hose as it rested on the lip of the can – and successfully held the nozzle inside.

"Well done!" cried Brother Melvin.

Father Terry felt like a kid basking in his teacher's praise, grateful and humbled that this old man should help him perform such a miniscule feat.

Encouraged, he reached forwards to switch on the tap. The hose tried to jump out of the can with the sudden force of rushing water, but he kept it in place with his foot, and with satisfaction watched the swirling liquid fill the receptacle.

When the water was near the top, he turned off the tap before removing the hose and flipping the nozzle switch to close it, all with his left hand.

Laughing, he picked up the full can. "Ta-da!"

With a chuckle, Brother Melvin clapped him on the shoulder. "Bravo, Father! But before you water the poinsettias, let me show you around the garden."

Brother Melvin now led the priest to another area, and shared his excitement over the progress of his winter fruits and vegetables. "I *knew* the Sacred Heart would ensure they thrived!" He pointed to the statue overlooking impressive rows of broccoli, cabbage, carrots, leeks, parsnips and Brussels sprouts, blackberries, strawberries, and rhubarb. "Our Lord has never let me down yet."

Moved by the old man's confidence in the Divine and ashamed at his own lack of faith, Father Terry asked, "Have you never had the feeling that Christ has abandoned you?"

Brother Melvin's eyes filled with knowing. "Of course! Everyone goes through those times. But what matters is that we don't believe that He actually *has* deserted us."

"How do you do that?"

"I always tell myself that He has a better plan for me than I've devised." The old man grinned. "And so far, I've been right."

"But He's allowed my right hand to become useless. I can't celebrate Mass anymore, so how can I be a priest? I'm no good with the ponies, now, either. What else can he be asking me to do?"

"Remember that you are a priest forever, Father, and always will be."

"But how can I be a priest, if I can no longer celebrate the sacraments?"

"One thing I've learned, Father, is that nothing shall be impossible with God. *Nothing.*"

Chapter Twenty-Eight: Revelation

Sunday, 20th October 2030

Father Godfrey was in the chapel praying for Father Terry.

It wasn't the first time his priest friend had suffered a crisis of faith. Each of the Angelscombe priests went through spiritual hell when they were cancelled – betrayed by Holy Mother Church and, seemingly, by Christ Himself. They'd felt lost, useless and abandoned.

Through long weeks of prayer and fasting, they had discerned their new role in the Lord's plan. He was calling them to remain faithful to the traditions of the True Church, as holy priests, separate from the false version.

Once they realised that their work with the ponies at Angelscombe was really about preserving the Deposit of Faith, they found new reserves of energy to carry out this adapted version of their vocation.

When the current lunacy was over, these priests, and others all over the world like them, were going to emerge from hiding and lead Jesus' flock. They were going to gather the lost sheep, the faithful Catholics persecuted by the wolves in the Church, and lead them to salvation.

But now that Father Terry had been rendered incapable of fulfilling that noble mission, how was he going to cope? In the Land Rover on the way back from hospital, he'd said he was battling an overpowering thirst for vengeance against Father Doyal. Was there any way Father Godfrey could help him fight his anger and repair his trust in Our Lord?

Would assisting Brother Melvin in the kitchen garden be of any use? Or was it too lowly a job for his friend?

He confided his concerns to Our Lord, asking for guidance in directing Father Terry towards inner peace, if not actual reconciliation with Father Doyal. For Father Godfrey, too, was having trouble forgiving that man.

Father, I ask You for the grace to even <u>want</u> to forgive him. He has done such damage to Father Terry, as well, and we cannot trust him. Therefore I ask You to help both of us.

When he looked at his watch, thirty minutes had already elapsed. *I'd better check on Terry.*

He left the chapel, and shortly afterwards was knocking on the door in the kitchen garden wall.

"Come in, it's open!"

He pressed down the old-fashioned black latch, and the hinges creaked as he pushed open the heavy door.

Right arm in its sling, Father Terry was on his knees in the vegetable section. He was pulling up carrots with his left hand, vigorously shaking the earth off and placing them in a wicker basket. He looked up with a mournful expression. "As you can see, Brother Melvin put me to work right away, with no sympathy for my sad condition."

The brother grinned. "Those who do not work, do not eat," he said cheerfully.

"See what I mean?"

Father Godfrey laughed. "I came to see how you were getting on and if you deserve a break from your travails."

Father Terry squinted at Brother Melvin. "I don't know. Do I?"

The old brother nodded with a grimace. "Off you go. Although I can't say you're the best worker I've ever had."

Father Terry rose to his feet and brushed the dirt off his trousers with his left hand. "See what I mean? No compassion."

Laughing, Brother Melvin waved a dismissive hand. "Away with you, Father. But I expect to see you back soon, ready to put more elbow grease into it."

"Yes, sir." Father Terry gave an awkward salute with his good arm. "I'll be back." He fetched his coat, which hung on the corner of the greenhouse door.

The old man chuckled. "Enjoy your break."

Father Godfrey held the door for his friend, and closed it behind them. "Was it really that bad?"

To his relief, Father Terry beamed. "No, it was jolly good fun, actually."

Father Godfrey pointed towards the garden wall. "But just now it sounded as if you'd been having a grim time. I was beginning to wish I hadn't suggested you work with him."

"We were just messing around. It was a great idea. Brother Melvin is most calming to be around, and he's a wise old egg."

"So he was helpful?"

"Yes, he was."

Since Father Terry wasn't forthcoming with details, Father Godfrey said, "Let's do the rounds of our sick and injured ponies and see how they're doing, shall we?"

"Is this your plan for helping me realise I'm not the only one on the list of ailing and wounded?"

Father Godfrey laughed. "I hadn't even thought about that, but it's a good angle. I like it. Our suffering helps us be more compassionate about others' suffering. We'll see if it works in your case."

Father Terry rolled his eyes. "Whom are we visiting first?"

"You've not seen Trudy for a few days, and I'm curious to know what you think about her condition. We've started using Brother Melvin's magic potion on her."

"The monk's pepper?"

"Yes. She's only been on it for a short while, mind, so there'll be no dramatic change. But see what you think."

They ambled in comfortable silence to the large paddock, which Trudy shared with three other older mares.

Father Godfrey waited while Father Terry inspected the four ponies.

"Which one is Trudy?" the priest finally asked.

"I was hoping you'd ask that!" cried Father Godfrey. "This means outsiders won't be able to spot her, either."

Father Terry nodded slowly. "You're right. Maybe Brother Melvin has saved her from being culled by our zealous masters." As the ponies walked expectantly towards them, he added, "I can now see that one of them has a thicker coat than the others. But she's not bug-eyed or cresty."

"Thankfully we caught it in time," said Father Godfrey. "It's autumn now, so she'll likely hang on to her coat for the winter. But I'm hopeful that she'll shed it normally next spring after being on the herb. I don't want to put a grazing muzzle on her, because that would give the game away immediately. So we're monitoring her to see if she can go out during the day with the others, instead of eating hay all alone in her stable."

Father Terry made a Sign of the Cross over himself. "God willing, she'll have many happy years yet."

"I'm not sure how we're going to explain her infertility, if this disease prevents her having foals."

"We'll leave that up to the Lord."

Father Godfrey grinned. "We're leaving a lot up to the Lord, aren't we? There's Ruby's paddock. We'll visit her next."

"Was Brother Melvin able to help with her milk production?"

"Oh, yes. That marigold has made a huge difference."

They leaned on her fence and watched the leggy foal suckle. Ruby still had a bandage on her left foreleg, but she was putting weight on it normally, and when the colt was done, she wandered over to the two priests.

Father Terry remarked, "She's totally sound, isn't she?"

"Her wound is healing at a tremendous pace. Pastor John is over the moon that we've been able to tend to our ponies without incurring the expense of calling in Dr. Tilman."

"It seems that between the minister and Brother Melvin, we're able to take care of most equine health issues."

Father Godfrey smiled. "Yes, God really knows how to make good come out of bad for those who love Him, doesn't He? Brother Melvin got kicked out of his retirement home, so we could benefit from his exhaustive knowledge of herbs, as well as his amazing skills as a gardener and chef."

Father Terry laughed. "He was totally wasted in that home!"

"Amen to that!"

"I wish I knew how God was going to make good come out of the evil *I'm* experiencing."

Father Godfrey smiled gently at him. "I think part of His plan is that we learn to trust Him *because* we don't know what He has in store for us, don't you?"

"You're right, of course. But I'm not sure what I'm supposed to be doing while I wait for my future to become clear."

"Perhaps He wants you to continue helping Brother Melvin in the kitchen garden? He must get lonely in there by himself. Yet he does his humble work without complaint, in imitation of Our Lord." Father Godfrey added wistfully, "I often think that makes him the real martyr among us." He so wanted that crown for himself!

"I beg to differ, Godfrey. You're the *real* martyr."

Father Godfrey was confused. "What on earth do you mean?"

"I saw how hard you fought your attraction to Father Doyal."

Father Godfrey was stunned. His face turned crimson. This was terrible! Had anyone else worked out the truth?

Maybe sensing his discomfort, Ruby came over and nudged his chest with her muzzle. He stroked her nose, grateful for the distraction.

Father Terry continued in this embarrassing vein. "Witnessing that, I realised I was right in thinking how for many years you've been battling an inclination you're not proud of, without ever letting on."

Utterly ashamed that his secret was out, Father Godfrey closed his eyes and pressed his forehead against Ruby's.

"The reason I'm telling you this is not to make you feel uncomfortable, Godfrey. It's because I want you to know that *you* are a true saint and martyr, my friend," said

Father Terry. "The new directive from the pope has made it even harder on you, I know. But you continue to stay true to Christ's teaching and bear your cross without complaint."

Father Godfrey was unable to reply. His heart was too full.

Chapter Twenty-Nine:
Embarrassment

Sunday, 20th October, 2030

Ruby slowly pulled her head away.

Father Godfrey swallowed hard, eyes on the ground. "I don't know what to say."

Father Terry smiled. "That's O.K. It's going to take time for it to sink in that you're one of the good guys, not one of the bad ones."

Father Godfrey gave a derisive snort. "If only!"

"As I said, it's going to take time for you to accept that I'm right."

Father Godfrey glanced at him. "There's also the possibility you're wrong."

"That's Satan messing with your head. Don't let him!"

Father Godfrey was all too familiar with Satan's games. He was worn out from repelling the Evil One's accusations that he wasn't good enough to be a priest – that no one at Angelscombe would like him if they knew the truth.

He frequently despaired of God's love, exhausted by the effort of throwing himself on God's Mercy, feeling unworthy to receive It, and doubting It had been bestowed. Followed by crushing guilt for not trusting God.

He was too ashamed to admit this to his brother priests in the Sacrament of Reconciliation, despite the seal of the Confessional meaning they couldn't repeat it to anyone.

Neither was there a priest beyond the walls of Angelscombe to whom he could confide, for an outsider might use this knowledge against him.

But now, a wonderful truth revealed itself. If Father Terry really *had* suspected him of experiencing same sex attraction for a long while, he'd never appeared repulsed by it. Father Godfrey had never sensed an inkling of distaste from him, or been made to feel inferior as a priest. In fact, the opposite was true; even after discovering he was right, Father Terry still liked him.

Father Godfrey realised here, finally, was someone to whom he could make a complete, honest Confession and come to for spiritual guidance. What a blissful release!

He felt a strong urge to hug Father Terry for being such a great friend, but it might convey the wrong message. He would also wait a while before asking him to hear his full Confession. But not too long. It was so overdue!

In the meantime, Father Terry had already given him good spiritual counsel, by saying he mustn't heed the Evil One.

Father Terry cut in with, "How's our strangles pony?"

"Looking a lot better, and there've been no more cases, thank the Lord. But we have one more pony on the sick list to visit."

"Oh? Which one is that?"

"Poppy. Nothing serious, but if you recall, she had conjunctivitis and our herbal wizard concocted eyebright tea to apply to her eyes."

"Did the remedy work?" asked Father Terry.

"It most certainly did."

"Then do I really need to check on her? I'll take your word that she's better."

The reluctance in his voice made Father Godfrey say, "Sounds as if there's something else you want to talk about."

Father Terry nodded his head slowly.

Father Godfrey's heart sank. "I've a feeling I'm not going to like it."

"We-ell, it's not going to be a comfortable conversation."

"I don't see how any conversation can be more uncomfortable than the one we've already had."

With a fit of exuberance, the colt left his dam's side and took off rearing and bucking around the paddock.

"That marigold must have some kick to it!" quipped Father Terry.

The two priests leaned on the fence and laughed at the youngster's antics while his mother stood with eyes half-closed.

"Do we know how many foals Ruby's had?" asked Father Godfrey.

"The stud records show this is her third one."

"No wonder she's not interested in watching her offspring show off."

"I'm glad of it," said Father Terry. "That leg needs more time to heal before she's ready to gallivant around after her baby."

"That's true." After an awkward pause, Father Godfrey asked, "So what did you want to talk to me about?"

"I know this is asking a lot, Godfrey, but I think you're the only one who can show Father Doyal fraternal charity by telling him he's on the wrong track."

Father Godfrey blinked rapidly in disbelief. "How can you suggest such a thing! I don't want anything more to do with that man! Just the thought of him fills me with dread after what nearly happened!"

Father Terry put a hand on his shoulder. "No one can *make* you talk to him. But we both know that obeying his progressive masters will not lead him to heaven. The charitable thing to do is try to dissuade him from his current path."

"Since you feel so strongly about it, why don't *you* talk to him? You're better at standing up to him than I am."

"Last time, he caught you in a moment of weakness."

Father Godfrey blushed deeply.

His friend smiled reassuringly. "But you've recovered now. God and His angels are standing with you and will ensure you're in no danger."

Father Godfrey's heart was beating so rapidly, he was about to pass out. "I'm not that heroic, Terry." He clutched the top fence rail with both hands to steady himself. "How can you possibly think I could do this? You're the strong one, not me!"

"We can do all things through Christ, Who strengthens us."

"I'm no Saint Paul."

"God's strength makes us perfect in our weakness."

"Stop spouting Scripture at me!" Father Godfrey wailed.

Father Terry commented wryly, "My *priest* friend is telling me to stop quoting Scripture?"

Reddening, Father Godfrey said, "Alright, I know that sounded bad. But come on! You're asking me to go into the lion's den."

"For a good cause."

"I repeat, why can't *you* do it?"

"I can, if you want me to. Although, if he goes for me, I'm a bit handicapped with this broken arm. And it would be a real triumph for you to see how, with God at your side, you can overcome him."

"That all sounds wonderful in theory. But it's for the saints of this world, not the likes of me."

"You don't realise how strong you are."

"You're just saying that to make me do this, so *you* don't have to."

Father Terry threw up his good left arm in mock despair. "Alright, have it your own way."

"*Thank* you. I trust I can rely on your discretion not to say anything to the others about this whole mess? I'm already worried about how much they may have guessed."

"Of course, Godfrey. You know that." Father Terry grinned. "And now I'm off to lend Brother Melvin some more unwanted assistance with his vegetables."

Father Godrey waved a cursory good-bye, then watched the mare settle down to graze with the now quiet foal at her side.

He went back over this unnerving conversation in his mind, and winced at how cowardly he'd come across to his friend.

He needed a spell in the chapel to think and pray.

Chapter Thirty: An Impromptu Meeting

Monday, 21st October 2030

The topic of confronting Father Doyal was not mentioned again.

Yet Father Godfrey found himself frequently contemplating Father Terry's comment, that his struggles with chastity were making him a martyr. At times he dared to think it might be true; perhaps this really *was* the path God had chosen for him to fulfil his dream of martyrdom?

Sometimes he even believed he did possess the strength to confront Father Doyal without being overpowered by the man.

Could he honestly call himself a martyr, if he wasn't willing to brave saving the man's soul without succumbing to the desires he'd successfully held at bay for so many years? Did he trust God enough to believe he would prevail?

But the test was going to be so hard! Afraid of failure, he shrank into himself, glad Father Terry didn't pursue the idea farther.

The priest did, however, take him to one side after Sunday morning Mass. "I'm always here for you, Godfrey. You can talk to me any time, night or day."

He was touched. "Thank you. That means a great deal."

And it did. He was relieved that his cowardice in refusing to confront Father Doyal hadn't diminished their friendship. Father Godfrey could still plan on going to Father Terry for the Sacrament of Reconciliation and spiritual direction.

As he watched Father Terry walk away, with his right arm in the sling, he recalled that he was supposed to be helping his friend come to terms with losing the use of his right hand. He felt mortified. This whole time he'd been worrying about his own problems and ignoring those of his closest friend.

Call yourself a martyr? I don't think so!

That afternoon the two priests carried the Eucharist under cover to 'tea' at Mrs. Prince's house. The ladies now learned of Father Terry's accident, and their abundant maternal sympathy made up in a small way for his own negligence.

During the consecration at Mass, Father Terry was unable to hold the ciborium in one hand and distribute the Host with the other. He had to stand back while Father Godfrey did the honours, and it was clear that he found it hard. Father Godfrey vowed to say extra prayers for him.

Driving them back to the monastery, Father Godfrey searched for a way to bolster his friend's confidence as a priest. He decided the time had come to make his request.

"Terry, would you be willing to hear my Confession? It's been so long since I was honest enough to recite a full and thorough inventory of my sins. It would be a real relief."

"Of course, Godfrey. It would be an honour. Let me know when."

On arrival at the farm, Father Godfrey went to his cell and changed into his work clothes. It was time to bring in the ponies from pasture and distribute afternoon feed and hay.

Father Terry left for the main building to look for Brother Melvin in the kitchen and, as he told his friend, perform mundane duties such as stirring the gravy and turning over slices of polenta in the frying pan.

When Father Godfrey arrived at the barn, the hay wheelbarrow was empty, so he volunteered to fetch more. The barn was half-full and he had to wheel the barrow deep inside.

A few bales had been pulled to the ground from a high stack, and, as he manœuvred the barrow next to them, he became aware of someone behind him. Their footsteps had been deadened by hay strewn all over the tiles of the original chapel.

He turned and saw Father Doyal standing two feet away, with an unpleasant grin on his face. "We meet again, Godfrey! And this time, Father Terry isn't here to protect you. Or, should I say, to prevent you from doing what I know you want to do."

A burst of loathing streaked through Father Godfrey – loathing of himself and of this man. He recoiled at the memory of how he'd been ready to give himself to him!

Then a flash of understanding replaced the hatred. God, Who had already let the scales of lust fall from his eyes, now allowed Father Godfrey to see the man exactly as He did.

Father Doyal was a child of God who'd gone badly off the rails in his priesthood. He needed help, not hatred, and God was calling Father Doyal to act *in persona Christi* to bring the misguided man back to repentance and the Truth.

So much for running away from this confrontation. It was clear that, in suggesting this meeting, Father Terry had conveyed God's wishes. Father Godfrey smiled at this evidence that his friend was a great spiritual director.

Misunderstanding that smile, Father Doyal took a half-step closer. "I see you're now ready to accept that we are meant to be together. All that fighting isn't good for a man, Godfrey. It's time to give in. You'll feel so much better after you do."

He stretched out his arms, and Father Godfrey shook off a renewed sense of repulsion. He stepped back, and almost fell into the wheelbarrow.

Father Doyal burst into laughter and advanced towards him. "Still determined to act coy, I see."

Father Godfrey instinctively dodged out of the way and, unable to halt his forward momentum, Father Doyal pitched headfirst into the empty barrow.

When he climbed out, Father Doyal's ire was going to be worse than his advances.

Father Godfrey longed to run out of there, but knew that escape wasn't God's will for him. It was his duty to preach His message to this man – even if he didn't want to hear it – and show Jesus' love through fraternal correction.

Holy Spirit, please guide me, please give me courage!

The furious priest was having trouble getting out of the wheelbarrow, which threatened to tip over every time he shifted his balance.

Fighting his repugnance, Father Godfrey grabbed the handles to keep it steady.

Glowering, the priest crawled out and, with both hands, angrily brushed strands of hay off his black suit. Pulling himself to his full height, presumably to intimidate Father Godfrey, he hissed, "You're going to pay dearly for this!"

"For dry-cleaning your suit?" Father Godfrey asked, astounded at his sudden temerity.

"No, you idiot! For humiliating a Catholic priest who, unlike you, is in good standing with the Church!"

"I venture to suggest that you humiliated yourself, without my help."

"You – ! I don't know what I ever saw in you, you worthless worm!"

"Your opinion of me is irrelevant. What matters, is God's opinion. And right now, God is not happy with you."

"How dare you!" Father Doyal lunged at him.

Being the lighter man, it was easy for Father Godfrey to side-step swiftly and avoid physical contact. He was thankful to God for choosing a large open space for this confrontation.

The other priest staggered to a halt and turned to glower at him.

Father Godfrey said sternly, "I repeat, God is not happy with you. You are on the road to ruin, Father Doyal. Unless you repent, you will spend eternity separated from God in Hell."

Fists raised, Father Doyal moved in closer.

A deep calm came over Father Godfrey; he felt sure the Lord would not let this man harm him as long as he faithfully carried out His mission.

"Blessed are the peacemakers," he said to the fists, "for they will be called children of God."

Father Doyal's eyes narrowed. He relaxed his hands, but flexed the fingers menacingly to make sure his foe didn't think he'd won. "I suppose you think *you're* a child of God, you, a cancelled priest? What a joke!"

"I was cancelled for being faithful to Christ, Who is Truth Itself," Father Godfrey responded. "It is His Truth that I'm telling you now. God has spoken; sodomy is a sin which cries out to heaven for vengeance. Father

Doyal, it is against God's natural law and is a *mortal* sin. Rome can try all it likes to twist that truth, to reduce sodomy to a venial sin or no sin at all, and attempt to rewrite the Bible. But none of that is from God; it all stems from rebellious pride, and pride comes from Satan."

Father Doyal stood with his arms akimbo, defiant and unrepentant. He tilted his head to one side, as though patiently waiting for a child to complete its ridiculous routine. Yet his demeaning attitude signalled to Father Godfrey that his words were having an impact.

"Are you finished?" Father Doyal ran his tongue under his top lip in disapproval.

"Actually, no," replied Father Godfrey. "I repeat, you will end up in Hell if you don't follow God's law, and instead choose to believe the errors currently being promulgated by Pope Lucius II."

Father Doyal wagged an aggressive finger. "You do realise I could have you laicised for this outrage?"

"I'd prefer to be laicised for doing the right thing, than go to Hell for obeying the wrong masters."

Is this really me saying these things? Holy Spirit, thank you!

"You are *impossible!*" shouted Father Doyal. He spun on his heels, nearly slipping on the carpet of hay, and strode out of the barn with furious choppy steps.

Father Godfrey bowed his head and prayed.

Lord, thank You for the courage to face him. I hope I fulfilled my obligation and shall pray for his soul.

Chapter Thirty-One: Aftermath

Monday, 21st October 2030

The whole episode had taken less than five minutes, and Father Godfrey hoped no one noticed his delay in fetching hay.

He hoisted four 50 lb bales into the barrow and wheeled them out to the barn. Mercifully, there was no sign of Father Doyal, and the other priests were too busy bringing in ponies to suspect anything sinister.

Physically and emotionally drained, he opened the hay bales and carried heavy flakes to the remaining loose boxes.

Spiritually, however, he felt wonderful. He hadn't wanted this clash with Father Doyal, but now it was over, he was elated. And he was dying to tell Father Terry that he'd done it – confronted Father Doyal and told him the truth. And not only that, but he was completely cured of any interest in the man beyond saving his soul.

After the last pony was in its stable, the next chores were to wash the feed buckets and prepare the animals' breakfast. The weary workers would then take a quick shower and change clothes for Vespers, ahead of going in for dinner.

So the earliest he could hope to chat with Father Terry was after the meal, but the long wait gave him time to think about his conversation with the troubled Father Doyal.

While he was getting ready for Vespers, he wondered why the Vatican was relaxing the rules about such a serious sin as sodomy. Countless souls, including Father Doyal's, were destined for Hell, thanks to so-called 'compassion'. How was it compassionate to keep silent about God's Truth, the only thing that could save them?

And where would that 'compassion' end? Would the pope decide it was unfair to tell kleptomaniacs it was wrong to steal, for fear of hurting their feelings? Should serial killers not be upset and 'marginalised', by telling them they were wrong to murder people and removing them from society? It was perfectly possible: he was already doing nothing to prevent the daily mass murder of unborn babies.

And what about priests like himself, who had gone to such enormous lengths to remain chaste? What torment their celibacy cost them! And for what? To be told their suffering was totally unnecessary? That sodomy wasn't a big deal, that it hardly even merited the status of venial, let alone mortal sin?

Rome was mocking the heroic struggles of faithful priests who refused, for the sake of Christ and their own salvation, to lower themselves to the base standards adopted by so many of their brother clergy.

Not only dedicated priests, but also laymen, who valiantly fought their inclinations every day in order to live pure lives, were being told their sacrifice was worthless.

None of this came from God; it could only come from the Evil One.

How he longed to speak with Father Terry!

When Vespers was over, Father Godfrey was filing into the refectory next to Father Terry and overheard Father Oliver remark to Pastor John, "I wonder what that Father Doyal was doing here today?"

Father Terry glanced at Father Godfrey, who blushed deeply. He knew what his friend was thinking, and was anxious to tell him what had really transpired.

At last the awkward meal was over. As the priests and brothers were walking out, Father Godfrey touched Father Terry on the arm. "Do you have a moment to hear my Confession?"

His friend's troubled look told Father Godfrey he feared the worst. "Of course. Let's go to the chapel."

The two men walked out into the black night in uncomfortable silence, triggering the automatic light at the front door. It illumined their path for a short while, then their guide became the subdued amber bulb at the entrance to the cloister-turned-stables. They heard the sounds of contented munching as they strolled past the ponies.

The hay barn roused mixed feelings in Father Godfrey, as they threaded through the stacked bales to the back wall, and entered the chapel.

"Is face to face O.K. or would you rather go behind the screen in the Confessional?" asked Father Terry.

"Face to face is fine," replied his friend. He wanted to see the priest's expression when he heard what really happened.

They genuflected and sat next to each other in the first pew.

Father Terry made the Sign of the Cross over Father Godfrey, who bowed his head. "May the Lord help you make a good Confession."

"Bless me, Father, for I have sinned. It is two weeks since my last Confession, and years since I made a full one." Father Godfrey looked at the folded hands in his lap, as he recounted all that he'd been too ashamed to say to his fellow priests at Angelscombe.

When he finished, he looked up. "That's it."

Father Terry's face was puzzled. "Is there nothing else you need to tell me? Is that the complete list?"

Father Godfrey smiled. "Yes. But I do have something else to tell you."

"I thought so."

"But you're wrong about what I'm about to say."

"Go on."

Father Godfrey related the events of that afternoon, and enjoyed watching his friend's face brighten, then break out into a wide grin. "Oh, you've no idea how happy it makes me to hear this! Today you overcame Satan, Godfrey, and fulfilled your mission by warning Father Doyal that he is on the road to perdition." He leaned forwards and placed a paternal hand on his friend's shoulder. "You're a good priest, Godfrey, don't ever doubt it."

Barely two seconds after they exited the barn, the night sky above them suddenly caught ablaze.

Chapter Thirty-Two: Now It Begins

Monday, 21st October, 2030

Many times larger than normal, the sun burst into the darkness, rotating at a dizzying pace and spewing out massive sparks of fire.

It was heading towards earth to consume the two priests – and set the whole planet on fire.

With a calmness that Father Terry found unnerving, Father Godfrey said, "Now it begins."

While both men stood rooted to the spot, trying to make sense of what was happening, the moon expanded and transformed into a second fiery orb. Spinning and whirling, it began hurtling towards the sun.

Father Terry tried to yell, "Watch out!" but had no voice.

The titans smashed into each other with a violent crash and flames flew out from the explosion, as if a volcano had erupted in the skies.

Father Terry closed his eyes and covered his head with his good arm, waiting for the terrifying flares to hit.

The ground trembled and groaned and he fell to his knees, expecting a hole to open and consume him.

Awkwardly balancing himself on his left arm, he opened his eyes and looked around for Father Godfrey.

When he couldn't see him, fear gripped his heart. This was it, the Warning, and he was alone.

He crouched in terror, waiting for celestial fire to strike him, and tried to pray. But terror blocked the recitation even of the Our Father.

He could only mouth, *Lord, have mercy on me, a sinner! Lord, have mercy on me, a sinner!*

Then a strange force drew his eyes heavenward.

All debris from the explosion had disappeared; in its stead hung – enormous and luminous – the Cross of Christ.

Then the roof of the sky peeled back and exposed seething, raging fires above. Father Terry squeezed his eyes shut against the awful sight, and his contorted lips begged more fervently for mercy.

When he dared open his eyes, Jesus appeared in front of the suspended Cross, but not nailed to it, and searing Light shone through the wounds in His Hands and Feet, penetrating Father Terry.

In a flash, the Light revealed every sin he'd ever committed, and its ripple effect. He saw sins he'd forgotten about, and ones he considered minor. Each was shown in excruciating detail.

On being shown the state of his soul, particularly where he'd fallen short as a priest, Father Terry felt such acute shame that he almost wanted to die – almost, for he knew where he would end up if he did.

Displayed with special clarity was how he'd used the cancellation of his public ministry to return to horses. God had not been his first priority for a long time, even when taking care of the ponies was clothed in the semblance of doing God's Will.

Father Terry had been a priest for many years, yet as soon as the opportunity arose to change direction back to equines, he'd questioned his vocation. He saw how 'double-minded' he was, according to the words of James 1:8; his loyalty was divided between God and horses, which made him unstable in all he did.

Yet, even while writhing in embarrassment, and wishing he could undo all the hurt he'd caused Jesus and His Father, he felt a powerful Love pouring over him.

Then he heard Christ say, "Pray, My son, pray and fast, in reparation for your sins and those of other priests against My Sacred Heart and the Immaculate Heart of My Mother.

"You are a priest forever. You are a priest above all else and shall love Me, the Lord your God, with all your heart, soul, mind and energy, and your neighbour as yourself.

"And, before you ask, no, the ponies aren't your neighbours."

Father Terry's face reddened. He had, indeed, hoped they were. "Then what *should* my involvement with them be?"

"Let your brother priests be your guides. Through them I will help you strike a balance between using them to maintain your cover in these dangerous times, and being a faithful shepherd of My flock.

"My priest, I need you to persevere in the Faith and be among the Remnant who will lead My Victorious Church after her passion and resurrection."

Father Terry understood that the ponies should be part of his life only inasmuch as they protected the ministrations of the cancelled priests from the eyes of the deep church. They were not an end in themselves.

But the obvious question had to be asked. "Lord, how can I be a priest with this paralysed hand?"

"Patience! Nothing shall be impossible with God."

The Cross vanished from sight and the twinkling stars returned to the night sky. The moon was normal again, as if her metamorphosis had never occurred.

Father Terry's Illumination was over, but Christ's final words echoed in his mind; they were the same as those spoken to him by Brother Melvin in the kitchen garden. *Nothing shall be impossible with God.* Could it be that the Angelscombe cook was a prophet?

Rising and shaking the earth off his clothes, he saw Father Godfrey getting up from his knees next to him.

The wonder in his friend's eyes, as they met Father Terry's, communicated that he, too, had experienced a powerful Illumination of Conscience, and he couldn't help wondering, had Father Godfrey fared better?

Looking away to shield his eyes from the flames bursting out of the exploding orbs, Father Godfrey noticed the strange behaviour of the pony mares in the paddock nearest to him.

They were staring at the sky with wide open eyes. Yet none of them moved, as if they recognised Who had come to visit His earth. Unlike him, they weren't afraid of what they were witnessing – their consciences were clear.

When he had the courage to raise his gaze upwards, the burning embers from the crashed giants had vanished. In their place, huge and glowing, was suspended the Cross of Christ. Above It, the sky abruptly furled up like a giant flag, revealing a heavenly ceiling of giant flames.

Knowing what was coming, Father Godfrey sank to his knees to beg for mercy. But he was unable to formulate the right words, and became anxious that Jesus would not show him mercy because of this.

Then the earth began to shake violently. Was it about to open up and drag him down to the netherworld? Was he such a bad person that Jesus had given up on him?

He desperately tried to summon enough faith to believe that Our Lord and Saviour would never abandon a soul that even *tried* to call on Him.

Then Jesus appeared on the luminous Cross, though not fastened to it. Light radiated from the wounds in His Hands and Feet and permeated Father Godfrey in a way that he could not later describe in normal language.

Suddenly, his soul was suspended in front of him, a softly glowing entity with patches of darkness that Father Godfrey recognised as areas of sin. How he longed to eradicate them!

Jesus revealed everything he had done to offend God during his lifetime, and he saw with horrifying clarity the effect of his sins on those around him.

But the one sin he expected to see was not revealed to him.

Suddenly, overwhelming Love enveloped him, and he heard the words of Jesus. "Father Godfrey, your daily struggles to overcome the temptation of giving into your unnatural attractions have been well-received by My Heavenly Father. He has accepted them in partial reparation for your sins.

"But stop striving to be holy in the eyes of others. Your quiet, daily battles against Satan are holy enough in God's eyes, and His Opinion is the only One that matters."

The Cross and the flames then vanished. The night sky returned, including a normal moon, leaving Father Godfrey overwhelmed with happiness.

Filled with a stronger determination than before to resist temptation, Father Godfrey rose to his knees and brushed the dirt off his clothes.

He saw Father Terry standing next to him and smiled broadly. "You were right, Terry, you were *right!*"

Brother Melvin was tending to his orchids in the greenhouse when the earth suddenly shook violently beneath his feet. Afraid the panes of the glass structure would shatter and fall on him, he hurried outside, only to be greeted by terrifying spectacles in the sky.

He watched helplessly as two fiery suns smashed into each other above him and sent blazing embers plummeting towards his precious kitchen garden.

All his labours were about to be for nothing! How was he going to be of use to the priests if he couldn't produce food for them?

The earth stopped shaking and with unsteady steps he reached the bench where he could sit and pray to the Sacred Heart of Jesus.

But several weird things happened. First, he couldn't formulate any words of prayer. Then a massive, radiant Cross appeared overhead. After that, the firmament slid back like a sun roof, and was replaced by a canopy of frightening flames.

He recognised these as signs of the Warning to which Father Godfrey had alerted them. But before he had time to worry about the state of his soul, Christ Himself materialised, suspended in front of His Cross, not affixed to it.

Through the holes in His Sacred Wounds flashed rays of light which thrust themselves into the deepest recesses of Brother Melvin's soul.

He saw inside himself, as it were, and watched helplessly as Jesus showed him every single thing he'd done wrong in his life, together with the consequences of his actions on others. He saw how deeply he had wounded Christ, and felt enormous sorrow. If only he'd realised before just how much pain his sins caused His Lord and Saviour!

Then the Voice of Jesus said, "Brother Melvin, stop being prideful and worrying whether or not you're making a difference to other people. Do your good works out of love for Me, not for human recognition.

"You are on the right path, if you do this. Love for your fellow man, done for My sake, will cover a multitude of sins."

Then the Voice was gone and the Cross disappeared. The sky reverted to its regular night time routine, scattered with stars and illumined by the full, gentle moon.

Greatly humbled by his experience, Brother Melvin recalled the words of Hebrews 12:6, which tell us that the Lord chastises those whom He loves.

He was now able to pray.

Lord, thank you for enlightening me with the Truth about my soul, and setting my steps on the right path.

Chapter Thirty-Three: Father Doyal Faces God

Monday, 21st October 2030

Father Doyal was sulking in his cell that Monday evening when the Warning overtook him.

He was furious at being ignominiously repelled by Father Godfrey, when he'd been so sure of success.

He was sitting on his bed, in the Catholic convent school confiscated by the New Church and turned into accommodation for the Fell Ponies and their staff. The previous pope had chased the nuns out for their seditious, traditional Catholic teaching of students, whose parents had no business sending them there in the first place. All children should be enrolled in state schools, where iron control could be exercised over their education.

Father Doyal's room was on the upper floor, with a view over the extensive grounds, now fenced paddocks.

He was pondering his next move against Father Godfrey, when he became aware of brightness outside.

Curious, he went over to the window and saw the phenomena witnessed by the residents at Angelscombe. Unlike them, he hadn't been warned what was coming.

He went into shock at the sight of the sun spiralling in the night sky and throwing out flames. When the moon turned into a second fiery planet and catapulted towards the sun, terror shut down his breathing.

Clutching his throat, he gasped, "It's the end of the world! I'm going to die! I'm not ready to die!"

His fear intensified as a huge cross rose in the sky – and Christ appeared, larger than life, suspended in front of it. No nails attached Him to the glowing crucifix, but Father Doyal could see the hollow marks from the wounds in His Hands and Feet. Rays of light poured out from the holes, straight through the priest's window and into his heart.

The pain was unbearable.

No, Lord, no! he tried to cry, but the words stuck in his gullet as an eerie, charred form took shape before him and a stench of sulphur filled his nostrils.

Flames were licking at the monstrosity's feet and Father Doyal knew he was seeing his soul.

He wanted to cover his eyes and nose, but his arms wouldn't move.

Nor could he block out the words of Jesus thundering in his ears. "Abnus, you have not behaved as befits a shepherd of My flock. You have led My sheep astray, and therefore your punishment will be far worse than theirs.

"Remember it is written that it would be better for a millstone to be tied around your neck and you be thrown into the sea, than that you should cause the least of My little ones to stumble."

Still unable to speak, he could only think the words, *Lord, when have I caused anyone to stumble?*

"Hypocrite! You know the answer. Scripture says that men who practice homosexual acts will not enter the kingdom of God. And again, it is written, they shamelessly proclaim their sins and do not hide them, just like Sodom, and have brought evil upon themselves. Remember the words of St. Paul about men committing shameless acts with men. I say to you, it will be more tolerable for the land of Sodom than for you on the day of judgement."

But, Lord, the new pope has downgraded sins below the waist! They're not even really sins anymore. And he's Your representative, so what he says goes for the whole Catholic Church!

"Do not concern yourself with him or follow his errors. I, and I alone, will deal with him.

"Concern yourself with *your* soul. Do not persecute the faithful of My Church, but discern your path back to a holy priesthood and save the souls of others. For the rest of your days, you must make reparation for your sins, if you wish to avoid the fires of Hell.

"Satan eagerly awaits your destruction. Avail yourself of My Mercy while there is still time!"

Father Doyal watched with alarm as the flames rose higher up his blackened soul, still hovering in front of him. They increased in height and intensity with each of his questions, as if fuelled by Jesus' Anger at his attempts to feign ignorance of God's Commandments.

The apparition was writhing in agony, engulfed in that pitiless sulphurous blaze; there was no doubt what fate awaited the priest, if he did not mend his ways.

Lord, Lord! Do not abandon me!

The Voice boomed in reply, "Not everyone who calls Me 'Lord' will be allowed into heaven, but only those who do My Father's Will. Repent, Abnus! Repent, before it is too late!"

Now almost consumed by fire, Father Doyal's soul faded away. The brilliant Cross and rays of Light receded, giving way to the star-studded night sky and the moon returned to its regular form and size.

The dazed priest was on the hard floor, although he didn't recall going down on his knees. Trembling, he rose and peeked warily out of the window, pressing his hands to his temples, trying to erase the vision of his tormented soul.

This was the worst night of his life.

Reassured that the world outside was back to normal, he sat down on his bed. "I need a drink!" he said out loud.

Reaching inside his bedside table, he pulled out a brandy bottle and snifter. The glass, cut and handcrafted in France, was a gift from his father upon his ordination, together with an original bottle of fine brandy which had long since been consumed.

Not being a religious man, Mr. Doyal's words of wisdom to his son that day were, "You're going to need these, Abnus."

Father Abnus Doyal's nerves were shot, and he was in dire need of strong alcohol to help him process what had just happened.

He mulled over Christ's words, telling him to discern his path back to a holy priesthood. What did that even *mean* and how was he supposed to achieve it?

Deep down, he knew the answer. But it demanded he give up too much; his current lifestyle was very dear to him, *and* was earning him the praise of his superiors. Surely, they couldn't all be wrong in what they were advocating?

He should have asked Jesus what He thought about the *Nova Theologica Populi*. And yet, hadn't He admonished him not to follow the pope's errors? That must include his latest document, for look how Christ had reacted to his mention of demoting sins below the waist! Father Doyal shivered at the remembrance of the way the flames eating his soul had leapt higher when he uttered those words.

Yet what was the alternative to obeying the dictates of Pope Lucius II?

His only other option was a return to the traditional church – and becoming a misfit like those Angelscombe priests. Worse still, he'd have to go to one of them for Confession.

And Christ had made it clear he must save souls. Otherwise … he didn't want to contemplate the 'otherwise'.

He emptied the brandy glass and buried his head in his hands with a loud groan.

No longer could he pretend that following the whims of the progressive Church was obeying God's Will. In quoting Scripture, Jesus made it abundantly clear that His Word was as true now as it had ever been, and no linguistic acrobatics could change that. The Bible was not open to rewriting.

Father Abnus Doyal faced two choices, just like the Israelites, whom Moses had warned before they crossed over into the Promised Land. A blessing or a curse: life everlasting in Heaven, if they obeyed God's Word, or the eternal fires of Hell, if they obeyed their twisted version of It.

He could either serve God and save his spiritual self, or serve man and save his worldly self, but he couldn't do both.

But why not? It wasn't fair! How could a good God put him in such a position? It was all God's fault that he had these unholy inclinations. Why was he expected to bottle them up, like that oh-so-saintly Father Godfrey?

He had very clearly given that priest special graces that were denied to him, who needed them more. He was poor Cain, whose offerings weren't acceptable to God, while his goody-two-shoes brother Abel was welcomed as His beloved. As far as Father Doyal could see, there hadn't been a lick of difference between the value of each sibling's sacrifice. It was blatant favouritism on God's part.

Alright, there *was* the small detail that Cain hadn't offered God the best. But not everyone could be perfect like Abel or Father Godfrey!

He cupped his chin in his hands and stared up morosely through his window. The twinkling stars seemed to outline the form of his black soul, and he imagined he saw flames swirling around it again.

A deep despair took hold of him.

God had made Himself clear: He despised Abnus Doyal.

Chapter Thirty-Four: Science Speaks

Tuesday, 22nd October 2030

At Matins the next morning, the priests' furtive glances told Father Terry that they'd all witnessed last night's frightening heavenly phenomena, and were wondering how their fellow brethren had fared in their Illumination of Conscience.

Who was on the road to sainthood and who wasn't?

His sleep had been fitful after Jesus' revelations and messages. His mind wouldn't stop churning. Try as he might to pray and switch off disturbing thoughts, he eventually gave up and checked his mobile phone for something – anything – to distract him.

And there was plenty!

With such titles as 'Is This the End of the World?' and 'Are You Ready to Die?', the internet abounded with articles gleefully describing terrified reactions on social media to 'weird celestial activity'. The overload of posts was causing many popular sites to crash.

Only on the Christian channels was there correct coverage of Christ's Mercy in coming to warn the world to repent of its iniquity and humbly beg Him for forgiveness.

The media were also quick to post a united response to the events, evidently crafted by the global elite to deceive the world populace. No reason to panic, this was nothing 'spiritual', for such things don't exist. The phenomena were easily attributed to natural causes.

In the cold light of dawn, Father Terry could easily have been persuaded – would almost have preferred – that the whole fantastic experience not have come from Heaven.

However, the faces of his brothers at Matins betrayed that they, too, had gone through the same life-changing events and Father Terry felt it his duty to discuss them openly.

First, he conferred with Father Godfrey, and while they were all at breakfast, the two priests made a joint statement, announcing that both had seen the phenomena in the sky and been visited by Our Lord.

"Did any of you experience those same events?" asked Father Terry.

Everyone's arm shot up.

Relief caused them all to talk at once, eager to communicate how Jesus had come to them in person with an overwhelming love, while not revealing the contents of their conversations with Him.

Father Terry noted his priests' happy spirits, which suggested to him that they were in good standing with Our Lord.

I bet they're in much better standing than I am, he thought ruefully.

He continued, "We all know what we saw was real, but, as you'd expect, the media is doing its best to explain the strange behaviour of the skies in secular terms, as well as the 'apparent' reliving by everyone of their past lives."

"Of course, they are," grumbled Brother Melvin.

"Those guys never sleep," complained Father Harry.

"Unfortunately not." Father Terry tapped his phone. "The propaganda machine is alive and well. As you've probably seen, this is all over the internet.

"'Scientists at NASA and the British Space Agency have explained that yesterday's phenomena were foreseen by them months ago, but they didn't want to alarm people by alerting them ahead of time.'"

"How very kind of them," observed Father Fred.

Father Terry grinned. "Listen to this. 'The explosion of two suns in the sky was an optical illusion, formed by magnetic forces working on the light from our sun and producing its mirror image. Proof that the crash was only an illusion is supported by the fact that no fiery embers fell down to earth from it.

"'The cross hanging in the sky, seen by so many, was caused by mass hysteria in the old-fashioned believers in Christ, who claim they also saw His body hanging next to it. Bad consciences are the reason so many reported seeing the state of their souls and hearing Jesus chastising them – an inevitable result of rebellion against the authorities.

"'There is nothing to be afraid of. Everything is under control.'" Father Terry's grin widened. "And there you have it, gentlemen, all neatly explained away."

Brother Melvin said, "Yet, I notice the scientists haven't manufactured an explanation for the sky turning dark, and peeling back to reveal flames."

"You're right," said Pastor John, who'd been very quiet, Father Terry observed. "That was really terrifying."

Father Godfrey smiled at the Lutheran. "But remember that Jesus foretold the skies would be peeled back like a roof to reveal the flames of His Divine Mercy. The fire wasn't intended to swallow us up, but to wake us up."

Pastor John shook his head. "God's Mercy is rather overwhelming, isn't it?" he said.

"Amen to that," agreed Father Godfrey.

Brother Melvin cleared his throat. "I find it insulting that we're supposed to swallow the idea of 'magnetic forces working on the light from the sun to produce its mirror image.'" He put air quotes around the absurd statement. "Isn't anyone going to challenge the scientists for not warning the public that this frightening event was going to happen – or rather, make them admit that they actually had no idea about it?"

"It's a load of hogwash," exclaimed Father Harry. "How can they deny that *everyone* saw the Cross and Christ hanging in the sky, not just naïve believers, and that *everyone* saw the state of their soul – including themselves? The state media may try to hide it, but it's all over the Christian networks. Just you watch; no one will dare question the authorities' version."

The clergymen nodded disapprovingly. Deep in thought, they then set to eating breakfast.

Later that morning, Father Terry was in the tack room, having a cup of tea with some of the priests, before going back to 'help' Brother Melvin in the kitchen garden. Father Godfrey sat opposite him, pulling apart a bridle in preparation for thoroughly conditioning the leather. Father Harry was stitching a piece of harness where the thread was coming away.

Father Fred was checking his phone, and burst out laughing. "You have *got* to hear this. The Vatican has made a pronouncement on the Warning." The priest put on a solemn voice. "'Relating to yesterday's events, we wish to apprise you of the following. Jesus Christ came to tell you to obey His commandments, as interpreted by the Supreme Pontiff, who is in daily communion with Our Lord. Christ's Peace will descend upon you, if you follow His Will as outlined by His Holiness Pope Lucius II.'"

The four men shook their heads.

"What has become of Holy Mother Church?" Father Terry wondered sadly.

"What indeed," replied Father Harry.

Father Terry spent the remainder of the morning uprooting vegetables for Brother Melvin with his functioning left hand. He was struggling not only with stubborn carrots and parsnips, but also his pride.

God's instructions were to allow his brother priests to guide him in balancing his use of the Dales, to maintain a secular cover in these dangerous times, against being a faithful shepherd of Christ's flock.

He was still the manager of the project – for the time being – but knew he must soon allow others to take over that role, so he could attend more to his priestly duties.

Although his crippled hand didn't let him do anything physical with the ponies anymore, it would still be hard to distance himself from the day-to-day equine operations. He must pray daily for the humility to carry out God's wishes.

His thoughts wandered to Father Doyal. How had that priest fared during his Illumination of Conscience?

Father Terry hoped, despite his bad hand, that he could still keep that man away from Father Godfrey. For he had a nasty premonition that Father Doyal might try to exact revenge on the priest for recently repelling him.

His back ached from bending over to pick the produce, and he rested on the bench next to the Sacred Heart. Keen to see the latest reactions to the Warning, he lay his mobile phone on the stone slab and took off his garden glove. Scrolling through the feed with his good hand, he found an absorbing piece of information on the Catholic Index, a 'subversive' underground Catholic news channel, broadcasting through its independent communications network.

The pope had allegedly confided what happened during his Illumination of Conscience to a close cardinal friend, who in turn conveyed the information to a trusted friend. That man, unbeknownst to the cardinal, was secretly an orthodox Catholic, who leaked the stunning news to the Catholic Index.

At lunch that Tuesday, Father Terry read this latest post to the others. "This has come through several channels," he began, "So I can't be absolutely sure it's accurate. However, where there's smoke, there's fire.

"Pope Lucius II allegedly fainted when he saw the state of his own soul. He is reported as saying that Jesus revealed Hell to him and warned him, that to avoid ending up there, he must resign from the papacy and retreat to a monastery to pray and do penance for the rest of his life."

An awed hush fell on the assembly.

Father Oliver spoke. "Do you think he'll do It?"

"Hard to say," Father Terry replied.

Later that afternoon, when he joined the priests in the tack room for afternoon tea and biscuits, accompanied by the smell of leather and saddle soap, Father Harry cried, "Oh, my, did you see this latest from the Catholic Index?

"Apparently, millions of Catholics have been flooding their local priests with demands to have their Confessions heard. However, they want to confess deeds that are no longer considered sinful in the New Church and the priests are in a bind. How can they absolve sins that are supposedly not sins?"

"Here's an article related to that," said Brother Melvin, looking at his mobile. "Catholics around the world are furious with the Church for lying to them about what's a sin and what isn't. Their Illuminations of Conscience have warned them that they're on their way to Hell if they don't repent and return to the traditional teachings of the Catholic Church."

Father Terry shook his head. "I'm not surprised. And the clergy and members of the entire Church hierarchy will have also had *their* Illuminations of Conscience.

"So their eyes have been opened and they have no more excuses. They must choose between secular riches and power, and the riches of Heaven that await them, if they repent and turn back to God and preach the Truth. It will be interesting to see who makes the right decision."

"Let's hope our pope does," said Father Godfrey.

"Well, to answer that, here's a statement from Pope Lucius II on the Vatican network," said Father Harry. "He's supporting the official line about 'natural phenomena' and making veiled comments about mass hysteria among the deluded faithful causing them to believe they were signs from God."

"But didn't he say earlier that Jesus Christ came to tell us to obey His commandments, as interpreted by the Supreme Pontiff? How can he do an about-face like that?" objected Father Godfrey.

"Sounds to me as if he's in total denial about the truth," said Father Harry.

"That'd be a first," joked Father Fred.

There followed a shaking of heads and grunts of disapproval. A few moments' silence ensued, while the priests drank their mugs of tea and feverishly scrolled through the news feeds on their mobiles.

Father Terry was surprised to find that even the mainstream media were having to report on people's reactions to the Warning, which could no longer be ignored. It wasn't enough to spout scientific platitudes.

While balancing his biscuit plate on his knee and trying to drink with his left hand, he saw a new item pop up on his phone: *Pope Lucius II in Trouble with His Own People.*

Intrigued, he put the plate down and opened the tab.

"A petition asking the pope to resign has been signed by thousands of priests and members of the hierarchy in the Catholic Church, including prominent cardinals and Vatican officials.

"'The main points of the document are:

"'1. Your Holiness, your attitude towards your own flock with regard to last night's Warning and your attempts to explain it away in scientific terms, are most insulting.

"'2. We have all received the same personal message from Christ, including you, Holy Father. He has told us that we have deviated from the Truth and are leading the flock, not to salvation, but to perdition. And we are also headed there ourselves.

"'3. You must repent and return the Church to traditional Catholic teaching before it is too late for all of us.'"

"Good on them!" said Father Fred.

"Better late than never," Father Harry added wryly.

"Do you think he'll resign?" asked Pastor John.

"He has a lot to lose in this world if he does," Father Harry pointed out. "How strong is his faith? Does he care about the destiny of his own soul and the souls of his flock? Does he still believe in God and eternal life?"

Father Fred said, "His cronies won't stand for him deserting the cause for which they elected him."

"He is in a very difficult position," agreed Father Godfrey.

Father Terry looked at his fellow brothers in Christ. There was so much at stake!

His voice was charged with emotion. "For better or for worse, the winds of change are coming."

Chapter Thirty-Five: A Lucky Discovery

Tuesday, 22nd October 2030

Father Doyal woke up the next morning with a hangover and a firm resolve to exact revenge on *all* the cancelled priests of Angelscombe.

He was certain *they* hadn't been forced to watch their blackened souls burning. *They* hadn't been told they were on the path to Hell.

Self-righteous S.O.B.s! Why should he go down on his own?

First he needed coffee to clear his head and a hearty breakfast to fuel his brain. Then he'd formulate a mighty plan for their ruin.

He phoned through to the kitchen chef, and told her to bring to his office a steaming mug of black coffee, two English muffins with melted butter on top and a pot of marmalade. "Oh, and a plate of crispy bacon and two fried eggs – with ketchup."

Exercising control over his staff soothed him somewhat. Here, at least, he still held sway.

After a few sips of coffee and biting into an English muffin dripping with butter and marmalade, his brain was once more firing on all cylinders.

What were the chances those holier-than-thou priests still prayed the Liturgy of the Hours? Under the terms of their cancellation, they weren't allowed to carry out *any* duties that could be construed as priestly. The previous pope was smart; he'd effectively laicised them and was paving the road to their excommunication. What a brilliant way of getting rid of those rebellious clergymen!

Why would they pray alone in their cells? I bet they meet for communal prayer, to bolster their revolt against the Church.

If he was right, he should catch them praying together this evening. Since he didn't actually pray the Liturgy of the Hours himself, he had to look up the time for evening prayer on the internet and arrived at Angelscombe in time for Vespers.

There was no activity outside except for Pastor John, whom he found doing night check on the ponies in their stables.

Without preamble, Father Doyal asked, "Where are the others?"

"Probably in their cells." Pastor John said with equal curtness, pointing at the main building.

"I don't see any lights on in the upstairs rooms."

"Not all their cells are upstairs."

Father Doyal found the minister's tone disdainful. "But there's a light on in the hay barn. What's that all about?"

"Looks like someone forgot to turn it off. I'll go do that now."

The man's shiftiness told Father Doyal he was trying to hide something. "I'll do it for you." He smiled beatifically and enjoyed the look of consternation on the pastor's face.

"As you wish," the Lutheran said, and continued down the row of stables.

When the priest entered the barn, he heard muffled voices at the rear of the building. Making his way to the back through the high piles of hay, he discovered a door in what he now saw was a false wall.

He tried to turn the knob, but the door was locked. He raised his fist to bang on it, but Pastor John, who had quietly followed him in, tried to prevent him.

Father Doyal shook him off and gave three loud raps. "What are you doing in there?" he yelled. "I demand to be let in!"

The door was opened a fraction by Father Terry.

Father Doyal pushed past him into the chapel. "Well, well!"

The prayers stopped abruptly and all eyes turned towards him. Fathers Fred and Oliver rose from their pews and rushed towards the interloper.

Taking one arm each, they marched him, protesting, back into the hay barn. They maintained their iron grip as Father Terry closed the chapel door and asked, "Have you come to pray with us, Father?"

Father Doyal laughed. "Don't play the innocent with me. I know you're saying Vespers in there, against the conditions of your cancellation."

"Oh, you know the prayers? Do you pray them yourself?"

This further outraged Father Doyal. How dare this man suggest he didn't recite the Office – even if he was correct. He tried to shake off the two priests. "Let me go!" he yelled.

Suddenly, the crackling of roaring flames filled his ears, and the reek of sulphur repulsed his nostrils.

Terrified, he stopped struggling.

Father Terry told the two priests to go back in and finish Vespers. "Thank you for your help, but Pastor John and I have got this."

"If you're sure," said Father Fred.

The two priests let go of the intruder and returned to the chapel.

The awful sounds and smells of his burning soul vanished, and a relieved Father Doyal made a big show of rubbing his arms where he'd been held.

Father Terry said, "Pastor John, could you please stand by, in case this man attacks me physically?"

Pastor John nodded. "With pleasure, Father."

"Ha! There's no need for me to get physical." Father Doyal knew he'd won. "I can't wait for Bishop Hardy's reaction when I tell him about your secret chapel and communal prayers. You're finished! He'll excommunicate you and take away your precious ponies. You're done for, Terry, you *and* your divisive band of ideologues!"

Father Terry's voice was steady. "Did you enjoy your Illumination of Conscience?"

That was a low blow!

Father Doyal hissed, "That's none of your business!"

"Oh, but it is. Because saving souls is my business, and that includes your soul, *Father* Doyal."

The reminder about saving souls was too much.

Father Doyal shrieked, "I'm going to *destroy* you!"

He clenched his fists, and Pastor John moved a step closer.

Yet Father Terry seemed unmoved. "Do you honestly think you can destroy *two thousand* years of tradition in the Church founded by Jesus? Are you more powerful than God? And do you really believe that your attempts to crush Christ's Church are leading you on the path to Heaven?

"Stop and think about it, Abnus. Your mind has been taken over by the Enemy and you are on the broad path to Hell."

Father Doyal gave a start. This conversation was going in completely the wrong direction; he was being spoken to the same way Father Godfrey had talked to him, not to mention Jesus.

But Father Terry was a *cancelled priest*, for Goodness' sake! Who did he think he was? Jesus Christ Himself?

"Don't you preach to me, you self-righteous has-been!" Father Doyal turned on his heels. "You'll be hearing from the bishop!"

Father Doyal strode out of the barn, furious. What gall the man had, acting like God's spokesperson, when he wasn't even in active ministry!

Hadn't he, Father Doyal (who *was* in active ministry, thank you very much) just scored a big coup in discovering the illicit chapel and communal priestly prayers? The bishop would be thrilled. He'd been hoping for a reason to put the priests on the fast track to excommunication, and here was his perfect excuse.

He would reward Father Doyal handsomely for this.

Yet despite his elation, Father Terry's words rang in his ears all the way back to Lambcot. 'Your mind has been taken over by the Enemy and you are on the broad path to Hell.'

He shifted uneasily in the driver's seat. Not to believe those words would be to presume that Fathers Terry and Godfrey *and* Jesus were lying.

When Father Doyal walked into his building, two women on the staff bombarded him with bizarre questions about sins and Confession. "Later! I'm busy!" he shouted, and made a bee line for his cell. He needed to think.

With trembling hands, he poured a generous quantity of brandy into his snifter and slumped, half-reclining, onto the bed.

Aiming to take a large mouthful, he missed the glass rim and spilled alcohol over the bedspread. With a loud curse, he sat upright and slid away from the wet spot. He inhaled deeply to steady his nerves, then took another (successful) draft of brandy and settled down again on the bed.

Last night's events, coupled with Father Terry's words, indicated a serious need for honesty about his situation. He was forced to see that the progressive edicts of Pope Lucius II, not to mention those of the pope before him, had lured him away from the teachings of Christ and the true mission of His Church.

Father Doyal realised that his whole priestly ministry was propped up by the lie he'd been fed; that Christ had no problem with him acting out his innate tendencies, because 'Jesus accompanies everyone, no matter where they are'.

Like everyone else in the New Church, he'd taken this talk about 'accompaniment' to mean that everyone was heading for Heaven, regardless of their lifestyle, 'because God is merciful and wouldn't be so mean as to throw people into Hell.'

Also, like everyone else, he'd been more than happy to ignore Jesus' final words, after not condemning the adulterous woman: "Go and sin no more" – that inconvenient call to obey the Commandments, which impinge on man's freedom to do what he wants.

Father Doyal now saw the arrogance of man in presuming that God was fine with rejection of His demands, and that He welcomed unrepentant sinners into His Kingdom.

But the Prodigal Son behaved atrociously! And yet he was welcomed back with open arms by his father. How unfair! Here I am, not behaving anything like as badly as he did, and yet Jesus warns me I'm on the road to Hell!

But he was well aware that the Prodigal Son had repented of his sins, and therein lay the big difference. He'd abandoned his pride and shown humility.

Pride. How misconstrued that word had become!

Father Doyal sat up and poured himself another glass. This business of self-reflection was painful. His whole priestly life had been one of deception and sin. How depressing! Did he have one single redeeming virtue in the eyes of the Lord? Was it even possible to reverse the damage and claw his way to Heaven?

Jesus told him to discern his path back to a holy priesthood; to save the souls of others and, for the rest of his days, make reparation for his sins, in order to avoid the fires of Hell. Even though he believed God despised him, those words did suggest reconciliation was possible. But what a long journey he had ahead of him! Did he have the strength to undertake it?

He rose from the bed and walked, brandy in hand, to the window. He needed a break from deep thinking.

His good view over the paddocks was obscured by the dark outside and, with a shudder, he remembered the events of the previous evening.

Lord, please don't show me my soul again! I beg you, show me the right path!

How could the Church to which he subscribed have led him so horribly wrong?

His thoughts turned to the latest Synods' constant emphasis on 'dialogue,' where the discussion was about the *process* and not the *outcome*; there was no clarity on the goals.

He was beginning to understand the dangerous vacuity of the New Church of Accompaniment and Dialogue. Where was the clear teaching about the four last things: Death, Judgement, Heaven, and Hell?

With frightening clarity, he saw that keeping people ignorant of sin and the eternal consequences of unrepented sin wasn't compassionate at all. Sparing their feelings now would not get them to Heaven.

He winced at his stupid question, 'Lord, when have I caused anyone to stumble?' and Christ's swift response, 'Hypocrite!'

How had he, a priest, fallen for such falsehoods? Father Terry was right: he'd made a pact with the Devil, and it already happened in the seminary.

After a long draft of brandy to deaden this unhappy thought, he let his mind drift to his confrères down the road.

Those Angelscombe priests must be feeling smug and virtuous; they'd stuck to the old rules, and not succumbed to the errors of the New Church. He envied them; they had each other for encouragement in keeping the faith. Here at the Fell Project, he was all alone with a bunch of women, none of whom cared about him.

But once Bishop Hardy knew about that secret chapel, Father Doyal wouldn't be alone anymore. He'd get the recognition he deserved – who knew, maybe a good word from the bishop would ensure he took over when the prelate retired? Or perhaps there was a vacancy in Rome?

He needed to be among his own again, to feel comfortable in his skin. He was a good person. He shouldn't have to agonise like this.

Tired of worrying about his standing with God, he drew the mobile phone from his pocket.

All over the internet was the government's scientific explanation for yesterday's phenomena. That was it! Being a Catholic priest, he'd been susceptible to the suggestion that Christ really had spoken to him. What a relief to know it was all bogus!

He couldn't wait to burst those Angelscombe men's bubbles. Tomorrow he'd call Bishop Hardy and spill the beans.

He fell asleep drafting the upcoming conversation with His Excellency.

But he wasn't destined for a peaceful night. He dreamed that his sooty black body was plummeting into a fiery abyss.

The acrid smell and heat from the flames became unbearable as he drew closer to the netherworld, and he knew it wouldn't be long before they swallowed him completely and burned him for all eternity.

Chapter Thirty-Six: The Search for Compromise

Wednesday, 23rd October 2030

Father Doyal woke up in a cold sweat and his face muscles were aching, as if he'd spent the whole night screaming.

He well understood that God was warning him not to side with the Devil and squeal on the Angelscombe priests to Bishop Hardy today.

But did it *have* to be all or nothing? Surely, there was a middle course?

How might he use this new information about the priests to his advantage, while not causing them to be laicised or thrown out of the Catholic Church?

Father Terry was in the kitchen, emptying the dishwasher with his left hand, when Father Doyal walked in uninvited.

It wasn't safe to be alone with the intruder here. There were too many long knives, and Father Terry's one functioning hand was his weaker one. Even though he was the taller, stronger man, he was at a physical disadvantage – thanks to this priest, he reminded himself bitterly.

Father Doyal leaned in and pulled a plate from the dishwasher. "Where does this go?"

Father Terry snatched it from him. "What do you want?"

"A truce." The priest smiled insincerely.

Father Terry doubted such a thing was possible, but it was better to talk than to fight. Nevertheless, it would be a good thing to get away from sharp objects and be visible to others.

He placed the plate on the rack by the sink and wiped his left hand on a kitchen towel. "Then let's take a walk."

Father Doyal shrugged his shoulders. "Suits me. But I don't want anyone to overhear us."

"Fine," said Father Terry.

Father Doyal followed him towards the paddocks, then stopped in full view of Fathers Godfrey and Harry, who were throwing hay over the fence to two pony mares. Each of them had a new foal at foot.

"Looks like you've had two more babies since I last checked," remarked Father Doyal.

"Yes, they arrived on Monday night." Father Terry looked meaningfully at the priest. "Something about the events of that evening triggered the births."

Father Doyal's face was deadpan. "I heard it was a full moon. That often causes a rash of births."

"Interesting," said Father Terry. "All I remember is seeing two suns in the sky."

Father Doyal's cheeks flushed.

The two priests watched the foals take off on a wild gallop around the large paddock, kicking up their heels and squealing for the sheer joy of being alive.

It did Father Terry good to see such happy innocence. "And we have two more mares about to give birth," he couldn't help bragging. "Have you had any foals this year?"

"We don't believe in autumn births. We're planning ours for the spring."

"Oh, I see. How many mares have you covered?"

"Covered? What do you mean?"

"It's the term for getting them in foal."

Father Doyal laughed. "How quaint. You trads are so prudish with your terminology!"

Father Terry knew he was embarrassed at his ignorance of horse parlance. "You'll find that all equestrian people use that 'prudish' terminology."

"Well, I didn't come here to talk about the ponies."

"You wanted a truce, if I remember correctly?"

Father Doyal nodded. "I do." He cleared his throat. "Look, there's no need for us to be enemies. We do belong to the same Church, after all."

Father Terry arched an eyebrow. "Do we?"

"Well, of course we do!"

"Go on."

"The new pope is simply trying to bring everyone together. Isn't unity what Jesus wanted?"

"He wanted us to be united to the Father, as He is united to Him. And the only way to do that is by obeying His Will. The new pope is not obeying God's Will."

"In what way isn't he?"

"Father, you don't need me to point out how far Rome has strayed from the Truths of the Faith. Setting aside the issue of Sodomy, let's look at the Fourth Commandment."

Father Doyal looked at him blankly.

Father Terry prodded his memory. "Remember to keep the Sabbath day holy."

"Oh, that! Well, it doesn't say you have to go to *church* that day – just rest and not work."

"You know as well as I do that to skip Mass on Sundays is a mortal sin in the Catholic Church. And now your pope is telling us we only have to go to a *state* service once a month."

Father Doyal grinned. "And that is exactly what he means about the errors of the traditional Catholic Church. She's made up all sorts of rules and regulations that aren't even in the Bible."

"If you believe that, then why are you a Catholic priest? Surely another denomination would have suited you better?"

This appeared to anger Father Doyal. Perhaps because he knew it was obvious to Father Terry that he'd chosen this vocation as a vehicle for indulging his baser inclinations?

"I shan't dignify that question with an answer. But I will tell you, that my offer is still open not to tell the bishop that you have secretly maintained the chapel and are performing priestly activities in there."

"If – ?"

"If you submit to the new pope, as obedience obliges you to do."

"You're saying that we have to give up our chapel, and our 'priestly activities' – in order not to get into more hot water with the bishop?"

"That's pretty much it. Then you'll get to keep your ponies, and you and your priests won't risk being laicised, or, even worse, excommunicated."

"You're fine with throwing all of us at the wolves, then, not just me?"

"Look, if you play ball, you could all get reinstated."

Father Terry looked surprised. "Oh, so you're now able to get *all* of us reinstated?"

"I thought that might sweeten the deal." Father Doyal pointed to Father Terry's right claw. "By the way, how's the hand?"

Father Terry glowered at him. *Lord, preserve me from hating him!*

How dare this man waltz onto the property, believing he could make a deal with the priests and bribe them into renouncing the Deposit of Faith!

Father Terry had no idea how to be an effective priest with his deformed hand, but his trust was in God, not the human beings in the Vatican. The Lord would find a way. "Nothing doing, Father. Go ahead, do your worst. We are not for sale."

Father Doyal's face registered disbelief, then disappointment, and finally, fury. "You are dealing with powers far beyond your imagining, you ape! You have no idea what's about to be unleashed on you!"

One of the mares was looking over the fence at the priests, hoping for attention. Father Doyal took a swing at her head with his right fist. "Stupid pony!"

She narrowly avoided the blow, and his hand punched air as she cantered off in surprise with her colt.

Indignant at his vicious behaviour, Father Terry yanked him back with his left hand. "How dare you attack our ponies!"

Eyes snakelike, Father Doyal shouted, "I'm done with you!" and tried to get out of his grasp.

Father Terry continued clutching his arm. "Remember the wicked man in Ezekiel, who repents and saves his soul, Abnus."

"What are you spouting off about now, you relic?"

Seizing his last chance to make the man see the truth, Father Terry kept tight fingers on his coat sleeve, and his voice became more earnest. "I beg of you, repent like that wicked man, before it's too late! I know it takes humility, and that's hard. But Satan hates humility. It's the quickest way to reject him and all his lies, Father."

"Are you calling me a wicked man?" Father Doyal angrily shook himself free, and brushed imaginary germs off his sleeve. "Who are you to judge me?"

"I'm not judging you. Scripture warns us not to judge. But I *am* telling you truths you don't care to hear, and you're confusing them with judgement."

"I know the difference, thank you!"

Father Terry's voice became very soft. "I'm not sure you do." He extended his good hand towards the priest. "Come over to the good side, Father. God gave you free will; use it for good, not evil."

"Ugh!" Father Doyal rolled his eyes. "As usual, there's no reasoning with you. I've tried to help you and your cronies, Terry, but you're beyond help. I am not responsible for what happens to you."

"Yes, you are. As you will find out in the next life, if you expose us for being faithful Catholic priests."

Father Doyal threw up his hands in disgust and stormed over to his car.

He drove off with a squeal of angry tyres, bitter that his hopes of reaching a compromise had been thwarted.

But Father Terry's words hounded him all the way back to Lambcot, and he was again forced to admit that the New Church was not aligned with the teachings of Jesus Christ.

Father Terry talked of saving souls. Pope Lucius II talked of saving Mother Earth and 'accompanying' our fellow humans – regardless of their behaviour. But to where?

Father Doyal had never paid attention to the teachings on Heaven and Hell at the seminary; he was there for a totally different reason.

Therefore Father Terry's quote from Ezekiel struck him forcefully. True to his vocation, that priest was trying to get him to repent and save his soul.

He recalled last night's dream. Was he willing to lose his soul and end up in that infernal abyss, in order to satisfy his carnal desires in this life?

Once again, he faced the truth that repentance meant curbing his natural inclinations and giving up the lifestyle he treasured – and had been led to believe was sanctioned by God.

Did he have the strength to summon the humility for that and repel the Devil, like the heroic Father Godfrey? Or was he doomed to remain a servile servant of Satan, and suffer the eternal consequences?

Where was God, Who was supposedly so loving? If he really existed and loved Father Doyal, why had He made him the way he was? Didn't He care that His priest was going through torture? This was His chance to prove He was real and show His much-touted love.

But Father Doyal felt no love, just a dull void.

There was no God.

And if God didn't exist, then neither did Satan, and last night's dream had been just a nightmare, not a warning from on high. The whole Illumination of Conscience thing had already been satisfactorily explained away by science, and his naturally sensitive nature had imagined the sulphurous smells and crackling of flames. He had nothing to fear or look forward to on the other side of death.

The final straw was being preached at by that Father Terry. How dare the man tell him he was wicked? And how dare he put the blame on *him* for what might happen to those do-gooders in Angelscombe, if he fulfilled his duty to tell the bishop what they were doing behind his back! He'd had enough of that priest treating him like an inferior, and pointing out the emptiness of the New Church and its teachings.

He couldn't join the traditional Church. He didn't have enough goodness in him to follow the example of the likes of Father Godfrey. And why bother trying to please a God Who might not exist?

Becoming a priest had been a huge mistake. It was supposed to have been a cover, but thanks to Father Terry's jibes, he was no longer at home in the fraudulent New Church. And if he left the priesthood, what else was he good for?

It was time to end this miserable state of confusion – and arrange it so Father Terry would feel guilty for the rest of his life.

Chapter Thirty-Seven: In the Garden

Wednesday, 23rd October 2030

Brother Melvin was pottering in the kitchen garden after lunch, when a movement on the roof caught his eye.

Father Doyal was standing perilously close to the edge, and it took a few seconds before it registered that he was preparing to jump.

The brother's heart was pounding dangerously fast in his old chest. He begged the Holy Spirit for assistance, then yelled, "What are you doing up there?"

"What does it look like?"

"It looks as if you're about to jump on my vegetables. Why? What have they ever done to you?"

Father Doyal gave a derisive laugh. "Who cares about your vegetables? I've got bigger problems than a few squashed carrots."

"What kind of problems?"

"What do you care?"

"I see a soul in need of help, and I'd like to offer mine."

"It's too late for that. God has given up on me."

"God doesn't give up on anyone. It's we who give up on Him."

Brother Melvin was glad to notice him pause at this. *Holy Spirit, please give me the right words to help this man!*

"Fine! Then I've given up on Him. He's never given *me* anything, anyway."

"You can't say that! He gave you life. And he ordained you a priest, to be an example of holiness to His flock and lead them to Him. That's a huge privilege."

"You're delusional, old man. Asking a priest like me to be an example of holiness is like expecting the proverbial pig to fly."

"You're selling yourself short, Father. God made you; therefore you are wonderfully made."

"No offense, but you know nothing about me. If you did, you wouldn't be talking like that."

"I may not know your background, but I do know your potential."

"Oh, really? What's that?"

"The potential to turn your life around and become the priest God wants you to be. And you can use anything unholy in your background to show others that, with God, all things are possible."

"That all sounds wonderful, but it doesn't apply to me. My time is up." He edged forwards.

Sudden anger welled up in Brother Melvin at the danger to his lovingly grown vegetables. "Would you *please* let me help you find a good landing spot? Somewhere that will suit you, but not hurt my food crop? People have to eat after you're gone, you know."

Father Doyal grimaced. "Fine. I've got nothing against you, old man." He moved along the rooftop a few feet. "How about here?"

Alarmed, Brother Melvin yelled, "Not on my green onions!" *I beg you, God, bring help fast!*

Father Doyal slid along a bit farther.

But Brother Melvin shrieked, "Don't you *dare* jump on my brassicas!"

Father Doyal looked confused. "What are brassicas?"

"Cauliflower, Brussel sprouts, cabbages and broccoli!"

Father Doyal huffed loudly: he was running out of space. "Then I'll go round the corner."

"Wait, there's a spot of soft earth over here." Brother Melvin indicated a small, uncultivated patch of ground. "We can bury you there, and you'll fertilise next year's crop of kale."

"I will *not* help you grow kale! I hate kale!"

"Then don't jump!"

Father Doyal had just closed his eyes in preparation for jumping on whatever vegetables he might land on, when his arms were seized and pinned behind him.

Fathers Fred and Harry grabbed his shoulders and hauled him off the parapet.

"Let go of me!" He struggled to get free, furious at being tricked into a conversation with that old brother which lasted long enough for the priests to climb onto the roof and stop him from hurtling into blissful oblivion. "I want to die!" he screamed.

"No, you don't," said Father Terry's calm voice. He'd clearly led the ambush. "You'd better come quietly, or we'll have to tie you up."

"What with? Your Rosaries?"

Father Terry showed him a couple of the ponies' lead ropes. "Nope, with these."

Father Doyal had to admit defeat – for now. "Fine!" He relaxed his body. They let him go and he accompanied them down the stairs.

When they reached the ground floor and his handlers still didn't leave his side, he said pointedly, "Good-bye."

"Not so fast, Father," said Father Terry. "We're not done with you yet – and neither is God."

Father Doyal's eyes narrowed suspiciously. "What do you mean?"

"Since you already know about our chapel, let's go in there and pray."

Wearily, Father Doyal covered his brow with the palm of his right hand. "I'm done talking to God. It doesn't do any good."

"Ask Him for forgiveness, Father, and mean it. Beg for His Mercy, and He will shower It upon you."

Father Abnus Doyal was too tired to argue. The decision to take his own life today had taken a lot out of him, and he was depressed he'd not succeeded. Maybe he could pretend to be praying while he worked out a new method for leaving this life?

With Father Terry leading the way, Father Doyal was accompanied to the first pew, and knelt between his captors.

"Do you have your Rosary?" asked Father Terry, still standing. His plan was to have all four of them recite it together.

Father Doyal's face reddened. "I – I – left it in the car."

Father Terry fetched a spare one from the Confessional booth to the right of the chapel. It was made from simple wooden beads, with a large Benedictine cross.

He saw panic in Father Doyal's eyes at the sight of it.

"Get that thing away from me!" he cried.

Pausing in mid-step, Father Terry glanced at the other two priests with raised eyebrows, and they nodded in understanding. *We all know who's afraid of the Rosary.*

Father Terry placed the beads in his pocket, and Father Doyal appeared calmer. "Close your eyes," he said. "The three of us will retire to the pew behind you and leave you to pray in peace."

Father Doyal shut his eyes, and Father Terry motioned to the others. They filed into the second row, and he mouthed, "Prayer of Liberation" to them. Taking a book from the pile at the end of the bench, he carefully turned the pages until he found the one he wanted. He showed it to the others, who picked up their own copies and opened them to the same prayer.

They knelt in unison and made a silent Sign of the Cross. For the next few minutes they quietly said prayers of deliverance over the priest in front of them.

Afterwards, Father Terry rose and quietly approached Father Doyal, who appeared to be asleep. He pulled the spare Rosary out of his pocket and held it next to the priest. When there was no reaction, he placed the beads around his neck with another silent prayer.

Mother of God, Protectress of the Faith, please watch over him. Drive Satan and all his evil spirits away and lead Father Doyal safely into the Catholic fold. May he recognize Your Son as his Lord and Saviour and bring his own and others' souls to eternal life. Amen.

Having thus consigned him to the care of Our Lady, the three priests slid out and left Father Doyal alone in the chapel.

Chapter Thirty-Eight: Reactions
Wednesday, 23rd October 2030

Brother Melvin sat on the garden bench next to the Sacred Heart of Jesus, wiping his brow with an old-fashioned white handkerchief. His knees were shaking, his heart was still beating too fast, and sweat soaked his black soutane.

Lord, that was a close one! Thank you for bringing my brothers to save that poor man. I hate to think how it could have ended if they hadn't intervened.

"And God has saved *you*, too, for the time being," he informed the vegetables which had narrowly escaped harm. "Thank you, Lord, for saving me from having to plant a whole new batch."

Thirty minutes later, his pulse had returned to normal. He was ready to work on the evening menu, when he heard voices outside the garden wall, belonging to the trio who'd subdued Father Doyal.

He got up and opened the heavy door. "Come in, come in! Tell me how it went with our would-be jumper." He ushered them to the bench he'd just vacated.

"We prayed over him and he's resting in the chapel," said Father Terry.

"That sounds good. I've just been thanking the Lord for your timely intervention," he told them, pointing at the Sacred Heart of Jesus statue.

"And we came to congratulate you on keeping Father Doyal talking," said Father Terry.

"Arguing with him over which vegetables to jump on was a master stroke, especially telling him he'd be useful for pushing up kale," said Father Harry, grinning.

Father Fred added, "I wish I'd seen his face when you told him that."

Brother Melvin chuckled. "He did look foolish. I mean, why worry about where you'll be buried once you're dead?"

"You saved a life today," said Father Terry.

Brother Melvin blushed. "It was a team effort, Father."

"It *became* a team effort because of your quick thinking."

"I give credit to the Holy Spirit. Believe me, I was praying my socks off to Him the whole time!"

Father Terry nodded. "We all were. And on the way here, we were citing examples of how you've helped us, too."

The brother looked confused.

"We've all benefited from your impromptu counselling in this garden," Father Fred waved a hand over the impressive produce.

Surprised, but pleased, Brother Melvin said, "And I thought you'd all come here to admire my green thumb!"

"That, too," protested Father Terry. "And we mustn't forget to let you know, yet again, how much we appreciate your fantastic cooking."

"Speaking of which," said Brother Melvin, "I need to get busy preparing dinner for you lot."

The clergymen rose hastily. "We don't want to get in the way of that!" said Father Fred.

They exited the garden, leaving behind a happy Brother Melvin. God had just let him know his strivings to be useful were not in vain.

As he looked at the Sacred Heart of Jesus, an inner voice warned him not to expect – or want – to be reassured about it again. Once was enough.

Brother Melvin nodded his understanding.

Noticing Father Doyal's car still parked at the farm, Father Terry decided to check on him.

He was in the chapel, awake and kneeling in the pew. As Father Terry drew closer, he noticed that the Rosary no longer hung around the man's neck. Instead, he was fingering the beads with a puzzled expression.

Father Terry hesitated. Should he let him know he'd seen him?

While he was deliberating, Father Doyal turned around. Father Terry froze. Was the priest angry with him for placing the beads around his neck?

But Father Doyal held them up and said, "Father, I was never taught how to pray this."

Hiding his extreme surprise at such deficient formation, Father Terry sat next to him and pulled out his own Rosary. "It's actually not complicated – on purpose. The original Rosary was the recitation of all 150 Psalms – "

Father Doyal looked aghast. "What – *all* of them?"

Father Terry nodded. "But that was too much for the general populace, so it became the recitation of Hail Marys in place of each Psalm."

"That sounds boring!" wailed Father Doyal.

Father Terry couldn't help smiling. "On the face of it, yes. But there is a whole lot more to reciting the Rosary."

"You said it was simple," accused the other.

"And it is. But it's certainly not boring."

"I can't wait to find out how *that* works."

"Well, each decade – that is, each group of ten Hail Marys – depicts a major event in Christ's life. There are four groups of five decades, called Mysteries, and each Mystery is devoted to a particular aspect of His Divine Life."

"You've lost me already," said Father Doyal.

Father Terry chuckled. "I agree, it does sound complicated, but it really isn't. Let me see – today is Wednesday, so we recite the five Glorious Mysteries."

"If you say so."

Father Terry counted on his fingers. "The first Glorious Mystery is the Resurrection. The second Mystery is His Ascension. The third is the Descent of the Holy Spirit upon the Apostles. The fourth is the Assumption of Our Lady into Heaven, and the fifth is the Coronation of Our Lady as Queen of Heaven and Earth.

"We meditate on those events while we pray each set of ten Hail Marys."

"You mean, the Hail Marys are background noise for the mysteries?"

"I hate to call them 'background noise', but I'll settle for their being a backdrop."

Father Doyal thought for a moment. "But seriously, what do you get out of all this?"

Father Terry was no stranger to this question. "If only you knew the power of the Hail Mary, Father! Satan hates that prayer, because he hates Our Lady. He's the personification of pride, and she vanquishes him with her humility every time." Pleased the other priest was showing interest, he continued, "As the great Archbishop Fulton Sheen wrote, 'What the runway is to the plane, that the Rosary beads are to prayer – the physical start to gain spiritual altitude.'"

Father Doyal said, with a pained expression, "Why was I never taught about this? Anyone in my seminary who showed devotion to Our Lady was laughed at and told to stop it immediately."

Father Terry looked at him with deep compassion. "Satan has done a lot of damage, Father. But God has placed us at this moment in time to combat the evil which has permeated Holy Mother Church. We must answer His call and rally to our Mother's aid."

"Thank you for including me in that 'we'," said Father Doyal, "but since I have thrown in my lot with Satan, God wants no part of me."

"On the contrary, Father, God wants to use you as an example of evil reversed. Remember Saul, whom Christ accosted on the road to Damascus?"

"Vaguely. Remind me."

"He was sending the early Christians to their torture and death, when Jesus called out to him, 'Why are you persecuting Me?' With that 'Me', Christ made it clear that the Church is *His* Body. Saul converted and became the great St. Paul whose writings we use today as our guide in the Christian life."

Father Doyal looked at Father Terry with a glimmer of hope.

"Never forget, you are a child of God," Father Terry said. "He loves you and is always calling you back to Him." A twinge reminded him that God was also calling *him* back.

Father Doyal began fingering the wooden Rosary beads. "Would you recite today's Mysteries with me? Did you say they were the Glorious Mysteries?"

Father Terry nodded. "I'd love to."

They knelt next to each other, and Father Terry guided his fellow priest through each decade. Then he helped him recite the Hail Holy Queen, and the prayer to St. Michael for protection against the wickedness and snares of the Devil.

When they were finished, Father Doyal surprised him. "Would you be willing to hear my Confession, Father?"

Father Terry beamed. "There is more rejoicing in Heaven over one repentant sinner than a hundred righteous souls."

The priest looked doubtful. "Keep telling me that."

"When we find it impossible to love ourselves, it's hard to believe God *still* loves us."

Father Doyal gave a lopsided grin. "I suppose He must, since He wouldn't let me die today and fertilise Brother Melvin's blessed kale crop." His tone became more serious. "This is going to be difficult for me, Father. You realise that, don't you?"

"Yes, but I promise you, the whole of Heaven truly is rejoicing over your humility."

"Have you, as a priest, ever done anything you bitterly regret?"

Father Terry nodded sombrely. "Oh, yes!"

"Perhaps you'll tell me about it one day?"

"Perhaps." He pointed to the Confessional booth. "Shall we?"

Father Doyal's demeanour struck him as that of a lamb going to slaughter, when he entered the wooden structure.

Father Terry walked into his side, picked up the purple stole, kissed it, and quietly recited a prayer. Aloud, he said, "May the Lord help you make a good Confession."

During the long hour that followed, Father Terry hoped the penitent could sense Christ's loving, forgiving embrace welcoming him back into the Catholic family.

Before giving him his penance, he said, "Father, you are in a perfect position to help others who bear the same cross as you and whose consciences have also been malformed. By amending your life, you can show them that, with God's assistance, it is very possible to live a chaste life."

After a pause, Father Doyal said, "It does help to have a living example of that right here."

"Yes. I hope he can be a light for your path to holiness."

"I owe him an apology," said Father Doyal in a quiet voice.

"That is your penance."

"Is that all?"

"Isn't that hard enough?"

Softly, Father Doyal said, "Yes, yes it is."

"And now I will absolve you of your sins."

Outside the Confessional, Father Doyal reached out to shake Father Terry's right hand, but stopped mid-way, acutely embarrassed. "Ugh! I forgot to confess my malice in harming you, Father. That makes my Confession invalid, doesn't it? Can we please go back in?"

"If you genuinely forgot, then, no, your Confession isn't invalid. Just remember to mention it next time."

"But I've robbed you of your ability to say Mass. Please forgive me. I don't know how to make up for it to you."

"Maybe you could start by hearing *my* Confession?"

Father Doyal looked shocked. "But I'm a terrible priest, Father!"

"Saul wasn't a good Christian, either, but look how *he* turned out. And neither am I perfect. Don't forget, you are *in persona Christi* when you're hearing Confession."

"If only you knew how humbling it is, for you to ask this of me."

"It's humbling for both of us, Father. But that is what we are all called to. Confession – *true* Confession – isn't easy."

He handed his stole to Father Doyal, who kissed it and placed it around his neck – mouthing the correct prayer, Father Terry was glad to note. He entered the penitent's side of the booth and confessed to Father Doyal all the feelings of rage and disgust he had harboured towards him.

"Your reactions were justified," said Father Doyal, "but you have viewed them with charity."

Father Terry smiled in the darkness on his side of the grille. Father Doyal had a great future ahead of him, if only he could stay the course.

"However, for your penance," continued his confessor, "I would like you to say a decade of the Rosary for the priest towards whom you harboured those negative feelings."

"Gladly!" responded Father Terry.

"Now please say the Act of Contrition."

Father Terry recited the prayer and Father Doyal absolved him of his sins.

As the two men exited the Confessional, Father Doyal smiled. "I don't ever remember feeling so much like a real priest as I do now."

Father Terry beamed.

Father Doyal's eyes were moist. "You've been a true friend to me. Thank you."

Father Terry nodded, then looked grave. "This was the easy part, Father. You now have to negotiate a difficult path with your superiors if you don't want to get cancelled."

"Believe me, I've been thinking about that – a lot. I suppose this is when virtue becomes its own reward."

Father Terry sighed. "I'm afraid so. But I and the other priests at Angelscombe are here for you, if you need us."

"I wish I could come and live in your community!"

"We both know that's not possible. We need you to stay on the right side of the progressives as long as you can, and protect our secrets. Ironically, you are more use to the world as a priest in good standing with the current regime than as a cancelled one, like us."

Father Terry was also a realist; his heart told him the man wasn't ready to live among a group of males just yet – especially around Father Godfrey. It would be asking too much of him at this early stage in his reform.

"But please," he told Father Doyal, "protect yourself from the evil influences trying to ruin your soul. Take up the duties you gave an oath to carry out at your ordination. Pray the Hours and say Holy Mass every day. Say the Rosary daily, and go frequently to Confession – at least once a fortnight."

Father Doyal reddened. "Father, I don't know where my Breviary is. I have no Book of the Gospel, Sacramentary or hosts for consecration – nor the objects and vestments needed to celebrate Mass. If I order those items, I'll come under suspicion."

Doing his best to hide his astonishment, Father Terry pulled out his mobile. "Here's where you can find the Liturgy of the Hours online, for free, as well as the Book of the Gospels and the Sacramentary. Regarding the hosts, we'll give you seven each week for your private celebration of the Holy Eucharist. I take it, you have access to red wine, at least?"

Father Doyal nodded.

Father Terry continued. "If you come back tomorrow, I'll also lend you the basic items you need – a chalice, paten, pall, purificator and decanter. But treat them with reverence, please; they are sacred items. And you can come here for regular Confession. How does that sound?"

Father Doyal shook his head. "I won't recognise myself anymore!"

Father Terry chuckled. "Is that such a bad thing?"

"Bad for Satan, good for me."

"And for everyone around you," added Father Terry. "Your project staff will see a positive difference in you."

The priest's face fell. "Supposing they ask me why that is? They might squeal on me."

Father Terry patted him on the shoulder. "Let's take it one day at a time, shall we? 'Sufficient unto the day is the evil thereof.' Pray to the Holy Spirit for strength and He will see you through. Remember, today all Heaven is rejoicing, and God will not abandon you, I promise."

"Thank you, Father."

Father Terry accompanied him to his car and said a prayer as he watched the man depart.

Lord, please protect his newly cleansed soul. Our Lady, please inspire him to say the Rosary daily and faithfully carry out his priestly obligations for the glory of Your Son and the Father. Holy Spirit, guide him towards ever increasing holiness!

Chapter Thirty-Nine: An Apology
Wednesday, 23rd October 2030

Dinner that Wednesday was a lively affair.

Everyone relished telling and retelling the 'Incident in the Garden', as they dubbed the aborted suicide attempt. The narration of Brother Melvin's brilliance in keeping Father Doyal arguing about vegetables enjoyed considerable embellishment each time it was recounted.

Father Godfrey was pleased to see how happy it made the old man to be appreciated for more than his culinary expertise.

But he himself felt uneasy. Immediately before dinner, Father Terry had told him that Father Doyal wished to speak with him.

"What about? I don't want to talk to *him*." Contact with that awful priest was the last thing he wanted. It didn't matter how profound a conversion he had supposedly undergone, there was no forgetting their shared past.

"I'm not at liberty to say. But please give him a chance," Father Terry said. "He's trying to mend fences, and you're the person he most needs to do that with."

Father Godfrey was torn. "I want to do the charitable thing, but how can I be sure it's not just a big ruse to get what he wants by another route?"

"My gut tells me his contrition is genuine. But I agree that he needs to be kept out of temptation's way while he adapts to a new and chaste way of life."

"Thank you, Terry. I feel like a mouse being delivered into the cat's paws."

Father Terry chuckled. "I hardly see you as a mouse! You can be very ferocious when you choose."

"A ferocious mouse, then," Father Godfrey said wryly, "but nevertheless a mouse in harm's way. No, thank you."

"I have a suggestion, if you don't want to meet him on your own. Would it help if I stand in the background? Out of hearing, but not out of sight, and with Father Doyal's knowledge."

"That changes everything! Why didn't you say that to start with?"

Father Terry texted Father Doyal with the details of when and where, and informed him that their rendezvous would be under observation from a distance. He received a swift reply in agreement.

But Father Godfrey was dreading it, even if his friend was going to be present. It had been his fond hope that all contact with Father Doyal would cease. In fact, he'd been uncharitably optimistic the man would be sent to a home for priests with mental issues, thereby ensuring he couldn't bother the Angelscombe residents again.

Unfortunately, once again, God wished Father Godfrey to confront the problem, not run away from it.

And so, he writhed uncomfortably in his chair at the dinner table, trying to join in the laughter and forget his meeting on the morrow.

Thursday, 24th October 2030

The two Angelscombe priests were waiting outside the front door of the main building after lunch the next day. On the ground next to Father Terry was a large suitcase.

"Planning on leaving us?" quipped a nervous Father Godfrey. "Are you expecting this meeting to go badly?"

Father Terry grimaced. "Very funny. I might as well tell you, as you're going to find out anyway. Our progressive priest is not in the habit of saying daily Mass, nor does he have the accoutrements needed to do so."

Father Godfrey was astounded. "And you're giving him the family silver?" He pointed at the case.

"I am *lending* him the necessary items, as a fellow priest and Christian who wants to encourage him on the right path."

"I'm sorry. I'm just on edge about this – this – get-together. You're right, we need to do all we can to help him be a good priest."

Father Terry smiled. "Shall we pray to Our Lady of Success for a good outcome?"

Father Godfrey nodded vigorously; Our Lady had never yet let him down.

As they were finishing the *Memorare,* Father Doyal's electric car drove up and parked a few yards away.

Father Godrey clasped his hands in agony and his friend gave him a reassuring smile, as their visitor exited the vehicle and walked towards them.

Trying to form a smile of his own, Father Godfrey forced himself to look directly at the man – and was startled.

Father Doyal was dressed in a long black soutane, not the close-fitting black shirt and trousers he habitually wore, and his face had lost its hungry, prowling expression.

Is this part of the ruse? Father Godfrey asked himself. *If so, it's very convincing!*

The ensemble made Father Doyal look more handsome than ever, yet not in a seductive way; he had an almost angelic aura about him.

Nevertheless, I shall proceed with caution, Father Godfrey told himself. *Handsome is as handsome does.*

"Hello, Father." Father Doyal quietly stretched out his hand.

Father Godfrey shook it wordlessly, then indicated Father Terry. "You don't mind my friend being here, do you?" It sounded like a challenge, although he didn't mean it that way. Or did he?

But Father Doyal remained calm. "Not at all. I completely understand. In fact, I prefer it." He smiled ruefully. "My past behaviour has made it desirable."

He exuded none of that previous smugness, Father Godfrey noted, and he was glad the reformed priest wasn't bothered by the presence of a monitoring third party. Especially since that third party was his former nemesis.

Father Terry has performed a miracle on him, he thought. *I hope it sticks.*

"I won't shake your hand for obvious reasons," Father Terry said, with a dry smile, "and will leave you to your tête à tête while I remain out of hearing."

Father Doyal nodded. "Thank you for your discretion, Father." He pointed at the suitcase with hopeful eyes. "Did you bring the items we discussed?"

"Yes. When you and Father Godfrey have finished talking, I'll give them to you."

"Wonderful, thank you!" He smiled at Father Godfrey. "Shall we?"

With a quick glance at Father Terry, who smiled encouragingly, the young priest said, "There's a grotto nearby that will serve well."

"Excellent, lead on!"

Father Godfrey prayed three Hail Marys on the way there, to ward off his renewed anxiety at being together with the priest who had tried to assault him not so long ago.

Remember also that he tried to kill himself, Godfrey. Have compassion.

Their route led them down a fine-gravelled path between oak trees and elms to a large, semi-circular clearing on their right. In the centre of the arc stood a large statue of Our Lady of Lourdes. She was clothed in a white robe, with a white veil over her tumbling brown hair, and a blue sash around her waist. A long Rosary was draped over hands clasped in prayer, and she looked down serenely at the two priests.

Wordlessly, they sat on the stone bench in front of the life-sized image.

Father Doyal said, "Shall we say a prayer first?"

"Yes," said Father Godfrey, who'd not stopped praying since the man's arrival.

They made the Sign of the Cross over themselves, and Father Doyal prayed, "Mary, Our Loving Mother, please look favourably upon us, your priests, as we work to reconcile our differences and become united to Your Immaculate Heart and the Sacred Heart of Your Son, Jesus. Amen."

"Amen," said Father Godfrey, beginning to glean what this meeting might be about.

Father Doyal had left a large gap between himself and his neighbour, and now folded his hands demurely on his lap, to indicate – so Father Godfrey hoped – that he harboured no evil intent.

Father Godfrey pretended to twist his head from one side to the other to relieve tension in his neck, as a means of checking for Father Terry's presence.

He caught a glimpse of his friend in the trees.

Mary, Protectress of the Faith, watch over me!

"Thank you for meeting with me," began Father Doyal. "I know this is very uncomfortable for you, so I'll keep it short.

"Father Terry heard my Confession yesterday, and my penance is to apologise for my behaviour towards you."

Father Godfrey stared stolidly at Our Lady, not wanting to be reminded of how nearly he'd succumbed to evil.

Father Doyal continued, "I am deeply sorry for threatening you. And for trying to make you capitulate to wrongful desires, which, unlike me, you have heroically not yielded to.

"Father Godfrey, I'm inspired by you. You've shown that it *is* possible to live chastely and avoid temptation, with the help of the Holy Spirit and the support of fellow priests.

"You have a valuable friend in Father Terry. He brought me around after my near-fatal brush with despair, when Satan tried to snatch my soul from eternal life.

"He's promised to help me be a good priest, and I hope you'll afford me the privilege of being able to call you a friend in Christ, too, and allow me to be encouraged by your example."

Flattered as he was, Father Godfrey nevertheless was tempted to ask exactly what form that 'encouragement' was expected to take. Did this mean more shadowing?

"I see you're unsure of my sincerity," said Father Doyal. "I don't blame you, but over time I hope to prove to you that I really have changed."

Father Godfrey felt churlish for his unkind thoughts. "Thank you for your understanding. And thank you, too, for apologising. It means a lot."

"Then that must be sufficient for me."

The priest's humility moved Father Godfrey to add, "Bless you, Father Doyal. I forgive you and am confident you will make a truly good priest."

He rose and turned to see Father Terry approaching them, suitcase in hand.

Chapter Forty: The New Assistant

Thursday, 24th October 2030

When Father Terry watched his friend rise from the stone bench, he deemed the conversation over.

He saw Father Doyal's expression of regret, as he observed Father Godfrey leave the grotto, and trusted it was regret at his disgraceful recent treatment of the young man.

Father Godfrey was smiling as he drew near.

"Good meeting?" Father Terry asked quietly.

"I'd say so. Everything was said that needed saying. I'll leave him to you, if I may. I have to catch up on my chores."

"Of course. I'll see you later. And thank you for doing this."

"God was determined I confront my demons. You were right to give him that penance."

"He told you about that?"

"Yes, and luckily for you, our discussion went smoothly. Otherwise, I'd be really mad at you now." Father Godfrey grinned, taking the sting out of his words, and walked down the path back to the barn.

Father Doyal waited respectfully for Father Terry to finish speaking before getting up from the stone bench. He looked peaceful, a good indication that he and Father Godfrey had indeed reconciled in Christ.

Father Terry tried to flex the fingers of his clawed right hand as Father Doyal drew close. Here he was, about to give the priest the items needed for celebrating the Eucharist, while he himself was unable to perform that essential rite without assistance.

He was struck by the irony of helping the very person who'd caused his deformity, to say Mass on his own every day.

Forgiveness was hard. If only it were a one and done deal! But it was an ongoing action, and Father Terry must resign himself to daily asking the Lord to help him forgive the man who'd destroyed the most important part of his priesthood – being able to properly consecrate the Host, that Source and Summit of the Catholic Faith.

He forced a smile. "I take it, it went well?"

"I think so, and I trust Father Godfrey does, too."

"Yes, he does." Father Terry picked up his suitcase. "And now, let's go through the items you need. I'll put this on the bench, and you can tell me if you need any reminders of what they're for."

"Thank you, Father. This is extremely embarrassing. But I know you're aware of the *Ordo Fraternitas* Mass – the new Mass."

"As if we didn't already have a new Mass," muttered Father Terry.

"You do say the Novus Ordo, correct? Not the Traditional Latin Mass?"

"I regret to say that, unlike our confrère Brother Melvin, who was raised in the Latin tradition, I was only taught to say the new Mass." He couldn't prevent himself from adding, "Or should I call it the *Old* New Mass?"

Father Doyal looked apologetic. "I'm sorry for what's happening in the Church right now, Father. But since I have no Latin, I am relieved that I'll understand your rite."

Father Terry sighed at the priest's overall lack of correct formation, but was glad of the chance to put him on the right path. He carried the suitcase over to the bench in front of Our Lady of Lourdes, to whom he sent up a quick prayer for guidance – and patience.

He opened the case and pointed to the sacred items inside, explaining their function whenever Father Doyal expressed the need to 'be reminded.'

He sensed a growing uneasiness in his companion, until, with a self-conscious cough, Father Doyal said, "Might I come to a Mass here at Angelscombe? I'd like to see it done properly."

"Why don't you assist me at Sunday Mass?" He held out his deformed hand. "It's my turn to preside, with the help of another priest – who will be you."

Father Doyal beamed. "Thank you for the opportunity."

"Say Mass tomorrow in your cell and acquaint yourself with the Novus Ordo Rite. That way, you'll be better equipped to help me on Sunday. And be here early!"

On reaching the barn, Father Godfrey discovered the other priests had already turned out the ponies and cleaned their stalls.

Fathers Fred and Harry were in the feed room, making up the evening meals.

"Need any help?" he asked.

"Nope," said Father Harry, peering closely at him. "Are you O.K.? We saw you go off with Father Doyal."

Father Godfrey saw an opportunity to put the aborted suicide in a better light. "Yes, thanks. He wanted to apologise for a few things." He hoped they didn't know the exact nature of those 'things,' and wouldn't ask.

"Good man!" cried Father Fred. "There may be hope for him yet."

"Yes," said Father Godfrey, "I think he's turned a corner."

"Then we shall continue to pray for him as he journeys towards being a good and holy priest," Father Harry said.

These responses rather suggested they *were* aware of Father Doyal's inappropriate behaviour. But there was nothing to be done; it was a cross from Christ that Father Godfrey must bear silently.

He nodded. "Well, if you don't need me, I have a few things I'd like to take care of."

"We're fine. See you at noon prayer," said Father Harry.

"Yes!" Father Godfrey continued on to the kitchen garden, which led him past the paddocks. Watching the dusky mares munch on fresh hay, he recoiled at the recollection of Father Doyal threatening him – right here – daring him to abandon his priestly vows and embrace the upside-down morals of the new regime.

He knew the memory was a trick of Satan to depress him. With great effort, he replaced it with Father Doyal's apology. All the signs were good that he had nothing more to fear from the man.

And he had the friendship of a wonderful priest; Father Terry, who knew about everything. He was concerned for the salvation of Father Godfrey's soul and would do all he could to help him achieve it. If only he could repay the favour!

He passed Ruby's paddock, where she stood contentedly with her fast-growing foal, and couldn't resist slipping through the fence rails to check on her leg.

He was amazed at how well it was healing. New skin covered the wounded area, and black hairs were already beginning to grow through. Soon there would be no evidence that she'd ever had an injury. Brother Melvin truly worked wonders! In a short time, he'd become a valuable member of their community.

Exiting the paddock, he made his way to the kitchen garden and rapped on the door.

"Ah, Father Godfrey!" said the jovial brother, as he let in his guest. "Have you come for that orchid to help you sleep at night?"

"Actually, I came to tell you I don't think I need it anymore."

"I *am* glad to hear that. I hope that means you're getting to sleep faster, and staying asleep?"

"I have a strong feeling I shall be from now on."

"Care to share why? Perhaps you've found a secret that I can pass onto anyone else with the same problem?"

Father Godfrey laughed. "It's called resting in the peace of the Holy Spirit."

"Ah." The brother made the Sign of the Cross. "That'll do it every time."

Father Godfrey was grateful to him for not probing further. Smiling, he said, "Yes."

Chapter Forty-One: A Holy Sacrifice
Sunday, 27th October 2030

Father Terry was pleased; Father Doyal arrived in plenty of time on Sunday morning. It was a good start.

Together they went through the Order of the Mass, and he explained the visiting priest's duties, including where he needed help.

"I know this sounds ridiculous," Father Doyal said, "but despite offering Mass in my cell yesterday, I'm nervous. I'm sure to get it wrong. I got into some lazy habits, even when I was a parish priest and said Mass regularly."

Father Terry said kindly. "Think of this as a refresher course from Our Lord."

Soon after, the two priests processed up the truncated aisle to the hymn 'Amazing Grace,' which Father Terry felt was appropriate for the occasion.

With their backs to the pews, both priests kissed the altar, built in the traditional style against the wall, and began the Novus Ordo Mass *ad orientem*.

Father Terry knew how Brother Melvin longed for the return of the Traditional Latin Mass. He himself looked forward to a day when the monastery would be restored to its proper use, with the whole barn once more becoming a chapel. Then he would learn to say Mass in the ancient language used by the saints throughout the past two millennia.

But for now, they must make do with this hybrid version.

He thought Father Doyal was probably glad not to be facing the tiny congregation. This was his first public appearance since his suicide attempt on the roof. Also, any mistakes he made while saying Mass would be less obvious to his more practised fellow priests.

He seemed to grow in confidence as the Liturgy progressed, and exhibited an excellent speaking voice during the First Reading.

Then Brother Melvin's deep mellow tones led them in the Responsorial Psalm, and Father Harry was the second lector.

Father Terry read the Gospel and gave the homily.

During the intercessions, he added a petition to the Lord to watch over all priests struggling to do God's Work and obey His Word in these difficult times.

Now came the part which Father Doyal told him he was dreading. But Father Terry was adamant: he must prepare the gifts on his own, and say the blessing over them.

Standing by the side table, Father Terry awkwardly picked up the drying towel with his right claw and placed it over his left arm, for his broken arm was still in a sling. He was unable to carry both the bowl and the jug to the altar for the washing of hands, so Father Doyal walked over to him and held his hands over the dish while Father Terry poured water over them with his good hand. Father Doyal then took the towel and dried his hands. After reposing the bowl, jug and towel on the table, Father Terry joined him at the altar.

While Father Doyal was reciting the Prayer over the Offerings, Father Terry was seized by a sudden conviction that could only have come from the Holy Spirit.

The certainty filled him that his decision to join the priesthood had *not* been born of a misjudged desire to appease his family by replacing his dead cousin in the seminary.

With brilliant clarity, he understood that Cousin Vincent's death was the catalyst, not the cause. That sad event had resulted in him following the path that God had always intended for him, and which he wouldn't have taken otherwise. Whether his cousin had lived or died, Terry Talbot was always meant to become a priest.

But with this revelation came confusion. The question remained as before: how could he function properly as a priest if his right hand didn't work? Was Father Doyal meant to assist him at *every* Mass he said? Was that part of God's plan, too?

Lord, I don't know what You intend to do with either of us, but please show me the path I need to take.

Father Doyal was leading the Eucharistic Prayers. He moved to one side, so Father Terry could also read a paragraph. He then handed the wine chalice to Father Terry, who held it high with his left hand.

Father Doyal raised the Host and proclaimed the final words of consecration, which Father Terry said quietly with him: "Through Him, and with Him and in Him, O God, Almighty Father, in the unity of the Holy Spirit, all glory and honour is Yours, for ever and ever."

As the small assembly gave the "Amen," Father Terry sensed a slight tingling in his right fingers.

Afraid he was imagining things, he carefully placed the chalice on the altar in front of Father Doyal, who broke the Host in half over it and dropped a small piece into the wine, now become the Blood of Christ.

It was time for the Agnus Dei.

Father Terry pressed his withered right hand to his chest for the first "miserere nobis," and found he could move his fingers into a complete fist, instead of their being stuck in the usual ugly talon.

In astonishment, he drew the hand away, ready to strike his breast for the second "miserere nobis". He tried to unfurl his fingers before making another fist, and they straightened out easily.

Thank you, Lord, thank you! his heart cried out.

By the third strike of his breast, for the "dona nobis pacem," he knew his hand was completely healed and wanted to shout, "It's a miracle!"

Unaware of what was happening, Father Doyal lifted the Host with the prayer, "Behold the Lamb of God, behold Him, Who takes away the sins of the world. Blessed are those called to the supper of the Lamb."

Father Terry had never meant his response as sincerely as he did now, when he repeated with the others, "Lord, I am not worthy that You should enter under my roof. But only say the word, and my soul shall be healed."

When Father Doyal handed the chalice to Father Terry with the words, "The Blood of Christ," his eyes widened in shock at seeing the priest take it with *both* hands.

"Amen," said Father Terry, eyes lowered to hide his excitement, as another rush of thanksgiving filled his heart. *Lord, I am not worthy,* he told Christ again, aware of how little he merited this extraordinary grace after his near-defection from the priesthood.

Father Doyal was experiencing a miracle of his own.

At this Mass, everyone was truly worshiping God. With fitting reverence, they were offering Him the supreme sacrifice made by His Son to expiate the sins of mankind.

How different from the *Ordo Fraternitas* Mass feverishly being drawn up in Rome!

An early draft had been circulated among the clergy in good standing with the Vatican. It was a flat, vanilla affair, crafted to be acceptable to people of all religions, including pagans, with the aim of gathering all mankind into a global church, parading under the banner of Catholicism in the universal sense. It bore no resemblance to the Mass of the Catholic Church founded upon Peter by Christ!

The New Church considered Our Lord to be one prophet among many, and His teachings were no truer or more binding than those of any other spiritual leader. He was no longer believed to be the Son of God, Who saved mankind by dying an excruciating death on the Cross. His sacrifice was meaningless in a world that did not recognise His authority.

Therefore, neither the liturgy previously celebrated by the Catholic Church, nor the consecration of the Host were valid. The *Ordo Fraternitas* was a communal meal and all were welcome to partake of it, regardless of their faith.

Pope Lucius II was rapidly making the Holy Sacrifice of the Mass extinct, and Father Doyal had been helping him – and Satan – achieve their goal. But Christ had mercifully intervened, through the priests of Angelscombe, and set him right before he'd died a faithless priest by his own hand.

Had the Vatican hierarchy heeded *their* warnings? Had Pope Lucius II listened to Christ during his Illumination of Conscience? Was he going to rescind his awful *Nova Theologica Populi* and not impose the *Ordo Fraternitas?*

With Father Terry at the altar, he was celebrating the real Mass. Even if it wasn't the traditional one, it contained the essential elements. Begotten of the Father, not made, Jesus was and always would be, the Son of God, the Saviour of the World, Love Incarnate.

No pope had the authority to deny that, and how foolish of him to try!

As Father Doyal raised the Host and declared, in the words of Christ, "This is My Body, which will be given up for you," he knew with every fibre of his being that he was speaking the Truth – a Truth that Pope Lucius II could never eradicate. While eating the Host and drinking the Blood of Christ from the chalice, he thought with remorse of how, in his whole priestly life, he had never truly believed that, through the power of Jesus working through him, the bread and wine actually turned into His Body and Blood. It had all seemed so utterly fantastic – childish wishful thinking – a necessary pretence for entering the priesthood.

But all that was before Jesus illuminated his conscience.

A short while ago, he'd tried to take his life, and almost followed Judas in committing the ultimate act of despair in God. Yet today, the Lord had bestowed on him the privilege of offering the Holy Sacrifice of the Mass – and Father Doyal would never again doubt His Divinity and Merciful Love. With Father Terry and Father Godfrey's help, he would strive to reject his unholy desires and be worthy of his vocation.

After Father Terry's support in the aftermath of his suicide attempt, he'd been praying fervently for his former enemy. Guilt at handicapping the priest was eating away at him.

Then, during Mass, he saw the fingers on Father Terry's deformed right hand open normally and close around the golden stem to take the chalice from him.

Not only had Christ forgiven His wayward priest and given him the gift of True Faith, but He had also answered his petition for Father Terry's healing!

He wanted to sink to his knees in awe and thanksgiving. For the remainder of Mass, it was hard to conceal his joy.

When the service was over, he gave the final blessing and solemnly processed the short distance to the back door of the little chapel with Father Terry. There they waited for the others.

He was gratified when they all clasped his outstretched hand with a smile as they exited, a token that they accepted him as a *bona fide* brother priest.

On the other side of the doorway, Father Terry opened his slinged hand in greeting, and Father Doyal delighted in the delayed reaction as each realised what he was doing.

Father Terry chuckled mischievously at the puzzlement and surprise of his fellow priests when they grasped the fact that they'd just shaken his right hand.

"What the – !"

"Isn't that your bad hand?"

"It's a miracle!"

Father Terry made the Sign of the Cross over himself with his left arm. "Yes, praise be to God."

"Praise the Lord, indeed!" exclaimed Brother Melvin. "I look forward to seeing you use both hands at breakfast." With that, the cook scurried off to finish preparations for the meal.

"This is wonderful!" cried Father Godfrey. "I have my fellow rider and trainer back."

"About that," said Father Terry, warily, "I think the Holy Spirit wants me to cut back on my involvement with the ponies' training."

Father Godfrey peered closely at him. "Did He give you some kind of message?"

Father Terry nodded. "I'll tell you about it later."

"O.K.," said Father Godfrey. "See you in the refectory."

Father Terry turned to Father Doyal, who was standing hesitantly in the chapel doorway after the others left. With a smile, he said, "That was quite some Mass. Want to talk about it?"

"Only to say thank you, more than I can express, for allowing me to celebrate it with you. I need time to process the many blessings I've received – blessings I don't deserve."

"We never deserve our blessings, Father. But thankfully, we have a God Who will not be outdone in generosity."

The two men retired to the makeshift sacristy in the far corner of the chapel, and removed their vestments in silence.

Father Terry closed the chapel door behind them and they walked through the hay barn. "Would you like to join us for breakfast? You did, after all, just celebrate Mass for us. And I need to celebrate my miracle with everyone!"

"I appreciate the kind offer, but I need to be alone for a while. However, I do have one request."

"What's that?"

"Might I be allowed to come back here for Mass sometimes? You know I daren't openly celebrate the *Novus Ordo* at Lambcot. I can only do it in private and hope no one finds out."

"You're welcome any time, Father. You saw that the clergy here consider you one of us now."

"Another reason for gratitude. But we both know I'm in a precarious situation. I need to tread carefully if I'm to be of any use to the True Church."

Father Terry grinned. "You'll be our man on the inside, a sort of double-agent."

Father Doyal grimaced. "God certainly works in mysterious ways. As long as I'm an instrument in His Hands."

"It wouldn't be a bad idea to sound out the ladies there, and see if any of them are real Catholics in need of your ministrations."

The priest's face brightened. "Perhaps they're as subversive as Angelscombe."

"Maybe!"

"For the time being, if I ever call to arrange a visit, it'll be my way of asking to attend Mass here with you. Nothing more sinister than that." He paused. "May I ask for your blessing before I leave?"

As a result of this discussion with Father Doyal, Father Terry arrived late to breakfast.

He was greeted by loud cheers, and shouts of "He's a living miracle!" and "Let's see it again!"

He sat down, and with a dramatic flourish, picked up a knife in his healed hand and held it as high as his sling permitted, to loud applause.

At that moment, Pastor John burst into the room. "Michaela and Gabriela gave birth while we were at Mass, the sneaky things! Two beautiful, healthy foals, suckling for England."

Father Terry burst into happy laughter; the Lord was truly favouring Angelscombe. "God was *very* busy today while we were at worship," he remarked. Putting the knife down, he lifted his coffee cup in his right hand. "God is good!"

The others raised theirs and echoed, "God is good!"

Brother Melvin's breakfast was enjoyed more than usual.

Afterwards, everyone rushed to see the new babies and their dams in the large foaling stables. Michaela was the proud mother of a handsome colt, and Gabriela was nursing a smaller filly foal.

"Any ideas for names?" Pastor John asked.

"I think the word 'miracle' should be included somewhere," said Father Terry. "Perhaps the colt could be Michaela's Miracle, Miracle for short?" he volunteered.

"What about Gabriela's Grace for the filly?" suggested Brother Melvin. "Grace, for short."

While everyone debated these names, the priests' phones pinged in unison.

Father Godfrey pulled out his mobile first and gasped. "Pope Lucius II resigned two hours ago!"

"What?" exclaimed the others.

Except Pastor John, who wailed, "Why don't *I* get these messages?"

"That's where being a Catholic priest comes in jolly handy," Father Harry said wryly.

The pastor grimaced at him.

"Do you think we'll get a more traditional pope now?" said the ever-hopeful Father Godfrey. "Someone who'll put us back in ministry?"

"Maybe. Or we could end up with an even more progressive pontiff," lamented Father Harry.

Father Terry was also concerned about who might be coming next. But as their *de facto* head, he felt obliged to remind them, "Worrying won't add a second to our lives or a hair to our heads, and it's not our business to look into the future. "

Father Fred was staring at his phone. "It says here, that 'the pope is retiring to a monastery for a quiet life of prayer and contemplation.'"

"Then we must pray for him," said Father Terry, forestalling any temptations to comment negatively on the new pope emeritus. "And let's hope the next conclave listens with true discernment to the promptings of the Holy Spirit. May the cardinals elect a pope who will steer the Barque of Peter back on the mission to save souls that Christ gave her."

"Amen to that," they all agreed.

Chapter Forty-Two: S.O.S.!

Sunday, 27th October 2030

Now that he'd recovered the use of his right hand, Father Terry longed to get back in the saddle as soon as his broken arm was fully functional again.

But his fingers had been restored for priestly work – not pony work.

Less involvement with the ponies would afford him the time to carry out Christ's exhortation to fast and pray, in reparation for his and other priests' sins against His Sacred Heart and the Immaculate Heart of His Mother.

This was going to be hard!

Remembering his promise to tell Father Godfrey about his message from Christ, he wondered whether his friend might be able to counsel him on how much he could interact with his beloved equines without offending Our Lord?

The very fact that he thought of them as 'beloved' revealed an unhealthy attachment. He already had his answer; he must hand over the reins, literally and figuratively, to his brother priests.

He groaned. *Lord, I will need a <u>lot</u> of help with this!*

He wasn't working in the kitchen garden today. It was Sunday, a day of rest; the perfect opportunity to enjoy quiet time with Our Lady of Lourdes and implore her aid in distancing himself from hands-on operation of the Dales project.

Above him, an anaemic sun struggled to filter through the cloud cover on this crisp October morning. He wrapped the tartan scarf around his neck and drew up the collar of his heavy black coat. He was about to put on his leather gloves, when he remembered to switch off the sound on his mobile phone. He didn't want to be disturbed while in conference with Mary.

It rang as he was reaching into his pocket. Irritated, he fished it out to shut off the caller, but it was Father Doyal. He'd better take it.

"Yes, Father, what is it?" He winced at the impatience in his voice.

"Father, I need your help! I'm being ambushed by a mob of irate Catholics, including my staff. They're furious, because Christ revealed to them during their Illumination of Conscience that they're in a state of mortal sin. They've spent the last few days organising themselves into a united front to besiege me, as I'm the nearest active priest within fifty miles."

"What about my successor at St. Thomas More Church in the village? Why aren't they flocking to *him*?"

"Father Gerald? Didn't you hear? He had a heart attack during his Illumination of Conscience and died that night. The bishop hushed it up and hasn't had time to replace him. That's another reason these people are mad. Then they found out there was an uncancelled Catholic priest at the Fell Project. I'm it!"

Father Terry shook his head at this predictable result of closing so many Catholic churches in England.

"Are you listening?"

"Yes, Father. Go on."

"This crowd is terrified of going to Hell. They're blaming me and the whole Catholic Church for leading them astray. They want to confess their sins, but aren't even sure what those are anymore. I'm just one priest pitted against dozens – so far – of angry parishioners. What am I supposed to do? Can I give them General Absolution?"

"No!" Father Terry's tone was stern. "If you do that, they'll remain ignorant of where they've gone wrong.

They need to know the truth about sin. Plus, this situation hardly qualifies as a state of emergency."

That is the condition for General Absolution, which requires that the absolved penitents go to Confession as soon as they are able, once the emergency has passed.

"Maybe not for *you*, but it is for me! These people are about to rip me to pieces if I don't do something. I need help!"

Adrenalin rushed through Father Terry's body and his heart was pounding. He knew what had to be done, yet this was so sudden! Were he and his fellow priests ready?

But Father Doyal needed guidance right this minute. "You must instruct them on the truth about venial and mortal sins. Gather them together and tell them you're helping them perform a good examination of conscience, before making a valid Confession that will repair their friendship with God."

"I – I suppose I could do that. Hopefully, I can remember enough to be of help."

"Use your mobile to look up the Ten Commandments." It pained Father Terry to have to suggest this to a Catholic priest. "Then pray to the Holy Spirit and don't worry about what to say. He'll give you the right words."

"Then what? Am I supposed to hear each individual Confession? That'll take forever! And what are the others supposed to do while they're waiting? They need to eat and drink!"

Despite the urgency of the situation, Father Terry chuckled to himself. How reminiscent of the events leading to the miracle of five loaves and two fish.

His face then became sombre, for he, too, needed a miracle.

"Go and organise the catechism," he said. "I'll get back to you very soon."

"Please hurry!"

"Father Doyal, God has granted you this opportunity to save many souls."

"Yes, Father, I know. But please hurry – I need help! Wish me luck!"

"You don't need luck; you have God on your side. Those people are hungry for the Truth you can offer them, and will calm down when they realise you're helping them undo years of bad teaching. Your staff will assist you, if you explain what you're doing. We'll talk again very soon, I promise."

Father Doyal's "O.K." sounded more like a strangled squeal.

Suddenly weary, Father Terry placed the phone back in his coat pocket.

He felt sorry for Father Doyal, but the man was asking him to take a momentous step that would put all the priests of Angelscombe in peril.

Heavenly help was needed. He walked into the clearing and prayed to Our Lady of Lourdes, kneeling on the moist grass in front of her statue.

Once assured of her aid and intercession with her Son, he rose and returned swiftly to the main building, where he called for an urgent meeting in the refectory.

Brother Melvin and Pastor John were also asked to attend. Although this was a matter for the Catholic priests, the decision made at this session would impact them, too.

Sitting at the head of the long trestle table, Father Terry made the Sign of the Cross, and the others followed suit.

"Thank you all for coming at such short notice. I wish I didn't have to ask this, but I have a strong feeling this is why God brought us to Angelscombe.

"Having been removed from ministry, we've been lying low, keeping the faith – waiting to be vindicated by our superiors, and reinstated.

"In recent days since the Warning, we've been rewarded for our efforts to evangelise by the many villagers who've quietly let us know how grateful they are that they were ready for their Illuminations of Conscience. Thanks to our keeping them rooted in the True Faith, they were not shocked or upset by what Our Lord had to say to them. Nor were the many other people they were able to warn."

Father Terry paused. He was not looking forward to imparting this next piece of news.

"However, our brother priest in Lambcot has not been so lucky. Even as I speak, he is being besieged by a large and angry throng of Catholics with malformed consciences, who blame him and the Church for the terrifying messages they received from Christ during the Warning. Jesus made it clear that they are all headed for Hell, unless they repent of their sins and turn their lives around. The problem is, they no longer know right from wrong, what is a sin and what isn't."

The priests in his audience shifted uncomfortably in their dining chairs, beginning to guess what was coming.

Father Terry continued. "Father Doyal is appealing to me – to us – to help him. Those people need their Confessions heard. I asked him to try his best to catechise them on God's truth about venial and mortal sins and prepare them to make a proper Confession."

How Father Terry longed for a glass of water to soothe his dry throat!

"However, we are talking about *a lot* of people. When Father called me there were dozens, but word is getting out and that number may have radically increased in the meantime. He's the only active priest within a fifty mile radius."

"Why don't they go to Father Gerald?" yelled Father Harry.

"Unfortunately, he died during his Illumination of Conscience, and hasn't yet been replaced."

"They kept *that* quiet!" Father Harry said.

"So those poor people have to rely on Father *Doyal*?" cried Father Fred.

A murmur of incredulous sympathy ran round the table.

Father Terry sorely wanted to remind them that Father Doyal had since repented and come back into the fold. It then occurred to him that their reaction might soften them to his request.

"I now come to my question, my brothers in Christ. Are we willing to expose our carefully protected cover and help Father Doyal save souls – many, many souls?

"Are we prepared to accept harsh reprisals for publicly performing our duties as Catholic priests? You are well aware that we face severe punishment from our own Church if we do this – even possible excommunication."

He could see the agony in his brothers' faces. He was asking them to give up this life of comfort and instead embrace the cruel injustices that awaited them if they did as he – as God was asking.

"My brothers, we have to make our choice *now*. The angry mob may already be flaying Father Doyal alive.

"We can go to his aid and risk losing our tenuous status as cancelled priests.

"Or we can stay here, safe in Angelscombe, awaiting a pope who will reinstate us." He turned to the SSPX brother and Lutheran minister. "If we're evicted, you might both be allowed to remain here. But I can't guarantee it, so I'd like your vote on this, too."

Father Godfrey raised his right hand. "I say we go."

Immediately, the others' hands shot up, including those of Pastor John and Brother Melvin.

Father Terry's heart swelled. He was deeply moved by this response, and proud of his priests for remaining true to their vocation. Each man was accepting God's call to save souls, regardless of the sacrifice.

And in support of them even Brother Melvin and Pastor John were willing to give up their comfortable life at Angelscombe.

The winds of change had indeed come, but not the way he'd anticipated.

Lord, we are in Your hands. Thy Will be done.

THE END

Thank you for reading *The Triumph of Angelscombe!*

If you enjoyed this book, would you consider leaving a review at your favourite online retailer?

Reviews are the lifeblood of authors, and help to spread the word about our work.

Thank you again, and until next time, God bless. ☺

Nova Theologica Populi

Papal Document Issued by His Holiness Pope Lucius II shortly after his election in CE 2030

1. **The Pope Is Infallible in Everything He Says and Does**
   a) Our Extraordinary Synod, guided by an outpouring of God's Spirit, has corrected a grave error of the Old Church, which decreed that the sayings of the Pope were infallible only when spoken *ex cathedra.*
   b) The Pope is the head of the visible Universal Church and therefore imbued with His Spirit; as the President of the Universal (i.e. catholic) Church, he has the final say.
   c) However, this now being a democratic Church, (praise the Lord! See *Theologia* 2. below) the Pope is open to the counsel of his cardinals.

2. **The Church is a Democracy**
   a) The findings of the Extraordinary Synod, inspired by God's Spirit, have led us to correct another error of the Old Church.
   b) Her rigid hierarchy put all the power into the hands of a select few. She ignored her living stones, by preventing the faithful from contributing to the decisions and doctrines of the Church, thereby impeding her from moving forward with the times.

3. **Everyone Is Saved**
   a) This is the clear will of God, Who created us to be with Him for eternity. All He asks in

return is to believe that He exists and that He loves us all. He meets us wherever we are, and lovingly accompanies us on our journey through life, without judgement.

b) We have thus achieved universal fraternity, and man can now truly flourish – a goal which conspicuously eluded the Old Church.

4. Denying This Truth Is Hate Speech

Telling any individual they are not saved is an act of hatred, which will be punished to the full extent of New Church Law.

5. Prohibition of Evangelization

Any attempt to force the old religion on anyone will be punished to the full extent of New Church Law. All must be allowed the freedom to believe what they wish, as long as they believe in One God.

6. Revised Teaching on Sin

a) The notion of mortal sin belongs in the Old Testament, to which adherents of the Old Church lamentably still cling, despite the two-thousand-year existence of the *New* Testament.

b) The God of the New Testament is merciful and compassionate, not given to jealous fits of rage and outbursts of rough justice. For those still wishing to believe that Jesus Christ was the Son of God, an obvious exception is that God was cruel enough to kill His own son.

c) Thankfully, He is understanding of our human frailty, and excuses our weaknesses.
d) It is, therefore, solemnly declared that 'sins below the waist' – to use my predecessor's delicate phraseology – are no longer considered to be mortal, and it is up to the individual, with pastoral guidance, to decide whether they are sinful at all.
e) Further, *all* unions formed in love are recognised and can be blessed in the Church, and given the validity of marriage. Any priest who refuses to bless a same sex couple will be guilty of hate speech. (See Article 4. above)

7. Conservation of Mother Earth
a) Inspired by the Spirit of God, the Extraordinary Synod discerned that Mother Earth, bequeathed to us by God for the benefit of mankind, is in need of protection by her very beneficiaries, who are in danger of destroying her.
b) The Church is obligated to lead the way in reducing the human population in order to allow Mother Earth to restore herself and recover from the iniquities imposed on her by man.
c) It is therefore necessary to correct a further error of the Old Church, by declaring the need to rapidly decrease procreation, through the use of contraception and the termination of excess pregnancies.
d) Regarding the elderly, their advanced age automatically renders them ready to meet

their Creator. Their loving Father awaits them with open arms, and the Church sees no impediment to terminating their lives – with their consent, of course.

8. Abolition of Daily Mass
a) Daily Mass is no longer required of the clergy in the Synodal Church.
b) We do not want to put ourselves above our separated brethren by making them feel less worthy for not holding services every day of the week. It would be contrary to brotherly love, and unecumenical.

9. Abolition of Priestly Celibacy
a) The Extraordinary Synod further discerned no further need for celibacy among her clergy. This was considered necessary in the old Church because of an outdated requirement that a priest refrain from intercourse within twenty-four hours of celebrating the liturgy.
b) Since ordained clergy are not obliged to say Mass on a daily basis anymore, the requirement for celibacy is no longer valid.

10. Abolition of the Novus Ordo Mass
a) In compliance with Our Lord's request to His heavenly Father 'that we may all be one', the Novus Ordo Mass and the Extraordinary Form of the Latin Rite, which exclude so many of our separated brethren, will be phased out over the next six months, and

replaced by the *Ordo Fraternitas*, the new universal rite.

b) Thus the communal meal shared by Our Lord with His friends during Passover will be welcoming to all faiths.

c) Priests will be allowed to say Mass every Sunday, as long as they recognise that 'Eucharist' denotes 'Thanksgiving' and does not refer to the actual *corpus et sanguis Christi*, as was previously taught in error.

d) There will be severe penalties for any priest who violates this teaching.

11. The New Role of Confession

a) In recognition of the value, to certain sensitive individuals, of clearing their consciences to a minister of the Church in the privacy of the confessional, the Synodal Fathers have generously extended the time for phasing out this outmoded crutch.

b) As in the case of the Novus Ordo Mass (see Article 10. above), the so-called 'sacrament' of Confession will be abolished at the end of a six-month period.

c) During this period, no priest may refuse to absolve a person of their sins due to a perceived lack of contrition.

d) There will be severe penalties for any priest who attempts to continue this practice beyond the grace period.

12. Women's Role in the New Church

a) The Synodal Fathers wish to reassure women who feel called to the priesthood that we are working assiduously to make this a reality.

b) At the present time, however, we offer the position of deacon for those women wishing to take the first step to possible priesthood. In so doing, they will be of inexpressible help to their parish priests.

13. On Keeping the Sabbath Holy

a) The Extraordinary Synod, filled with the Wisdom of God's Spirit, has discerned that the requirement to go to church every Sunday puts too heavy a burden on the faithful.

b) Today's man is busier than in biblical days, and cannot always find time to attend every week. Thus, we declare a mandate to attend Church services one Sunday a month only.

c) To assist the faithful in keeping track of their monthly obligations, each church will have an electronic check-in system and will send the participant a text after the service to let them know they have fulfilled their monthly requirement.

d) On the intervening Sundays, it is strongly suggested that the faithful read through these precepts to thoroughly acquaint themselves with them.

e) Especially since the *Nova Theologica Populi* is subject to revision from time to time, as the Spirit reveals more errors from the Old Church that must be addressed, or doctrines that require updating, to accommodate the everchanging needs of the people.

Decreed in the year CE 2030, His Holiness

Lucius II

Resources & Notes

Introduction:

John Henry Westen's interview with Xavier Reyes-Ayralwith on Lifesitenews.com:

https://www.lifesitenews.com/episodes/book-of-revelation-is-pope-francis-the-true-pope-or-false-prophet-part-1/

Bishop Strickland's Letter:

https://www.lifesitenews.com/opinion/bishop-strickland-warns-of-apostasy-at-the-top-says-fatima-consecration-not-done-properly/

The full text of Archbishop Carlo Maria Viganó's sermon can be found on his website:
https://exsurgedomine.it/240707-in-sanguine-tuo-eng/

See my blog post regarding the October 2023 Synod:
https://hilarywalkerbooks.com/2023/10/25/did-someone-forget-to-put-gods-invitation-to-the-synod-in-the-mail/

Chapter One:

Roman Catholic priests are required by canon law to pray the whole Liturgy of the Hours every day.

There are three major hours:
1. The Office of Readings, formerly known as Matins, and still often referred to by that name.

In the book, I use the term Matins, as it is more traditional and consistent with my use of the term Vespers (see 3. below).
2. Morning Prayer or Lauds
3. Evening Prayer or Vespers. I use the term Vespers in the book.

For more details about the Liturgy of the Hours see:

https://divineoffice.org/liturgy-of-the-hours/how-to-pray-the-liturgy-of-the-hours/

Chapter Five:

This great article describes the items used at Mass, and explains their origin and use:
http://www.catholictradition.org/Eucharist/sacred-mass.htm

Chapter Thirteen:

The full quote attributed to Pope St. John XXIII is: "What do we intend to do? We intend to let in a little fresh air."'
It is, however, contested whether he actually said this. For more information go to:
https://sharonkabel.com/post/windows/

Chapter Thirty-Three:

Scripture references:
Luke 17:2
1 Corinthians 6:9-11
Isaiah 3:8-9

Matthew 11:24

About the Author

Now an American citizen, Hilary originally hails from England and lives in Hilton Head, South Carolina with her husband and Jeeves, the English Bulldog.

She is the bestselling author of Christian inspirational novels, Christian romances and short stories.

When not penning fiction, Hilary is down at the horse barn with Cruz Bay, her home-bred Welsh Cob/Thoroughbred Cross.

Acknowledgements

I am hugely indebted to the amazing people who helped and supported me during the writing of this book.

My heartfelt appreciation goes to the beta readers who gave their valuable time to proof-read the draft and final products, and provide suggestions for making this novel the best it could be. Thank you, Eleanor Bell, Wendy Emblin, Gail Gordon and Anna Rashbrook.

I extend deep gratitude to my Launch Team, especially Julie Barrett, Małgorzata Bernaś, Merlinda Craig, Luiza Lazarescu, Lia Lorimer and Rachael Smith. Your loyal support of my book launches have played a crucial part in ensuring their success, and I thank you with all my heart!

God bless you,

Hilary

Rubesca4@Gmail.com

https://HilaryWalkerBooks.com

Discover Other Books by Hilary Walker

Available at all major ebook retailers. For more details, visit https://HilaryWalkerBooks.com

CHRISTIAN INSPIRATIONAL

The Jack Harper Trilogy

(Also available as a box set)

Riding Out the Devil (Book 1)

Riding Out the Tempest (Book 2)

Riding Out the Rough (Book 3)

Riding Out the Turbulence (Companion Short Story to *The Jack Harper Trilogy*)

The Father Michael Trilogy

(Also available as a box set)

Riding Out the Wager (Book 1)

Riding Out the Regrets (Book 2)

Riding Out the Wreckage (Book 3)

The Laura Harper Trilogy

(Also available as a box set)

Riding Out the Return (Book 1)

Riding Out the Rift (Book 2)

Riding Out the Race (Book 3)

CHRISTIAN ROMANCE

Saving Prophecy: A Sinclair Island Romance (Book 1)

Dinny's Challenge: A Sinclair Island Romance (Book 2)

Friday's Folly: A Sinclair Island Romance (Book 3)

Rachel's Risk: A Sinclair Island Romance (Book 4)

Ivan's Choice: A Hilton Head Romance (Book 1)

CATHOLIC NON-EQUESTRIAN FICTION

Brittle Diamonds – a Christian Mystery Novel

A Modern Catholic Trilogy:

A Truthful Man – a Modern Catholic Novel: Book 1

A Divine Truth – a Modern Catholic Novel: Book 2

A Blazing Truth – a Modern Catholic Novel: Book 3

EQUESTRIAN GUIDES

A Step-By-Step Guide to Entering Your First Dressage Competition

The Beginner Rider's Guide to Stress-Free Horse Buying:
How to Purchase the Perfect Horse for a Beginner Rider without Going Insane

AUTOBIOGRAPHY

The Horse Bumbler Series: The Autobiography of an Awful Rider with Aspirations

Part One: First Catch Your Horse

Part Two: You've Caught Your Horse: Now What?

Part Three: The Aim of All This

Part Four: What Horses Do to You

SHORT STORIES

A Perfect Christmas & Other Horse Stories (A short story collection)

How I Lost My Husband's Horse

A Dog Named Blue

The Horse Inside